GREENWILD

THE
CITY BEYOND
THE SEA

Praise for *Greenwild: The World Behind the Door*

'If you don't believe in magic, you will after you've read *Greenwild*. It's phenomenal.' – A. F. Steadman, author of *Skandar and the Unicorn Thief*

'A spellbinding, enchanting read full of wildness and beauty.' – Hannah Gold, author of *The Last Bear*

'A glorious, page-turning adventure . . . Thomson has created a gorgeous, utterly believable world as magical and magnificent as the Amazon rainforest itself. I adored this book!' – Aisling Fowler, author of *Fireborn*

'*Greenwild* is a thrilling adventure that takes seed in your imagination and runs wild!' – M. G. Leonard, author of *Beetle Boy*

'I fell utterly in love with this sharply beautiful, contemporary adventure.' – Cerrie Burnell, author of *Wilder Than Midnight*

'A wonderfully whimsical story with a beautiful world – and lots of mystery and adventure – for readers to immerse themselves in.' – Aisha Bushby, author of *A Pocketful of Stars*

'Wildly thrilling and beautifully written, *Greenwild* is the most special type of adventure!' – Carlie Sorosiak, author of *I, Cosmo*

'I adored this wild and wondrous adventure!' – Maria Kuzniar, author of *The Ship of Shadows*

'A rare and wondrous treasure that had me spellbound from first page to last.' – Catherine Doyle, author of *The Storm Keeper's Island*

'A wildly inventive adventure, bursting with beautiful detail and a satisfying plot as twisty as magical vines . . . I loved it!' – Tamzin Merchant, author of *The Hatmakers*

'A spellbindingly magical book full of adventure, hope, and lessons for us all to learn here in our world.' – L. D. Lapinski, author of *The Strangeworlds Travel Agency*

'A beautifully realized eco-fantasy that will open a door in readers' hearts.' – Chris Riddell

Other books by Pari Thomson for
Macmillan Children's Books

Greenwild: The World Behind the Door

GREENWILD

THE CITY BEYOND THE SEA

PARI THOMSON

Illustrated by Elisa Paganelli

MACMILLAN CHILDREN'S BOOKS

Published 2024 by Macmillan Children's Books
an imprint of Pan Macmillan
The Smithson, 6 Briset Street, London EC1M 5NR
EU representative: Macmillan Publishers Ireland Ltd, 1st Floor,
The Liffey Trust Centre, 117–126 Sheriff Street Upper
Dublin 1, D01 YC43
Associated companies throughout the world
www.panmacmillan.com

ISBN 978-1-0350-2118-5

1 3 5 7 9 8 6 4 2

A CIP catalogue record for this book is available from the British Library.

Printed and bound by CPI Group (UK) Ltd, Croydon CR0 4YY

For Tom

Full fathom five thy father lies;
Of his bones are coral made;
Those are pearls that were his eyes;
Nothing of him that doth fade,
But doth suffer a sea-change
Into something rich and strange.
Sea-nymphs hourly ring his knell:
                    Ding-dong.
Hark! now I hear them — Ding-dong, bell.

from *The Tempest* **by William Shakespeare**

Chapter 1

It was a day like a freshly peeled orange: bright and zesty and sweet.

The smell of spring was in the air at Mallowmarsh, and Daisy Thistledown was feeling hopeful. All over the gardens, Botanists were hard at work, tending giant palm trees in the Great Glasshouse, harvesting football-sized plums from the orchards, and planting new lightning seeds in the Mallow Woods. Wild violets were blooming beneath the ancient yews, and the sky was filled with parakeets swooping from tree to tree, delivering the post and screeching joyfully.

A couple of apprentices waved at Daisy as they walked past, and she waved back, grinning. After three long weeks of waiting, the expedition to the Amazon rainforest would finally be setting off tomorrow, and Daisy felt the thrill of it racing through her veins like electricity.

She was standing at her usual spot on the edge of the lake, watching the Mallowmarsh shipbuilders put the finishing touches to their work. It had taken a team of trained Botanists two full weeks to lay the living beams and grow the mast from a seedling – but at last the ship was almost ready: proud and high on the water, with a hull of polished oak wood, a great white sail furled tight as a bud, and an elaborate system of rigging that used living green vines instead of rope. The ship strained at its moorings, as if eager to be on its way.

Daisy had observed the final preparations with mounting impatience and excitement: the deliveries of mosquito netting from Moonmarket and biscuit barrels from the Mallowmarsh kitchens; the piling up of no-glare marsh lamps and crates of phosphorescent mangoes on the shores of the lake. She had tried to help (and been waved away) as Botanists went staggering up the gangplank with heavy jars of healing chamomillion cream, packets of extra-sticky binding vine, and anything else that could possibly be needed for a voyage to the Amazon.

Of course, children weren't technically allowed on the dock, but she had so far managed to ignore this instruction.

'Back again?' asked Madame Gallitrop, who was supervising the loading of a caged Venus flytrap onto the deck of the ship. Her voice was resigned.

'I thought,' said Daisy, 'I'd come and see if you needed help.'

Madame Gallitrop, the head of the Intemperate House, was a plump and cheerful Frenchwoman with merry dark eyes and thick black hair swept back into an enormous bun. 'I see,' she said dryly. 'Well, ma chère, the ship is stocked, the provisions are loaded, and we are nearly ready to set off for Moonmarket tomorrow night.'

Daisy felt her fingers tingle, and she summoned a small vine from the shore to curl around her ankles. She could feel anticipation rise up in her like sap through a stem as she gazed at the floating ship. It looked very fine, with its portholes gleaming, flags fluttering, and its mast – a living oak tree – growing straight from the smooth wooden deck.

The ship was where Daisy felt closest to her mother.

This was partly because its jaunty pennants reminded her of Ma's own devil-may-care brand of confidence, and partly because the ship was Daisy's ticket to finding the person she cared about most in the world. Her mother was imprisoned somewhere in the heart of the Peruvian rainforest, and this was the rescue mission that was going to save her.

'Isn't there anything I can do?' she asked for the hundredth time. 'Perhaps I could polish the railings? Or dust the capstan?' The vine she'd summoned coiled eagerly over her left foot.

'No,' said Madame Gallitrop, shaking her head. 'We have everything under control, ma chère. You know you're not supposed to be here. Leave the preparations to the experts.'

'But—'

'Watch out!' It was a Botanist from the kitchens, toting a crate of ginger-root beer along the dock. 'Out of the way! Children aren't allowed near the ship.'

Daisy felt a wave of annoyance – and suddenly the vine at her ankle surged out of her control. It shot into the air,

ballooned to the width of a python, and snapped the landing stage in two with a great splintering crash.

Daisy leapt back onto the bank just in time, but the barrel went flying into the air and lodged in the ship's mast, showering ginger beer on the Botanists beneath. Madame Gallitrop toppled headfirst into the water with an almighty splash and emerged glowering, a frond of riverweed draped over one ear like an ill-conceived hairpiece.

She spat out a small water beetle. 'Enough,' she said, her voice unusually frosty. 'Kindly help me out of the lake, Daisy, and then make yourself useful somewhere else. You must learn to *control* your magic.'

Daisy Thistledown was a Botanist too – one who had only just discovered that she had green magic. As it turned out, using magic was one thing; keeping it in check was another.

'But,' she said, bracing herself against the bank to heave Madame Gallitrop out of the water, 'I want to do something. I want to *help*!' She heaved again, and the Frenchwoman collapsed onto the remaining half of the landing stage. She righted herself with dignity, straightening her sopping overalls.

'Non!' she said, reverting to her native French. 'That was the fourth accident this week. You can go and "help" elsewhere!'

'Oi! Get that child OFF the landing stage,' roared one of the shipbuilders, a grizzled man who was persuading the nearest mizzenmast to grow high enough to take a sail. 'What have I said about untrained children using magic near the ship?'

Madame Gallitrop, now standing on the shore and dripping from every inch of her hair and overalls, shot Daisy a pointed look.

Daisy slunk away, her cheeks hot. But she was still close enough to hear the shipbuilder's words as he surveyed the damage she'd done to the dock.

'That girl,' he said, 'is a lost cause.'

Chapter 2

Max Brightly was a lost cause. That's what the midwife had said approximately two minutes after he was born, taking one look at his furious pinched mouth and the way his small, angry fists punched the air. And people had gone on saying it all his life: 'That boy,' they said, 'is a lost cause.'

His mother's friends had said it wryly, flinching at his outraged infant roars. His teachers had said it despairingly, lifting their hands in defeat each time Max picked a fight or used a word so rude it made them feel faint. And so, finally, had the doctors – lots of them, after Max became sick and even breathing began to hurt. The tone was hushed now, but not so quiet that he couldn't hear the words from his hospital bed, where he lay with his skin very white – so pale that his birthmark stood out like a smashed strawberry beneath his right eye – and his hands resting on top of the starched cotton sheets. 'That boy is a lost cause.'

In fact, the only person who had never said it was his mother. 'There's nothing lost about you,' she told him fiercely. And she glared at anyone who dared to suggest otherwise.

here for a long time now – he wasn't sure how long – and hunger was blocking out his thoughts like white noise.

What he knew was this: he had been taken from the London hotel he'd been staying at with his mother ('Just for a few nights,' she had said, when they'd arrived from New York). They had been in the middle of an argument – the usual one, about Max not being well enough to start school – when a noise had sounded from the corridor. There had been a moment, stretched out in Max's memory, just long enough for them to look at each other, eyes wide.

Then the door had splintered and fallen inwards with a scream of wood, and suddenly the room was full of two men – big and tall and masked. Max's mother had shouted and then the taller of the two men had crossed the room in three steps and backhanded her across the face so that she fell to the ground and lay still. Her eyes were closed, and Max couldn't see if her chest was moving.

He roared and scrambled towards her; he tried to fling himself on the man – and then a sack was tossed over his head, and everything went dark. He felt himself being lifted bodily over the other man's shoulder. 'No,' he heard himself shout. 'Mom! No, please!' He flailed out wildly with his arms, straining to get free, and felt his fist strike something hard: the man's nose. Max's captor grunted, and then he knocked Max's head against something hard, and his brain became a firework that flared and then went dark.

Chapter 3

The shipbuilder's words echoed in Daisy's ears as she walked away. *A lost cause*. He was right, she thought miserably. She lost control of her magic every time she used it – but most of all, she was lost without Ma. Her hand sought out the daisy-shaped pendant she always wore around her neck. It had belonged to Ma, and though it usually calmed her, now she felt only a sharp, twisting worry.

Ever since the letter from her mother had arrived on the night of the Great Mallowmarsh garden party, Daisy had been waiting for nothing else but for the rescue mission to set off. Instead, she had been asked to wait, and wait, and wait some more.

Over the last few weeks, the Greenwild had been swept with attack after attack by a shadowy organization called the Grim Reapers. Daisy shivered at the name. The Reapers were driven by greed above all else – and, as Artemis said, the Greenwild was a treasure chest of priceless plants and animals that could make an unscrupulous person very rich indeed. Artemis White, the Commander of Mallowmarsh, had been working overtime, keeping track of the Reapers' movements and organizing defence measures.

'We survived our attack,' Artemis had said. 'And so far, the Reapers haven't been able to penetrate any of the other pockets. Even so . . .'

'What?' asked Daisy. She knew that only people with green magic could enter the Greenwild – which meant that the Grim Reapers couldn't get in; or at least not without help. They belonged to the outer world, or 'the Greyside', as Botanists called it.

'Even so,' said Artemis, 'there are people with green magic who support the Reapers. Botanists gone bad, if you like.'

Daisy nodded, and Artemis sighed, pushing her long silver hair away from her face. The fine lines around her blue eyes looked shadowed and creased. As the commander of Mallowmarsh, Artemis was responsible for every soul within it. She was also Daisy's grandmother, a discovery that both of them were still getting used to.

'My theory,' said Artemis, 'is that Botanists who misuse their power – who turn it against living things – poison the magic inside themselves and so lose access to the magical world. But it's only a matter of time before the Reapers find a way in.' She rubbed a hand over her eyes. 'And in the meantime, the Greyside is no longer safe. We have to assume that every port, airport and city in the outer world is being watched. It will be safer to travel to the Amazon via Moonmarket, instead of through the Greyside. And that way, we can convene with Botanists from other pockets – the ones brave enough to go against the Bureau.'

The Bureau of Botanical Business governed the many pockets of the magical world, and it had forbidden any rescue missions to the Amazon. Artemis was almost certain it had been infiltrated by Reapers. 'So, we'll have to be careful,' she said. 'The French are joining the search alongside us, along with Botanists from Italy, Japan and India. We meet at Moonmarket.'

Moonmarket, Daisy knew, was a vast crossing-place between all the pockets of the Botanical world, and it was open for just one night a month. Travellers going through Moonmarket could hitch a ride on boats heading all over the world, which meant that you could start the night in Melbourne and end it in Mumbai, or travel from Cape Town to Cannes in a heartbeat. It was by far the best means of international travel – as long as you didn't mind waiting for the full moon, of course.

Tomorrow, thought Daisy, with a skip to her heart. The ship would be sailing for Amazeria, the biggest pocket in the Peruvian Greenwild – and the one nearest to where the missing Botanists were imprisoned. She pulled Ma's letter out from her pocket and read the words she had read so many times that she knew them by heart:

My rascal. I'm alive.

That was all; but they were words to make hope burn like a candle inside her. Ma had vanished on an expedition to the Amazon rainforest when her plane had crashed back in December, and she had been reported missing, presumed dead. Now it was early March, and Daisy knew that Ma was alive, but imprisoned by Grim Reapers.

Daisy stood on the shore of the lake, remembering it all. How Ma had set off for Peru in pursuit of a dangerous news story. How Daisy had been left behind at a boarding school called Wykhurst – and how she had decided to escape and search for Ma when she'd gone missing. In the process, she had found a hidden silver door in the depths of the Palm House at Kew Gardens in London – and behind it, she had discovered a world where plant magic was real. A world that held the answers to the mystery of Ma's disappearance.

The Greenwild, thought Daisy. Her blood still thrilled at the name. It was a great hidden world: a place where all manner of things were possible. A place she hadn't known about until she'd stumbled across it by accident that day in Kew Gardens. Except, of course, that it hadn't really been an accident. Ma had given her a glowing silver paperweight (Daisy knew now that it was called a dandelight) and it had cast its beam of light like a compass needle, leading her to the hidden door. It was sitting in her pocket now, heavy and cool, with a dandelion puff trapped inside the glass like a silver firework – ready to light up when it was needed.

She felt an indignant movement from inside her other pocket and glanced down to see Napoleon looking back up at her, one feline eyebrow raised, white whiskers quivering.

'All right, I know,' she told the tiny cat as he leapt onto her shoulder. His fur was black and white, and his teeth were tiny and fierce and pointed. 'You got me here too.'

Napoleon was a kitten with fine whiskers and an even finer sense of his own importance. He had adopted Daisy soon after Ma had vanished, and it was true: she would never have reached Mallowmarsh without his help.

Daisy fingered Ma's letter, tracing it for clues. Ma was a journalist, a writer by trade, which made it even more frustrating that the note was so short.

There had been nothing strange about Ma deciding to go to Peru, since she often travelled to research stories. What *had* been different was Ma deciding to leave Daisy behind. Until then, they had gone everywhere together, and Daisy had spent most of her life moving from place to place, as Ma chased one breaking news story and then another. Daisy had celebrated her third birthday in Berlin, her fourth in Cairo, and her fifth in Mogadishu. She remembered her sixth birthday in Bolivia: a perfect summer day when Ma had bought a single rose from a street vendor and tossed it on the floor of their hotel room. Seconds later, the entire suite had been twined with roses up to the rafters, growing out of the overstuffed armchair, bursting through the shiny mahogany headboard, and rustling foot-deep around the walls. Daisy had been young enough to convince herself, later, that she had made the whole thing up. But arriving at Mallowmarsh – a place of lily-pad boats and magical glasshouses – had taught her that birthday roses were the least of the marvels green magic could achieve.

Even so, Daisy missed her mother so much that it was like having a constant stomach-ache. She missed Ma's bright brown eyes, crinkled with laughter at the edges. She missed the way that Ma took her out dancing, and sailing, and out for tea to eat giant cream puffs ('life is too short not to eat cream puffs,' she said), and stayed up half the night with her reading *The Voyage of the Dawn Treader*. She missed Ma's stories of growing up in Iran, and the way she spoke to Daisy in Farsi, the language of her childhood. She missed Ma's scent of ink and jasmine, and the way she made her feel that anything in the world was possible.

Ma had been her ally, her best friend, and they had told each other everything. That's how it had always been: ever since the death of Daisy's father when she was only three years old. Pa had been an English Botanist called Henry White – and he had been killed by Grim Reapers. Now, the Reapers had taken Ma too, and Daisy would do anything – *anything* – to make sure that she didn't lose her in the same way.

She turned back to the words in Ma's letter: words that made her want to shout, 'Hurry up!' to every Botanist who passed.

I'm alive, Ma had said. But for how much longer?

Napoleon meowed, and Daisy looked at him. 'Yes,' she agreed as they turned their back on the lake. 'Not long now. We'll be on that boat tomorrow. Come on,' she said, glancing at her watch. 'It's almost five o'clock.'

Chapter 4

When he woke, Max was very cold, and his blood felt slow and sluggish inside his veins. He was in a large, dark, damp room with no windows – a cellar, he guessed.

That was the start of the worst of it: the days passing with no way to mark them. Without his medicine he quickly became ill and feverish. The old pain came back, and it was so overwhelming that he vomited onto the floor. The larger of the two men came twice a day to leave a plate of bread and a cup of water. He was tall and thick with muscle, and his nose – thanks to Max's efforts – was broken. He was also, Max noticed with satisfaction, missing a tooth.

'I'll get you for this, boy,' he had said that first day, half spitting the words. 'Not now, but soon.' And he shoved the plate of stale bread towards Max with a violence that made his jaw feel loose with fear.

Max tried his best to force down the food, but after the third day he became too sick to eat. At first, he was infuriated to discover how much he'd relied on the medicine; how much his mother had been right. Then he became too exhausted for fury, and instead his brain fixed on the image of her lying on the hotel room floor, her arms flung out, eyes closed. Was she alive? That was all he wanted to know.

Max lay in the dark room, breathing heavily. The ground seemed to rock beneath him like the deck of a ship. He lost unknown chunks of time to unconsciousness and pain; great waves of pain that seemed to come from deep inside his bones and rise through his skin to shimmer around him in a haze of agony.

Days passed.

He wasn't sure when the first envelope arrived. He only knew that it was lying there next to his plate of stale bread, white and crossed with handwriting that made his heart stutter in his chest. Max, said the inscription in his mother's round, familiar script, with a row of three kisses beneath. It was the best thing he had ever seen.

In seconds the envelope was open, and its contents lay scattered on the floor: ten snow-white flowers that seemed to glow with their own silver light, and a single sheet of paper scrawled with this message:

> Max, my lovely boy – I'm going to get you out. Soon.
> Until then, eat these. Promise me, Max. Every single one.

Trembling slightly with weakness, wondering if he was

dreaming still, Max took the first flower and put it in his mouth. It sat on his tongue and then dissolved in a rush of sweetness that left a bitter aftertaste in his mouth – like a marshmallow, he thought, with a centre made of ash. For a moment he grimaced. Then he looked back at the note, and he ate another flower, and another, until they were all gone.

After that, Max fell asleep and didn't wake up for twenty-four hours. When he opened his eyes, he felt at once that the pain had begun to ebb – as if warm sunlight was coursing through his bones, chasing the agony away. He was still weak, but he suddenly became aware that he was very, very hungry – hungrier than he could remember being in his whole life. He crawled over to the bread and ate it in three gulps. It was stale and looked rat-nibbled around its edges, but it tasted like the most delicious thing in the world.

For the first time since he'd been captured, Max felt he could breathe properly. He didn't know how she had found him, or why she couldn't come right away, but he knew his mother was alive, and she was coming to rescue him.

So, when another envelope arrived three days later, and another a few days after that, Max ate the flowers without question. Each time, he slept for a day, and woke up feeling different, more himself. The changes were slow. His body was weak from two years of hospitals and medicines and night sweats, his muscles were easily tired, and his breath was short. But even so, being without pain felt better than being a king, or a millionaire. It was as if he'd been carrying an elephant on his back for two years, and now it had dropped away, leaving him suddenly weightless.

With this feeling came more hunger, not to be satisfied by the meagre daily lumps of bread. And with hunger something else returned: his fury. Fury at the men who had attacked his mother and brought him here. Fury at the two years he had lost to illness. It was a feeling so electrifying that not a second of it could be wasted. *Yes*, thought Max.

No matter how weak he remained; no matter how long or short this reprieve, he was going to seize it with both hands.

He was going to escape.

Chapter 5

It started raining in big damp gusts as Daisy walked across the Great Lawn, and she was soaking by the time she ducked through the door of the Five O'Clock shed.

'Avast there, matey,' said Indigo. He was the only other person who'd arrived so far, and he looked her up and down as she came in, dripping water all over the floor. 'Did you fall in the lake?'

'No,' said Daisy, shaking herself off and deciding not to mention what had happened to Madame Gallitrop. 'Just the rain.' It was drumming on the roof so that it felt cosy inside, with the stove glowing and the lamps lit so that the stained-glass panels of the tiny glasshouse shone out like magic lanterns.

Indigo grinned and stroked the parakeet on his shoulder, as Daisy hung up her sopping coat and dropped into one of the squashy chairs around the table with a relieved sigh. Indigo had come to Mallowmarsh when he was five, when his parents had moved from one of the largest pockets in the South American Greenwild. He was about the same age as Daisy – nearly twelve – and he was one of the four members of the Five O'Clock Club, so called because they met at five each afternoon to exchange news and snacks. Besides Daisy and Indigo, the club included Acorn, who was nine, and the Prof, who was twelve: both of them had lived at Mallowmarsh all their lives. When Daisy had first arrived, they had welcomed her into the gang and helped her solve the mystery of Craven: the man who had chased her across Kew Gardens.

Together, they had discovered that Craven was a Botanist who had been stripped of his magic – an unthinkably terrible punishment – for the crime of murdering a fellow explorer. In revenge, he had joined the ranks of the Grim Reapers, who were hunting down Botanists around the world. They were the ones behind Ma's disappearance, and the disappearance of many others.

Indigo pulled a handful of seeds from his pocket to feed Jethro, his parakeet. Then he extracted an eyedropper to feed the baby hedge-piglet that was curled on his lap. It was hot pink and about the size of a teacup. 'Found it in the bushes,' he said, answering Daisy's glance. 'It's the runt of the litter.' Despite the rain, Indigo looked, as always, like he'd been dipped in a vat of sunshine. His skin and eyes were the same gold-brown colour, like raw amber when you hold it up to the light. His brown curls sprang up in all directions, and he was wearing a pair of mud-spattered yellow overalls.

There was noise from the doorway and Daisy looked

around to see the Prof staggering through the door, soaked from head to toe. 'Ugh,' she said, peering into her bag. 'I think the rain got onto my books.' She took out a stack of thick volumes and placed them tenderly in front of the stove to dry. Then she took off her jacket and hung it by the door, revealing a pair of overalls with holes in the elbows. Her halo of dark hair was pulled back from her warm brown cheeks with an old green headband. She looked like an off-duty dancer, too elegant to care how she looked.

Just as the Prof was warming her hands in front of the fire, the final Club member staggered in, even wetter than the rest of them. 'Sorry I'm late,' she said, her voice slightly squeaky. 'Ivy barged in front of me, and I had to wait *ages* for a lilypaddle!'

Acorn Sparkler was younger than the others and very excitable, with bright red hair pulled back in two pigtails and a sweet pale face flecked with hundreds of fawn-coloured freckles, thick as the stars of the Milky Way. She bounced into a chair and began peeling off her socks.

Daisy put the kettle on.

The Prof turned to Daisy as the shed began to fill up with a pleasant warmth. 'I heard something on my way over about a shattered landing stage? Your name – er – might have been mentioned.'

'What happened?' asked Indigo, leaning forward and looking far too interested.

'Nothing,' said Daisy shortly.

Indigo and the Prof exchanged a significant look, and Acorn patted Daisy's hand sympathetically. The three of them knew better than anyone how she had struggled to control her magic over the last three weeks. Daisy had thought, for a long time after her arrival in the Greenwild, that she had no magic. She had also thought that her problems would be solved if only it showed up. She had been wrong on both counts.

'So, is the ship ready?' said Acorn, taking a sip of tea and tactfully changing the subject.

'Yep,' said Daisy. 'All set for tomorrow night.'

Indigo's eyes sparkled. 'And then we'll be on our way.'

'I wonder if I should pack my travelling library,' mused the Prof. 'It's only three suitcases, after all, plus a small handbag for the index.'

'Er . . . I'm not sure,' said Daisy, reaching for the teapot.

There was a contented silence as the four of them munched on teacakes and the Prof turned the pages of the *Greening Standard*, the biggest newspaper in the Greenwild. Then she paused, frowning. 'Listen to this.' She shook the paper and read from an article on the second page. '"An unknown Botanist died minutes after being found alone in the Brazilian Greyside yesterday. The victim displayed no visible signs of injury except a round burn mark on her throat, and a bleaching to the irises of her eyes. 'Like white ice crystals,' said a local man. 'No colour left at all.' The unknown woman's last word was reportedly 'mortal': a tragic reflection of her fate.

'"This is the third such body found in the area in the last two weeks, following the discovery of the remains of French Botanist Eugene Tulipe and Australian Alberta Wattle, both with the same bleached eyes. Local Greenwild authorities are investigating the deaths, but have so far found no significant leads."'

The Prof looked up at the others. 'It's odd, isn't it? Three deaths with no apparent cause. And in Brazil too – in the rainforest.'

'Yes,' said Daisy slowly. 'It is.' Botanists had been vanishing for months, but none had turned up dead – until now. She shivered, thinking of Ma, and felt fear scuttle up her throat like a spider.

'Maybe Artemis will know something about it,' said Indigo.

Artemis had left Mallowmarsh three days ago on a tour of the European pockets, gathering Botanists to join their rescue mission ('Germany will be crucial,' she had said, 'we'll want their support.'). She wasn't due back until late that evening, and Daisy felt her fingers itch with impatience and dread.

People were dying. There was no more time to waste.

Chapter 6

Escaping, Max soon discovered, was easier said than done.

He continued to grow a little stronger with each delivery of the magical white flowers, but it was slow. His legs were about as tough as noodles, and even crossing the cellar left him breathless. He began to train himself, walking from one end of the room to the other until he could do it five times in a row, then ten, then twenty. He tried not to think about whether he was 'cured'. Instead, he focused on getting stronger; a little more every day.

Sooner or later, he thought, the guards would make a mistake – and he needed to be ready. The moment his fever had lifted, Max had begun marking the passing days by scratching the brick wall of his cellar with a stray nail. By this reckoning, it was exactly two weeks after he first started feeling better that he finally had his chance.

Max loved two things: listening to music and picking locks. He had lost his heart to music in his cradle, and whenever he had gone missing as a small child, he had usually been found hiding near the concert hall in Bolderdash, or sitting underneath the gramophone in his neighbour's house, his face pale and ecstatic as he listened to reams of Beethoven and Bach.

The lock-picking was something he had acquired later, when he had needed to keep his hands busy in hospital. The days there seemed to last for centuries, and he had persuaded his mother to bring him a steady supply of different locks, picks and combinations. By the end of two years, there was very little he couldn't open. Like music, lock-picking required a sort of perfect pitch – a sense of flair and timing. Opening locks became a thing that could be mastered; something he could control when everything else was spinning away from him.

Anyway, Max hadn't been able to pick the lock on his cell because the nail he'd found was too thick for the job. But that morning, the broken-nosed guard (Max had heard the others calling him Jarndyce) had been careless. He had clattered down Max's morning bread ration with an unlovely smile, and hadn't noticed the badge falling from his cloak. It was black with a symbol of a scythe on it, and it had a long needle-like pin at the back. There was a second guard – a less terrifying one – posted outside his door at all times, so Max had to work quietly. A few hours later, he was ready.

As the second guard approached the door to deliver his evening ration, Max sprang forward with the nail in his hand and raked the man across the cheek. The guard gave a cry and fell backwards as Max leapt past him and away up the stairs. His legs were already burning with the effort, his lungs heaving for air. Somehow, he made it to the top and caught a blur of kitchen counters and clanging pans as he rushed through, sending a whistling kettle toppling in his wake. The guard chasing him cried out as boiling water splashed his arm, and he fell back cursing. Then Max spotted Jarndyce, who yelled and leapt to his feet. Max gasped and put on a burst of speed. Then he was in a dim corridor with a door at the end of it, and – *yes!* – it was open, and he was out on the street, beneath the orange glow of the streetlamps, taking in great gulps of fresh air for the first time in almost a month. It tasted like iced water, pure as the moonlight pouring down around him.

Max glanced wildly to both sides. Jarndyce and the other guard were already coming after him through the door. Max staggered down the street, reeled around the corner, and tripped over a grate in the middle of the road. It wasn't quite closed. Max glanced over his shoulder. The two men were gaining fast. His muscles were exhausted, and he knew he couldn't run any further. He pushed the grate aside, took a deep breath, and dropped down into the darkness.

He landed hard on the floor of a sewer tunnel. Jarndyce peered down through the grate and Max shrank back. 'Come back, boy.' His voice was a low snarl. 'Or you'll regret it.' He tried to squeeze his shoulders through the hole in the pavement, but it was too small. In almost any other circumstance, this might have been funny, but Max didn't wait to see if he'd manage it. Instead, he lurched on, down the long, black tunnel and into darkness.

That had been two days ago. Two days of hunger so consuming that it seemed to be eating him from the inside, until he was all air and nerves stretched tight as piano wires. Even the terrible, wretched smell – like being stuck inside a toilet bend with no way out – didn't seem to dampen his appetite. He'd spent the first day underground completely lost, shivering and cold. He'd spent the second day equally freezing, but he had managed to locate a second grate. There was a ladder bolted to the wall, and he'd climbed it, looking out for Jarndyce – and when he'd seen that the coast was clear, he pushed up at the grate with his aching shoulders and emerged into the air of London. It seemed to glitter around him with frost, each breath deliriously clean and sweet after the smell of the sewers. It was night again and the sparkle of city lights shimmered against the million cold fractals of the air.

Food. He needed food.

Glancing several times each way, Max took a deep breath and set off down the street.

Chapter 7

Daisy was quiet and distracted when they got back to the Roost, and accidentally put a teaspoon of salt into the mug of tea that Miss Tufton set in front of her.

'What's wrong?' asked the old housekeeper as Daisy spluttered and set down her mug. 'You look like you've had a bad shock.'

The kitchen was as cosy and warm as ever, the surfaces piled with chipped plates, flowerpots, wooden spoons and creased books, and the ancient roof beams hung with copper pots and fragrant bushels of rosemary and thyme. There was a gnarled old tree growing directly out of one of the wooden kitchen counters, half its branches covered with cherries, and the other half with ripe apples. It was called a larder tree, because it could produce any fruit you could imagine (as long as you asked nicely).

Daisy explained about the article as Miss Tufton set down a fresh cup of tea in front of her. The piece had been accompanied by a photograph of the dead woman: her open eyes as white as ice crystals.

'So you saw that, did you?' Miss Tufton tutted and

picked up her rolling pin. 'We don't know who's behind it.'

'But the bleached eyes – it seems so . . .'

Miss Tufton began rolling out pastry. 'It's not like anything I've heard of before – and not like any poison or curse that I've come across either. It's unnatural, like . . .' She paused and shook her head.

'Like what?'

'Nothing.' Miss Tufton stomped across to the stove, the knitting needles in her hair bristling.

Daisy took a deep breath. 'This changes things. People aren't just disappearing. They're dying.'

'I know,' said the housekeeper, looking suddenly very tired. She sat down in the rocking chair next to the stove and took off her slippers to rub wearily at her bunions.

'Ma's out there,' said Daisy. 'Every day she could be—' She stopped, unable to finish the thought. Instead, she said, 'But we're setting off soon. Tomorrow I'll be on that boat, on the way to the Amazon. Ma needs me.'

Miss Tufton looked up at her, surprised. 'But children are no longer coming on the expedition. Oh Daisy, did no one tell you . . . ?'

'What? Tell me what?' Daisy's forehead began to throb dangerously.

'Well,' said Tuffy carefully. 'The rescue mission is going to be dangerous and difficult. And with the Grim Reapers getting stronger, and this news of people turning up dead . . . well, the council has decided that it's not safe for underage

Botanists. This is a job for trained adults, Daisy; not eleven-year-old girls.'

'But I can be useful!' she cried. 'I've proved that, haven't I?' Ever since Daisy had defeated Craven and saved Mallowmarsh from being burned to the ground, people had looked at her a little differently, nodding at her as they ate lunch in the Orangery or calling out greetings as they hurried past on their way to the Seed Bank. Gulliver Wildish, the Head of the Great Glasshouse, had been extra patient as her newly discovered magic backfired on her day after day. Madame Gallitrop (though admittedly this was before today's disaster) had presented her with a beautifully illustrated book on the palm trees of Amazeria. And the terrifying head chef, Mr McGuffin, a Scot with a large, ginger moustache and a set of knuckle tattoos, had slipped her an extra slice of apple tart at teatime the previous day – an act so astonishing that Indigo had stared in disbelief.

But now, Miss Tufton shook her head slowly. 'I don't think the commander will see it like that,' she said.

'See it like what?' came a voice from the doorway. It was Artemis herself, looking tired. The lines around her eyes were deeper than usual, and her overalls looked crumpled. 'The Germans are on board,' she said. 'And I think I've persuaded the Albanian pockets too, but the others were more of a chal—'

'Artemis! You're back!' Daisy leapt up, spilling her tea.

'I can come with you on the ship, can't I? I need to be there, I can help, I can—'

But Artemis, unwinding a scarf from around her neck, was already shaking her head. 'No, Daisy. I'm sorry, but things have changed. This isn't an expedition for children.'

'But . . .' Daisy trailed off. She could see from Artemis's expression that it was no use arguing. It was just like when Ma had set out for the Amazon. She was being left behind all over again.

Daisy stayed silent as Artemis and Miss Tufton talked, but her mind was working furiously. Her worry about Ma felt like a giant hand pressing down on top of her head, impossible to ignore.

Whatever Artemis said, Daisy needed to be on that ship. Her palms itched again, and she rubbed them against her shirt.

It was time to take matters into her own hands.

Chapter 8

Max had never felt so cold in his life. He was still wearing the shorts he'd put on the morning they'd left New York all those weeks ago, and his T-shirt now had a rip in the hem. He realized, in a distant way, that he probably smelled quite bad.

This part of London was very quiet and eerie by night, and the street was empty except for a fox that trotted, stiff-tailed and confident, down the pavement before him. It paused to rummage in a pile of rubbish and extracted a tasty morsel before leaping along a neighbouring wall, eyes glinting in the streetlamps.

It was the fox that gave Max the idea.

He would need bins.

Not the small ones on the street, but the big skips that sometimes sat outside supermarkets, where they dumped leftover food at the end of the day. This meant crossing the long street with its dark trees and sleeping houses, then slipping onto the shuttered high street that lay beyond. It was spooky and deserted here, with the occasional car swishing up and down the road and plastic signs lit up in neon colours that left blue and red shadows across the inside of his eyelids. He darted down a side alley and – 'Bingo,' he said, looking at the open skip against the far wall. He could see several sandwiches on top, still in their wrappers, glinting enticingly as treasure. He reached inside and then heard a noise behind him.

Max was behind the skip before he'd had the chance to form a thought. He stood hidden, barely breathing, peering out from beneath lowered lids to stop his pupils catching the light. The man in the alley had thick, muscled shoulders and a shaved head that shone in the dim light. His broken nose was unmistakeable.

Jarndyce.

He held a device up to his mouth and spoke softly into it, his voice only a murmur in the quiet alley. 'Yes, that's right,'

he said. 'He can't have gone far on so little food. No, well – you tell me.' He paused. 'Okay, yes – I'll let you know when we find him. Yes – at Moonmarket, Wednesday midnight. I'll bring him with me through the entrance at West India Docks.' The man passed within a metre of Max's hiding place and for a moment he seemed to pause and narrow his eyes.

Then a rustle came from the end of the alleyway – the fox! – and the man turned, distracted, and hurried towards it.

Max stood there, shaking so hard that he had to clench his jaws to stop his teeth from chattering. Then he took a breath, ducked around the skip, stuffed three sandwiches into his pockets, and ran as fast as he could.

Max wasn't sure how long he ran for – but it was long enough for his legs to go weak and begin wobbling beneath him. Long enough for the streets to grow wide and tree-lined, with gracious steps leading up to gleaming front doors, and thick curtains drawn back from windows that shone with warm light. At last, he ducked through a brick archway onto a mews street of romantic little houses with flowers tumbling from their window boxes. The pastel-painted house fronts glowed softly in the streetlamps as he tore the wrapper from his first sandwich. He wolfed it down so fast he barely chewed. After the second sandwich, he paused and swallowed, then ate the third more slowly, savouring each bite. It was only cheese and tomato, but it tasted better than anything he could remember eating in his whole life. There was a fruit tree growing in the front garden of one of the nearby houses, and the owners had put out a box of leftover apples for passers-by to take. Max selected one, rubbed it on his grimy shirt, and bit into it with a giant, satisfying crunch. It had streaky red skin, and it tasted sharp and sweet, like the start of something new.

For a moment, he allowed his thoughts to turn to his mother; to her grey eyes and her unexpected, honking laugh that she saved mostly for him. Then Max remembered that he'd spent most of the last two years fighting with her – over his treatment, his medicines, everything. When he found her, he decided, the first thing he'd do would be to say sorry.

Max was just crunching into his second apple when he heard a noise behind him: a soft movement of leather boot on paving stone. He whirled round and saw a man coming through the archway of the mews. Not Jarndyce, but just as sinister looking. He was very tall, with dark eyes and a shock of bone-white hair swept back from his pale face. He walked with a slight limp, and by his side padded an enormous hound with drool dripping from its fangs. The dog growled and bared its canines. It sounded like a small motorcycle revving up.

'Max?' said the man as Max shrank back. 'Max Brightly. We've been looking for you. We—'

But Max had already ducked, turned, and was gone. All that was left was an apple with a single bite taken out of it, spinning on the pavement.

Chapter 9

'There's got to be a way to get on that ship,' said Daisy.

It was the next day, and she was striding up and down inside the tiny space of the Five O'Clock shed, while the Prof brewed tea on the small camping stove and passed around pieces of lavender shortbread they'd filched from the kitchen at the Roost. Acorn was perched in the corner, where she'd been watering the chocolate tree with fresh milk. It grew small balls of milk chocolate from its branches, each one about the size and shape of a blueberry. The more milk you used to water the tree, the lighter the chocolate became, so you could adjust it to your taste.

Acorn frowned, putting down the milk jug. 'Get onto the ship? But wouldn't someone notice?' Acorn was the youngest and quietest member of the Five O'Clock Club, but, Daisy thought, also the bravest. She had come with them to Moonmarket three weeks ago when they'd thought that Sheldrake – a terrifying Botanist with bone-white hair and a giant bloodhound called Brutus – had stolen Daisy's dandelight. The fact that the glowing glass orb acted like a compass, leading its holder to the nearest door into the

Greenwild, meant that it would be 'disastrous' (the Prof's word) if it fell into the wrong hands ('Understatement of the century,' said Indigo). In theory, only people with green magic could pass through the doors between the Greyside and the Greenwild – but the dandelight worked like a sort of master key, allowing you through even if you didn't have magic. It was also very rare. According to Artemis, there were only three known dandelights in existence – and one of them belonged to Daisy.

Anyway, it had turned out that Sheldrake hadn't stolen the dandelight after all. No, that had been a woman called Marigold Brightly, the brand-new Keeper of the Seed Bank. She had been blackmailed by Craven, who had kidnapped her son Max and promised her his freedom in exchange for the dandelight. That was how the Grim Reapers had got into Mallowmarsh in the end. And after the battle, when Craven had been defeated, Artemis had returned the dandelight to its rightful owner. 'I'm trusting you with this, Daisy,' she'd said, looking hard at her granddaughter. 'It belonged to your father. Carrying it is a great responsibility.'

Now, Daisy brought her attention back to the shed and the question of how to get onto the ship. 'The fleet is guarded night and day by the Mallowmarshals,' she said. 'Only grown-ups are allowed near it.'

The Prof wrinkled her forehead. 'There must be a way,' she murmured, sprinkling sugar carefully into her tea.

Indigo shrugged and spoke through an enormous

mouthful of shortbread. 'It can't be that hard, can it? We just cause a diversion and sneak on board when no one is paying attention.'

'We?' Daisy looked at him, eyebrows raised. 'You mean you still want to come?'

The other three members of the club stared at her as if she was being particularly dim-witted. The Prof was the first to speak. 'Of course we're coming, you idiot. My grandfather is out there, remember?'

'And my dad,' said Acorn, her voice small but determined.

'And I wouldn't miss this for the whole Greenwild,' said Indigo.

'Oh,' said Daisy. And despite everything, she smiled.

Then she cleared her throat and nodded at Indigo. 'All right then. What sort of diversion did you have in mind?'

Indigo looked thoughtful. 'There's a colony of piffleflicks that lives on the shores of the lake. They're a bit fretful at this time of year because they're busy building their nests.' He sipped his tea meditatively. 'They don't like being disturbed.'

'Well,' said the Prof, 'the full moon is tomorrow night. So, we'd better get planning.'

Ten minutes later, they had the outlines of a plan and Daisy was feeling cautiously confident. The Prof sat back with a sigh of satisfaction. 'Great,' she said. 'Now we can reward ourselves with a bit of revision.'

Indigo groaned. 'Now? Really, Prof?'

'Yes, really,' she said, spectacles flashing. 'Don't you *want* to get into Bloomquist?'

As Daisy had learned when she'd first arrived, the Mallowmarsh school only went up to the age of twelve, after which the best students were admitted into an elite academy for the study of plant magic, called Bloomquist. Selection was based on a series of three tests, and Daisy, Indigo and the Prof had already taken the first one (Acorn, only nine, was still too young). It had included a terrifying encounter with a snake-headed hydra plant – something that still gave Daisy nightmares, even though the three of them had passed.

Now they were busy revising for the second Bloomquist test – a written exam that would assess their knowledge of plant names and properties ('to the limit', Madame Gallitrop had said with relish) – which was due to take place in a matter of weeks. But Daisy found it hard to concentrate on this when there was so much else at stake. Who cared about getting into a magical school when Ma was missing and a rescue mission was about to set out to search for her?

To the Prof, however, a test was a test, no matter the circumstances.

'What are the main properties of venomous snake-root?' she asked now, quizzing Daisy from one of her immaculate colour-coded notecards.

'I don't know,' said Daisy, doodling an outline of the

Amazon River on her notebook.

'Come on,' said the Prof. 'The clue is in the name. *Venomous* snake-root? It's poisonous enough that a single bite from its fangs could kill a grown man.' She paused. 'Okay, how about this. What is bone coral and where is it most commonly found?'

Daisy shrugged. 'In the sea?'

The Prof sighed. 'Sort of. It's a coral that feeds on the bones of the drowned. It's most often found near big shipwrecks.'

'Okay,' said Daisy, interested despite herself. 'What does it do?'

Indigo grabbed the Prof's notecard and scanned the page. 'Ooh, listen to this! It says the coral is full of pearls made from drowned men's eyes.' He frowned and read aloud: '"The pearls are of such surpassing beauty and splendour that many risk their lives to bring them up from the depths of the ocean."'

The Prof shuddered and grabbed the notecards back from him. 'All right, that's enough. I say it's time for more tea.'

Chapter 10

The sun was setting as they walked back from the Roost, sinking beyond the line of trees and trailing bands of pink along the rim of the sky. Daisy looked up at the Heart Oak, which stood solid and magnificent at the edge of the lake. All the magic of Mallowmarsh was rooted in this ancient tree, which had flourished on this spot for the centuries since the pocket had been founded. Now, though, she saw that one of the branches was completely white, like a bone, with withered leaves.

She frowned and knelt among the tree's gnarled roots. The soil was white and dry when she rubbed it between her fingers, as if all the colour had been sucked away.

'Look at this,' she murmured as the Prof joined her.

'Strange,' said the Prof, frowning. 'I saw something similar in the Sump-Rose Garden yesterday. The earth there was bleached – and some of the roses had shrivelled up and turned white.'

Daisy was about to ask another question when Napoleon meowed from his spot on her shoulder. He'd seen it a split second before she had: a dot approaching from the west, getting larger with each passing second. It was a parakeet, with something tied around its leg. 'A message!' she cried as the bird came closer. Her pulse hammered in her throat. It probably wasn't from Ma, she told herself fiercely. She mustn't hope.

But now she saw that the parakeet was being pursued by two great ravens swooping down on it from either side, dwarfing it with their shadowy black wings.

'Indigo!' screamed Daisy. 'They're attacking! Do something!'

Indigo glanced up and took in the situation in a moment. He stood with his hands clenched, concentrating with every part of his body.

'I can't reach them,' he said at last. 'The ravens – their minds are closed off.' The parakeet gave an exhausted surge forward just as the closer of the two ravens swooped. The smaller bird let out a sharp little cry and one of its wings seemed to buckle. They all began to run, and Daisy saw

Jethro dart out under Indigo's command and dive-bomb one of the ravens from above in a manoeuvre that caused it to swerve, buying the other parakeet a few precious seconds. 'Come on,' Indigo was muttering. 'Come on, come on.' He sprinted forward, his cupped palms outstretched. The parakeet put on a last, desperate burst of speed, and collapsed into Indigo's waiting hands. The two ravens cawed furiously and swerved away, leaving great claw-shaped gouges in the roofs of the nearest treehouses.

'Vandals,' cried the Prof, shaking her fist at them. 'Hooligans. Ostrogoths!'

Daisy hurried over to Indigo and bent over the small bird, which was panting with tiny, rapid movements of its chest. She found that she was trembling, and her fingers shook as she removed the message from around the parakeet's leg.

My rascal, began the message, and Daisy's heart pounded. For a moment her eyes were too blurred to read, and she had to brush at them roughly with the edge of her sleeve. Then she took a deep breath and looked again at Ma's familiar handwriting, dashing and bold and inky on the rough paper.

I am sorry it took me so long to send this, it began.

Unfortunately, it is tricky to write when one is a prisoner in a bunker forty feet underground – let alone to seek out paper and pen, or to locate the single airshaft a parakeet might access. Even now that I have my bearings, I must keep this short. But first, Daisy, joonam, I am sorry for not being there to pick you up from school at Christmas. You can't imagine how I tortured myself with what you must have thought. When I woke up after the plane crash and found myself in this cell, I was weak and confused; and then I was weak and angry. I began to understand that there were dozens of other prisoners here: other Botanists.

Now I must take a deep breath and explain. Botanists, Daisy, are people who can do plant magic. I am a Botanist, and so are you. Forgive me for telling you none of this before. I thought I was keeping you safe, but I was wrong. Many of us are disappearing, and that is why I came to the Amazon: to find out why.

It turns out that getting captured myself was a rather extreme way of conducting my research, but it seems to be working. The organization behind the disappearances is called the Grim Reapers and they want to take green magic for themselves. I am hoping that by now you have followed my instructions and used your father's dandelight to get into the Greenwild. I hope that you have found Mallowmarsh and that you are learning about the world I kept from you. I visited Mallowmarsh once with your father – but I don't know who is in charge there now; so, I send this message to you to pass on:

Do not come after me, Daisy. The Grim Reapers are more dangerous than you can possibly imagine. Their numbers are bigger than I had conceived, their aims more deadly. This is a war, and the Amazon rainforest is the front line of *the battle. Tell the people of Mallowmarsh: come with help, or not at all. Find the people of Iffenwild and bring them here. Their power may be our only hope.*

Darling Daisy, joon-e-delam – the writing became hurried and scrawled here – *I am out of time, and I must send this. This may be my last letter for a while. It comes with all my love, always.*

Ma

Daisy blinked and looked up, surprised to find herself still on the Great Lawn of Mallowmarsh with the yew trees rising around her. She took a deep breath, dizzy with what she'd read.

Ma was alive, but she was in danger. Ma needed help. Daisy looked up again with dry and bright eyes and clenched the letter in her fist. She would find the people of Iffenwild, whoever or whatever they were. She would take them to the Amazon to help Ma. Then, together, they would fight to save the Greenwild.

Daisy lay awake for a long time that night, unable to sleep. Napoleon too seemed restless, sitting on the ledge of the round attic window and looking out across the sleeping grounds of Mallowmarsh. She had rushed to show Ma's letter to Artemis, along with its final instruction. 'Where is Iffenwild?' she had asked. 'What kind of power is Ma talking about?'

Artemis scanned the letter and asked her to describe exactly how and when it had arrived. 'Right,' she said, handing it back as Daisy finished talking. 'I'll discuss this with Sheldrake and the rest of the council.'

It was only after she'd gone that Daisy realized Artemis hadn't answered either of her questions.

Chapter 11

It was almost midnight now, but the sky outside was filled with an eerie glow. It was snowing. Daisy pulled her blankets around her and crossed to the window to watch as flakes settled in glittering drifts around the Roost, dusting every twig and branch of the great tree.

Napoleon curled up on top of her left foot as they gazed out together and she remembered the last time she had seen snow – over three years ago. She and Ma had been in Krakow, where Ma was writing a story about the Polish elections. Daisy had woken in their rented apartment to the sound of silvery bells ringing across the frozen air. She and Ma had breakfasted on hot chocolate and tangerines, sitting like marmosets in a nest of blankets while fat white snowflakes fluttered past the windows. Outside, the streets of Krakow were buried in snowdrifts and the air was diamond-dusted with ice. When they stepped into the street, the snow creaked under their boots and settled on their eyelashes. Ma grinned.

'Let's go!'

'Race you!' yelled Daisy.

With shouts and battle cries, they slid and sprinted through the snow to the top of the nearest hill. That afternoon was a blur of sledge-races and snowball fights and breathless cold. It had been perfect. But then, any time spent with Ma was extraordinary, as if someone had turned up the volume and colour on life.

Daisy sighed and shook herself. The snow outside was turning to rain now, and the window was spattered with silver drops. The treehouse swayed and Daisy's room in the canopy felt like a small boat floating on a dark sea. She tried to imagine herself stowing away on the Mallowmarsh ship, sailing for the Amazon – or perhaps, if Ma's letter was right, for a mysterious place called Iffenwild. What would happen if they were discovered? Or if she lost control of her magic again?

'We'll just have to risk it,' she told Napoleon. 'It's too

important not to try.' The little cat meowed in agreement and sharpened a claw on the windowsill.

Together, they looked out into the dark. The rain was slackening, and as Daisy opened the window to let in the cool air, she heard voices drifting up from the kitchen two storeys below. Artemis was saying something about travel timings and Daisy leaned as far as she could out of the window to listen. It was no use – the voices were too faint. Instead, she scooped Napoleon onto her shoulder and hurried into the corridor and down the stairs, skipping the tread that creaked, until she was crouched on the landing above the kitchen, close enough to make out the conversation over the soft murmur of rain.

'I lost him,' said a deep voice. Sheldrake, Artemis's second in command. Daisy pictured his white hair, the great form of Brutus slumped snoring at his feet. 'I tracked him all the way to Notting Hill, but he ran the moment he saw me. He wasn't fast, but I couldn't chase him with my leg the way it is. I caught it in a rabbit trap last week.'

'Are you sure it was him, Ferrus?' Artemis's voice was urgent, worried.

'Of course. Marigold showed me photos of him – those cheekbones, that hair. And the birthmark under his right eye – unmistakeable.' He paused. 'The boy ran before I could tell him that we only wanted to bring him to safety. I'm pretty certain he's being tracked by the Grim Reapers, though he's done a good job of evading them so far.'

Miss Tufton grunted. 'That'll be why he ran. How was the boy to know you weren't a Reaper?'

Artemis sighed and Daisy imagined her pressing her fingers together. 'Well, let's keep the search parties out. We've got to find him before they do.'

'Yes,' said Sheldrake. 'And it had better be before we leave for the Amazon.'

'I don't know, Ferrus,' said Artemis, sounding tired. 'Is that still the right thing to do? The reports we're getting out of the rainforest – well, they're bad. We'd be foolish to lead our people into a place like that without enough back-up. Even with the Germans and the rest alongside us, it may not be enough. These people have guns. It could end in a massacre.' She exhaled. 'Daisy's mother might be right. We need more support. We're going into the heart of a rainforest, remember. Their power could turn the tide – quite literally.'

Daisy leaned forward, knuckles white as she gripped the wooden banisters.

Whose power? Were they talking about Iffenwild?

'Ah, of course!' There was a sarcastic edge to Sheldrake's voice. 'Why didn't I think of that? Oh yes – maybe because it's a murderous nation that exists only in myths and stories for small children.'

'I don't think so,' said Artemis, sounding thoughtful. 'There's good evidence to show that it exists. And if that's the case—'

'No,' said Sheldrake. The rain had stopped, and his voice was clear. 'We don't have time to go chasing daydreams. We need to get to the Amazon as soon as—'

Daisy leaned forward again and this time the banister creaked.

'What was that?'

Daisy heard Sheldrake's heavy footsteps, one foot dragging slightly, as he moved towards the kitchen door.

By the time he reached it, Daisy was already halfway back to her room and the landing was as quiet as the tranquil sky.

Chapter 12

Max was very tired now, and colder than ever. The three sandwiches already felt like a long time ago and his tongue was dry and sandy.

Hearing that dog racing after him had been the worst thing of all. He shuddered, remembering its panting breaths, the drool dripping from its fangs. He'd darted into a doorway, too tired to run anymore, and pulled a stinking piece of cardboard over himself. Then he'd closed his eyes and prayed for the dog to leave him alone. Someone must have been listening, because a great torrent of water had rushed out of a nearby drainpipe, drenching the dog from nose to tail. The hound had leapt about a foot in the air, turned a few circles, and loped slowly back to the man at the other end of the alley.

Max sighed. His arms felt shaky with relief.

A plan, he thought. *What is the plan?* He heard his mother's low, determined voice, speaking to someone in the hospital corridor after another scan, another test. 'What are our next steps, doctor? What is the plan?'

It came to him with sudden clarity.

He wouldn't be safe for as long as he was in the Greyside. What he needed was to get into the Greenwild. He needed to find his mother. All the envelopes she'd sent him over the last three weeks had borne the same return address:

Marigold Brightly,

The Seed Bank,

Mallowmarsh,

British Republic of the Greenwild

Mallowmarsh, he thought. The word felt like a prayer. But how to get there? The doorways into the Greenwild were secret for a reason: to stop people like Jarndyce from finding their way in. Max knew where to find the entrance to Bolderdash, the American pocket where he and his mother had lived until he was ten. You got in through a golden door – one that only Botanists could see – in a great craggy rock in the New York Botanical Gardens. This had been before he'd become sick, before his mother had tried and given up on Greenwild medicine and turned to the Greyside for new treatments. But he had no idea how to get into Mallowmarsh, except that the entrance was probably somewhere in London.

Think, he told himself. *There must be a way*. He looked into the distance for a moment and then shook his head. It was a wild, ridiculous idea. But it was all he had.

Chapter 13

'Iffenwild?' said the Prof the following morning as they made their way out of the Orangery after breakfast. 'I've never heard of it.'

Daisy glanced at her. 'Artemis seemed to recognize the name. But then I asked Miss Tufton this morning and she said she had no idea.'

'Ugh!' The Prof raised her eyes to the sky. 'What is it with grown-ups and not telling us the things we need to know? I say we go to the library and find out for ourselves. There isn't much time. The ship leaves tonight.'

Daisy followed, thinking longingly of the Greyside internet.

'Right,' said the Prof as the Five O'Clock Club walked through the tall glass doors of the library. 'Remember, we're looking for any mention of Iffenwild, no matter how small.'

This was a daunting task. The library was the size of ten great cathedrals, with towering oak trees holding up the vaulted glass roof, so that it felt like a rustling indoor forest. The trunk of each tree was packed with shelves, and there were more shelves all the way around the walls, with hundreds of little staircases and ladders going up and down between them, and tall windows framing the blue sky outside. There were friendly round tables clustered in groups on the scuffed oak floor, and mismatched armchairs lit by green reading lamps, where Botanists sat leafing through volumes and making notes. Floating high in the air between the oaks were dozens of hot-air balloons in every shape and size, crossing and re-crossing the vast leafy space like lazy kites, with Botanists leaning out of their baskets, plucking books from the shelves as they sailed by.

'The balloons are a new feature,' said the Prof. 'They're enchanted not to get tangled up in the trees. Now come ON.' She tugged Daisy forward with one hand and Acorn with the other, leaving Indigo to trot beside them as they made their way towards a docking station at the centre of the room where several hot-air balloons sat tethered and waiting to be used.

Heading straight for the nearest balloon, the Prof fired up the burner and attached a small valve so that the blue silk began to fill with gas and strain against its rope. Her hands were quick and sure, and she called cheerily to the pink-haired librarian sitting at the desk in the corner of the library: 'Hello, Mr Monocot.'

'Hello, Prof,' he called back. 'Remember, the balloons have a fifty-kilo book-weight limit. We don't want a repeat of last time.'

'What happened last time?' asked Indigo, looking worried.

The Prof pretended not to hear. 'Come on,' she said, clambering into the woven willow basket. Acorn and Indigo followed. Daisy went last, glad that Napoleon was hidden inside her jacket. She wasn't sure pets were allowed on hot-air balloons, even in magical libraries.

Then the Prof released the sandbags attached to the basket and Daisy watched the leaf-strewn floor fall away as they soared towards the canopy of oak trees. The air smelled of new leaves and old paper, a delicious scent that was cosy and sharp and exciting all at once. Indigo called out the sections as they floated upwards and shelves of books came into view around them. 'General Fiction; Botanical Cookery; Arboreal Architecture; Green Music . . . Aha! The Greenwild Geography section. Let's start here.'

They were halfway up one of the tallest oaks, and the Prof showed Daisy how to turn down the balloon valve so that they hovered in place. Then she tossed a vine over the side of the basket and, with flawless control, directed it to curl around the branch next to the shelf they needed. Daisy watched enviously as the vine looped itself around the tree and tied itself into a neat sailing knot.

The four of them scoured the shelves and pulled out anything that looked promising. There were tiny books the size of Daisy's thumbnail, covered in ruby silk, and giant leather-bound volumes big enough to crush a rhinoceros, and everything in between. They soared five storeys up into the tower that housed Botanical History, stacking up books as they went.

'Right,' said the Prof when it was clear that they were struggling to stay airborne. 'That should be enough to begin with.'

'You think?' muttered Indigo.

The Prof ignored him. She spun the valve and the balloon sank gently back towards the ground.

They arrived with a soft bump and tumbled out of the basket, hefting their piles of books towards a group of green-leather armchairs beneath an oak tree.

'Okay,' said the Prof, allocating a stack to each of them. 'Focus, everyone.'

Indigo rolled his eyes, but the Prof got her way. The next hour passed in silence, apart from the noise of pages turning and the odd acorn falling onto the desk. Daisy had a stack of map books and atlases with gold edges, and she scoured each volume for clues. Napoleon helped, holding down the pages of the bigger books. But not one of them mentioned a place called Iffenwild.

She sighed and the Prof looked up from a book called *Islands of the Greenwild: A Botanists' Guide*. 'Any luck?'

'No,' said Daisy, closing a volume called *Pirate Botany: A Swashbuckling History* with a dispirited thump.

'Me neither,' said Indigo. Acorn, who had caught a cold after the rainstorm the previous day, shook her head and sneezed. The noise echoed around the hushed library and Napoleon jumped, sending a small mountain of books and pamphlets crashing to the floor. An apprentice reading at a nearby table turned and shushed them with a nasty glare. But Daisy wasn't paying attention. She was too busy staring at the slim volume that had fallen at her feet. It must have been wedged inside one of the bigger books, she thought, which was why they hadn't spotted it before. It was much older than the others, with a red cloth cover so faded it was almost pink, and worn edges that glittered dully with white crystals.

'Is that . . . sea salt?' whispered Indigo.

The faded gold lettering across the cover spelled out three words. Daisy squinted down at them:

The Wild Atlas.

The covers opened with a puff of dust and salt. There, in the index, sixth from the top, was a line that made Daisy's heart beat in double time.

Kingdom of Iffenwild: Capital of the Marindeep.

Chapter 14

Daisy couldn't concentrate that afternoon.

Iffenwild.

She rolled the name around in her head like a wish.
Iffenwild. Once they'd found the name in *The Wild Atlas*,
the Prof had leapt into action and fired up the balloon for a
second voyage around the library. This time, she returned
with a smaller pile of books. The spines, as she set them
down on their table, were dusty and faded from neglect,
with titles like *Memories of the Marindeep* and *Island
Commonwealth: The Lost Pockets of the Ocean.*

'My grandfather used to tell me stories about the
Marindeep,' she said, her eyes flicking over the pages as she
turned them. 'The story goes that there was once a whole
federation of ocean pockets – islands and lagoon cities –
whose magic harnessed the power of the sea, in the same way
that the Greenwild harnesses the green magic of the land.
Greenwild and Marindeep – the two halves of the magical
world. Equal and united.' She paused, her eyes scanning a
tightly printed page. 'Here we are.' She read aloud:

'"From the middle of the nineteenth century, the ocean

pockets of the Marindeep became increasingly distressed by the damage caused by humans to the world's oceans. Instead of trying to fight this damage, the maritime pockets decided to cut themselves off from the outer world in order to preserve their own safety."'

'That's the opposite to the Greenwild,' said Daisy, surprised.

'Exactly,' said the Prof. 'Most Greenwild pockets made the decision long ago to stand and fight the damage being done in the Greyside.' She paused, scanning the page in front of her. 'Listen to this,' she said, and read from the book.

'"The Marindeep turned their backs on the outer world once and for all – and they cut themselves off from the Greenwild for its refusal to do the same. Ever since, the coasts and islands of the Marindeep – from Atlantis to Lyonesse – have been known as 'the Lost Pockets', and their existence has slipped out of memory and into myth. They are not often spoken of among Greenwilders today, except in stories for children. Indeed, many believe that the Marindeep – and its marvellous capital city, Iffenwild – no longer exist, placing them in the same category as kelpies and krakens."'

Daisy looked at the others. Their eyes were as wide as saucers, and Acorn's mouth was hanging open slightly. '*This is it*,' said Daisy urgently. 'This is what Ma meant. She thinks that the Lost Pockets can be found, and that they can help us defeat the Reapers. Iffenwild is the capital – that must be why it's the one she wants us to find.'

'But . . . no one knows where these pockets *are*,' said Indigo. 'So how are we supposed to find them?'

'Aha! You're forgetting this map,' said the Prof triumphantly, snatching up *The Wild Atlas* and spreading it open on the page labelled *Iffenwild*. 'Oh,' she said, and frowned. The faded map showed an island in the centre of a lagoon that opened out its arms to the sea. There was a smattering of smaller islands all around it, and the edges of the page were decorated with tiny whales and hurricanes, as though the mapmaker had got caught up in fanciful doodles while he was drawing.

'Location Unknown', read the scroll at the top of the page.

They looked at each other. 'What now, genius?' said Indigo.

Daisy waited carefully for the right moment to talk to Artemis, catching her just as she was finishing a slice of treacle tart after lunch at the Roost.

'About this expedition,' she said hesitantly.

'Yes, Daisy?'

It came out in a rush. 'Have you had a chance to think about Ma's letter? Shouldn't we try to do what it says and find Iffenwild – before we go to the Amazon, I mean? We know it's the capital of the Marindeep. What if they can help us?'

'Ah,' said Artemis. 'I see you've done your research.' She rubbed her forehead wearily. 'No Greenwilder has entered the Marindeep for centuries, Daisy. And no one knows where the doorway into Iffenwild is, if indeed it still exists. We don't have time to sail the seven seas searching for it. Many Botanists have tried before, and failed.'

'But—' said Daisy.

'No,' said Artemis. 'I've discussed it with the council and we're in agreement. We go to the Amazon tonight. Isn't that what you wanted? You've been talking about nothing else for weeks.'

'I know,' said Daisy miserably. 'But that was before Ma's letter. If you'd met her, you'd understand. She doesn't make mistakes. If she says to do something, then she means it.' She was struggling to put it into words – Ma's journalistic instinct, her quicksilver sharpness on the trail of the truth. If she thought Iffenwild could be found, then Daisy knew it must be possible.

She called an emergency meeting of the club that afternoon.

'Right,' said the Prof. 'If the grown-ups aren't listening, then we need a plan B.'

Daisy nodded. 'I say we hitch a ride on the Mallowmarsh ship to Moonmarket. Then, we keep our eyes peeled for any information about Iffenwild and how to get there. The market is the biggest international crossing-place in the whole magical world. There are bound to be clues.'

Indigo nodded. 'Okay,' he said. 'And if we can't find a way to get to Iffenwild – well, then we go with the Mallowmarsh boat to Amazeria, like we planned.'

Daisy wanted, so badly, to be in the same country as Ma: to be moving towards her, instead of away. But Ma's words echoed like bells in her head:

Come with help, or not at all. Find the people of Iffenwild and bring them here.

Indigo clapped his hands. 'So, we have a plan. All we need to do is get onto that ship before it leaves tonight. We can worry about the rest once we're there. We've done harder things than searching for a hidden entrance to a lost pocket.'

'Like what?' said the Prof, raising an eyebrow.

'Hang on a minute,' said Daisy. 'If we're searching for a hidden door, then the dandelight can help us. If we can get ourselves to the right general area' – she ignored the fact that this could be anywhere in the world – 'then it should lead us straight to the door to Iffenwild.' She drew the heavy, cool sphere from her pocket, and it glowed between them, lighting up the shed.

'Yes!' said Acorn excitedly. 'Good idea.'

Indigo smiled and glanced at the angle of the sun through the window. 'It's almost dinner time,' he said. 'Come on. There's lots to do before midnight, so we'd better get started.'

Chapter 15

Max was hanging upside-down, and it wasn't very comfortable. Concealing himself in the rafters of the warehouse had seemed like a good idea five minutes ago. But that had been before his foot had slipped and he'd ended up clutching a roof beam like a terrified koala. His arm muscles weren't strong, and he didn't know how long he'd be able to hold on.

'You made it.' He heard a gruff voice below and looked down at two dark-cloaked figures. One was Jarndyce. The top of his shaved head was very shiny from this angle, and Max could almost see his own desperate reflection in its surface. He tried to lever himself back to an upright position on the beam, but only ended up slipping more dramatically. The world swung beneath him, and he closed his eyes, feeling sick.

In theory, it was a *good* thing that Jarndyce was here – it meant that Max had come to the right place at the right time. *Moonmarket, Wednesday midnight*, Jarndyce had said. *Through the entrance at the West India Docks*. He frowned, thinking about it. As far as he knew, the only way to enter

Moonmarket was from *inside* a Greenwild pocket. Once a month, when the moon was high, Botanists from every corner of the world came to exchange seeds and gossip, to sip glasses of plum wine and snisky, and to buy and sell everything from dragon-fruit (the fire-breathing variety) to floating rakes made from cumulus wood.

If he could just get into Moonmarket, thought Max, he'd be able to find a boat heading to Mallowmarsh – where, he knew, he'd find his mother. What puzzled him was how Jarndyce was hoping to get into the market from Greyside London. It ought to be impossible. But Jarndyce had said the West India Docks, and here he was.

Max swallowed, and gripped the roof beam tighter. He would see this through, whatever it took.

All the same, he knew there was a chance this plan was the stupidest thing he'd ever done. It meant following the very person who was trying to capture him, and heading straight into a market that children were expressly forbidden from visiting on their own. Max had gone only once with his mother, who had held on to his hand very tightly the whole time and told him not to go wandering off. 'The edges of the market aren't safe,' she had said grimly. 'Full of nasty characters you wouldn't want to meet on a dark night.'

Max looked down. Dark night? Check. Nasty characters? Double check.

His arms and legs were hurting desperately now with the

effort of clinging to the beam, and his hands were starting to go numb.

The great doors of the warehouse opened onto the river and through them Max saw the full moon shining on the smoothly swelling waters of the Thames, so that the whole river looked like a pathway of silver.

He shifted again. He wouldn't be able to hold on for much longer. His arms were shaking, and he could feel his fingers slipping one by one.

Then Max heard the bells of Big Ben ring out across the city: twelve slow, deep notes like ripples spreading across water.

Midnight.

'Ready?' said the Prof.

The four of them were crouching on the shores of the lake beneath a large flowering plum tree. A petal had just

landed on Daisy's nose and she was trying her best not to sneeze.

'Mm-hmm,' she said, sticking out her lower lip and trying to blow the petal off. Two feet away was the nest of piffleflicks that they had to avoid disturbing until the last possible moment. One of the baby flicks – already the size of a small alligator, with alarmingly sharp teeth – was pecking in the dirt.

'It's so cute,' said Indigo, sighing happily. The baby piffleflick swallowed a passing mouse in a single gulp and belched loudly.

'Ugh,' said the Prof. 'Can we focus, please?'

'Right, right! Of course.' Indigo grinned at them. 'Everyone ready?'

'Only for the last *hour*,' said the Prof.

'Acorn?'

'Ready!' she squeaked. She was clutching a trowel and looking fierce.

'Daisy?'

Daisy nodded.

'Right,' said Indigo, glancing at the ship. 'Wait for it . . . until those two guards reach this end of the dock . . . Okay. On the count of three. One . . . two . . . three!'

He nodded at Napoleon and the tiny cat bounded gleefully forward. The piffleflicks erupted from their nest as though they were fleeing a tiger.

There was an explosion of squawks, feathers and flying teeth over the deck of the ship that sent the guards sprinting for cover.

'Go, go, go!' whispered Indigo, and they ran, Napoleon on their heels, down the bank, up the landing stage and up over the side of the ship. There was a sort of storage space just below deck that was filled with – Daisy sniffed – something that smelled suspiciously like pickled herring. She held her breath, lifted the edge of its tarpaulin covering so the others could climb beneath, and ducked in after them.

They had done it.

As the twelfth and final note of Big Ben rang across the water, the two men in the warehouse looked at each other and nodded. Max watched, trembling, from his place in the rafters as Jarndyce took something from his pocket. It was a pale, round object about the size of a child's fist, and it burned with a chilling white light. He used it to trace an outline in the air, which shivered like pale fire and made the shape of a roughly arched doorway.

Jarndyce put the stone back in his pocket. Then, as one, the men turned and stepped through the bright arch: off the warehouse pier and into the river.

But the splash Max expected never came. As soon as their feet touched the water, the two men vanished.

Max gave a great gasp of shock and pain – and plummeted from the beam twenty feet onto a pile of tarpaulin.

For a moment he lay there, stunned, his head dazzled with pain and exhaustion. Then he closed his eyes and counted to three. When he opened them again, he forced himself to get up and staggered across the concrete floor of the warehouse to the doorway. The burning arch still glimmered like a wound in the air, making the hairs stand up on his neck. Just beyond it lay the doors of the warehouse, and the drop into the river.

Max took a deep breath, and stepped off the edge.

Chapter 16

Daisy could hear the others breathing beneath the tarpaulin of the storage compartment. The smell of fish was so overwhelming she thought she might faint. The space was very cramped and she was pretty sure she had someone's toe in her ear.

'Indigo,' she hissed. 'Is that you? Move, won't you?'

'Sorry,' he muttered.

She heard him trying to shift. 'Ow,' she said. 'That was my stomach!' Napoleon was curled around her neck like a tiny furry shawl, and he yelped in protest.

'Honestly!' said the Prof. 'All of you, be quiet, or we'll be found before we even leave Mallowmarsh.'

Daisy pulled the dandelight out of her pocket and shone it around the confined space. Its soft silvery glow lit up their pinched faces, full of fear, but also something like excitement. Acorn was pinching her nose against the fishy smell, but she looked bright-eyed and alert.

'Okay,' said the Prof, consulting her watch. 'Five minutes to midnight.'

They heard people on the deck, calling instructions to

each other and unfurling the sails as the ship prepared to depart. Artemis's voice rang out above the rest.

'That's it, Montague – a bit to the left. Careful where you stow it. Very good, Beechwise. Only a few minutes to go now.' There was a pause as the Botanists on deck stared at the moon rising above the lake and waited for the great clocktower of Chiveley Chase to sound out the hour of midnight. *Here we go*, thought Daisy as the first chimes rang across the grounds. Through a gap in the tarpaulin, she watched as a gust of wind rose and shivered across the water, turning it pale and shimmering.

Then she heard a great whooshing noise, a shift in pressure that seemed to squeeze the whole ship in a great pocket of motion. It spun them in tight arcs that tugged right behind her stomach, making her feel seasick. The ship groaned and the rigging creaked and for a moment she thought the whole thing would come apart at the joints. 'Oh no, oh no,' she could hear the Prof muttering. Napoleon dug his claws into Daisy's shoulder, and Daisy squeezed her fists so hard that her knuckles ached.

When she opened her eyes, the light coming through the gap in the tarpaulin was bright silver and the air smelled like spice. Daisy peered out and saw they had come to rest at the centre of a great dock that was full of ships from every nation of the world – Norwegian longboats and Chinese dhows and spiky, piratical-looking French ships with rigging as fine as a spider's web.

'Moonmarket,' whispered Acorn.

Artemis was already waving to some of the boats, and Daisy realized that these were the Botanists she had persuaded to stand with them against the Grim Reapers in the Amazon.

There was a small man in a bowler hat standing at the centre of the dock, who seemed to be overseeing the chaos.

'Welcome to the Greenwild Regional and International Travellarium,' he called, waving his bowler hat. 'Also known as GRIT. As you know, all boats will return to their pocket of origin at moonset. Any Botanist wishing to hitch their boat to another and return with it to its place of origin instead, please make your preference known at once to a travel representative and show your grassport at the border control booth over there.' He indicated a small cabin where a bored-looking official in a green uniform was sitting smoking a foul-smelling cigar.

'Leave this to me,' called Artemis to the others, and Daisy watched as she leapt down to the dock to speak to the official.

'Pocket of origin?' asked the bowler-hatted man, sounding bored.

'Mallowmarsh, England,' said Artemis. 'But my friends here –' she gestured to the other boats – 'come from many different pockets.' She listed them.

The man made a note on his clipboard. 'And your destination?'

'Amazeria,' said Artemis. Her voice rang out loudly and confidently enough to be heard on the decks of the ship.

There was a sudden hush on the other boats as people turned to see who had spoken the word. The bowler-hatted man cleared his throat awkwardly. 'I wouldn't advise it, madam. The Perilous Pocket is . . . well, very perilous just at present.'

'Oh really?' asked Artemis politely. 'I would never have guessed.'

'And even if it *wasn't*,' said the man, ignoring her, 'we haven't had any boats heading to Amazeria in weeks.'

He gestured to a row of trawlers lined up in the Travellarium, each with large signs indicating their destination. Daisy saw signs for dozens of different pockets, from Maplebrim (in Canada) to Tamariskie (in Sudan), but nowhere could she see a sign for Amazeria.

She frowned and saw that Artemis was speaking again.

'I don't think that will be a problem,' she said briskly. 'I have arranged private transport. Our escort will be here before moonset.'

Max felt a sick tugging sensation in his stomach, as if he'd been yanked with a fishhook behind his navel and spun upside down through silver and darkness. When he righted himself, he found that he was in a small, dark room that smelled of mothballs. He reached out an arm and encountered the softness of fur against his skin. He was inside some sort of coat closet, he thought – and judging by the swaying of the rotten planks beneath his feet and the sound of splashing water, it was located below the main deck of a ship. There was a door a few feet to the left, and he could just see Jarndyce beyond it, murmuring to a group of people dressed in shadowy costumes and masks. Max retreated into a corner, heart pounding. He noticed a grimy window at his elbow and saw through it a dock protruding out into the water, surrounded by a gathering of other ships with dark sails, and market stalls selling objects that glittered unsettlingly in the dim light.

This wasn't the market Max remembered visiting with his mother. That market had been bright and full of revelry, its stalls stocked with toffee apples and magical trowels and shining pyramids of bizarre and wonderful fruit. It was the first time Max had tasted a phosphorescent mango, and his hair hadn't stopped glowing for a week.

Here, though, everything was very dark, and the damp air smelled like decay. Max took a breath. He needed to get off this ship and search for a Mallowmarsh boat.

But even as he began to move, three people materialized at the far end of the closet in puffs of silver steam, shook off their black cloaks and strode through the door to join the gathering in the room beyond.

Max pressed himself back into the rails of coats, hands numb with fear. He realized now what he should have seen at once. There was no way off the ship except through the cabin where Jarndyce and a dozen others now stood.

He was trapped.

'It doesn't look like anything's going to happen any time soon,' said Indigo, after Artemis had been standing on the deck for half an hour.

'I agree,' said Daisy. 'I say we use the time to do a bit of investigating. Indigo, Acorn, you stay here, and send Jethro to find us if it looks like things are moving. The Prof and I will see what we can find out about Iffenwild.'

There were giant luminous goldfish that swam through the depths of the Moonriver, and Indigo coaxed them to create another diversion by jumping so high and dramatically through the air that the whole crew turned to watch in amazement.

With Napoleon on her shoulders and the Prof by her side, Daisy slipped from under the tarpaulin and over the right side of the ship, scaling a narrow ladder down to the landing stage below.

'Right,' she said, raising her hood to avoid being recognized by any of the Mallowmarshers on deck above. 'Let's go.'

Chapter 17

Two hours later, Daisy and the Prof had walked the length and breadth of the Travellarium without success. They took care to linger behind groups of adult Botanists, so it wouldn't look as though they were by themselves.

'Iffenwild?' asked a little man holding a box of silver trowels, scratching his head in bemusement. 'Never heard of it!'

They'd ventured further into the market too, listening desperately to every conversation they walked past, hoping to overhear something useful. 'The Marindeep,' said a woman by the fishmonger's boat, voice wistful. 'My father's grandfather used to tell stories about it. Beautiful fish, he said they had . . . The most beautiful fish in the world. But that's all it was, my dears: a story. And I've never heard of any Iffenwild.'

They'd passed through boats selling magical herb teas, and evil-smelling baskets of red garlic, and brooms made from buoyant wood that floated in the air. But they had found nothing that would help in their search for Iffenwild.

'Any luck?' asked Acorn, as they finally crawled back on

board the ship. But Daisy didn't need to say anything. The answer was on her face. Ma had given her one task, and she had failed.

'No progress here either,' said Indigo, sitting on the floor of the storage space with his chin on his knees.

Daisy watched as the man in the bowler hat called out greetings to other arriving ships and took their details. Passengers were busy negotiating, handing over small bags of gold moon pennies for their fares, and having their grassports stamped by the self-important official in the cabin, who chewed his walrus moustache in between large puffs from his cigar.

Artemis was standing at the front of the Mallowmarsh boat, playing with a pair of dice and looking utterly unconcerned whenever the bowler-hatted man scowled in her direction. More time passed, and Daisy began to think that they would never leave their hiding place and that the smell of herring would become part of her DNA for ever.

Then – 'Look!' she said. 'Someone's coming to talk to the commander. Over there, wearing a green cape.'

They crowded around the gap in the tarpaulin and strained to hear what was being said. The person in the cape, Daisy saw, was a girl – no older than fourteen. She had a sharp, decisive chin and pointed eyebrows that gave a determined expression to her smooth brown face.

Finally, their escort had arrived. Not a crew in a big trawler like the other transport boats, but a girl too young for Moonmarket, in a small boat that seemed to be made of leaves. It looked barely big enough to tow a dinghy, let alone the *Great Mallow*. Artemis leapt down from the deck to shake the girl's hand, and a cheer went up from the Mallowmarshers, although the noise was also tinged with fear.

'All right, everyone,' called Artemis, smiling. 'We're on our way to Amazeria.'

Daisy swallowed. This was what she'd been longing for, almost since the moment Ma had disappeared – but now her stomach felt oddly troubled. All around the ship, Botanists were springing into action, steering the *Great Mallow* towards the tiny craft, which bobbed in the upswells of the water like a leaf on a busy pond. The people aboard the other ships were doing the same – Italians and Indians, Germans and Chinese, and many others Daisy couldn't see. Then each of the Botanists disembarked to have their grassports stamped by the official with the walrus moustache, who looked at them dubiously from rheumy eyes. 'Amazeria, eh?' he wheezed, puffing at his cigar. 'Rather you than me. Good luck getting back alive.'

Daisy and the others exchanged glances. The Prof groaned and buried her face in her hands. 'It'll be okay,' said Daisy, patting her shoulder. 'We'll be fine.'

'It's not that,' said the Prof, yanking at the ends of her hair. 'It's travelling without our grassports. This is SO illegal.'

'I think that ship sailed a while ago,' said Indigo. 'Literally.' The Prof cast him a dirty glance.

'Look,' said Daisy. 'Something's happening.'

The Amazerian girl uncoiled a dozen lengths of long silvery rope and used them to hitch the ships to a small hook at the back of her leaf boat.

'How do we know that she'll take us to Amazeria?' asked Daisy. 'I mean, isn't it just as likely that our ship will end up taking *her* back to Mallowmarsh at moonset?'

'No,' said the Prof, shaking her head. 'It's old magic. You follow the boat you're hitched to.'

The moon was beginning to dip lower in the sky and Daisy watched it sink towards the horizon like a gold balloon falling to earth.

'Moonset in half an hour,' called Artemis at last, consulting her watch. 'Batten down the hatches. Everyone, to your stations.'

Daisy watched the Botanists making their final preparations, and resigned herself to going with the *Great Mallow*. This was what she'd wanted, she told herself fiercely. So why did it feel so wrong?

It was dark inside the closet, and Max shrank back and tried not to breathe too hard as more people arrived and the room beyond began to fill.

Time passed – he wasn't sure how long. Max's fear gave way to impatience, and then slid back towards terror each time someone new materialized and came past his hiding place. With every passing minute, his chance of finding a Mallowmarsh boat slipped further out of reach.

Suddenly, as if at some invisible signal, Jarndyce looked up and surveyed the company. 'All right,' he said, checking his watch. 'It is fifteen minutes to moonset, and we are all assembled. We know what we must do. Remember your positions. When I give the signal, we attack. Give no quarter, show no mercy, and leave no Botanist alive.'

Max crouched, trembling in the corner behind the coats. He felt cramp growing in his foot and tried not to move.

The doorway he'd come through was clearly a forbidden entrance used – by these people, whoever they were – to enter the Moonmarket. And tonight, they were going to attack a market full of innocent Greenwilders.

Suddenly Max was assailed by a memory of his mother talking to one of her friends by the side of his bed in hospital – one of those many conversations where she thought he was asleep. He had learned an awful lot like that, lying on his back, too exhausted by pain to speak or even open his eyes – but listening, hard.

'They're on the rise,' his mother had said, her voice hushed. 'They're growing every day – and Darkmarket is the centre of their operations.'

'Who's on the rise?' he had asked later, when he was feeling a bit better. 'And what's Darkmarket?'

'Oh, just a nasty corner of Moonmarket,' she had said

breezily. 'And the only thing on the rise right now is my craving for a cup of that disgusting hospital coffee.' Max had laughed, despite himself. Only later did he realize that she'd never answered his question.

Well, it looked like he had found the answer at last. This was Darkmarket – and somehow, he'd landed himself in the middle of the greatest attack on the Botanical world he'd ever heard of.

The cloaked figures were checking their weapons now and downing tumblers of amber liquid that glinted in the light of grimy lanterns. Then, one by one, they began filing out through a small door. The cramp in Max's foot was becoming unbearable. He had to stretch; he had to move. He shifted infinitesimally, and the boards creaked below him.

'What was that?' Jarndyce looked around, nostrils flaring. He paced towards Max's hiding place. Their eyes met for a split second, and Jarndyce's pupils went wide with surprise.

'You!' he said, and lunged.

Chapter 18

Daisy stroked Napoleon's paw and looked out of the gap between the tarpaulin and the deck. The market was bustling with shoppers making last-minute purchases before moonset, and the boat to the left, she saw, was busier than most. It was an enormous barge, selling different varieties of magical apples from polished wooden carts. There were gleaming pyramids of tiny Pink Duchesses ('The apple of grace – dance like a duchess, results guaranteed!'), barrels of lurid green Granny Buckthorns ('Give yourself the gumption to speak your mind!'), and sparkling arrangements of Golden Greenwilds ('The apple of fortune – for eaters seeking the favour of Lady Luck!').

'That last one's a fraud,' said the Prof scornfully. 'Everyone knows that.'

Botanists milled back and forth across the decks of the boat, looking at the displays and buying apples by the bag, sack and barrel.

Daisy heard a raucous laugh and looked down to see three people standing next to one of the apple stalls.

'But I must, darlink,' said a woman wearing a flamboyant

scarlet turban and what appeared to be a gold silk jumpsuit. She sounded Russian and spoke with great emphasis on certain words. 'I know it's nonsense, but I'm *fond* of my superstitions. I *must* have a Golden Greenwild before every performance. I simply *must*. The last time I forgot, our Hamlet tripped over the stage cat and broke both his arms. *Vot* a disaster!'

She swooped towards the stallholder and proffered a handful of moon pennies, while her two companions watched with wildly contrasting expressions. The first – a man who was as big as a bear, with a small, sleeping baby in a sling across his chest – was looking on with amused grey eyes. The second – a lady in an elegant waistcoat, with a bundle of curling black hair tied up in a scarf – was watching with one peevish eyebrow raised. She kept checking her pocket watch ostentatiously.

'Calm yourself down, darlink,' said the woman in the turban, now triumphantly bearing her bag of apples. 'The moontide is still twenty minutes away – and anyway, shopping, it is good for the soul. We will get to Iff—'

'Please!' said the other woman, interrupting. 'Honestly Rozaliya, not so loud.'

'Oh pfffft!' she said, waving a dismissive hand at the surging crowds. 'No one is paying attention to us.'

'Fine, fine,' said the woman, raising her hands theatrically. 'Let's get back to the ship. I knew it was a mistake to moor so near Darkmarket – it's too far away from the centre. It'll take us at least fifteen minutes to walk back.'

'Fewer people ask questions there . . .' said the bear-like man, his voice fading as they walked to the other side of the apple barge and across the gangplank to the neighbouring ship.

Daisy glanced at the Prof. 'Did you hear that?' She felt dizzy, heart beating as hard as if she'd just run a race.

'Iffenwild,' breathed the Prof. Her eyes were wide and shining. 'It's got to be.'

For a moment, Daisy hesitated. It was less than twenty minutes to moonset. If she stayed on the *Great Mallow*, she'd be in Amazeria before the end of the night. Closer to Ma; closer to everything she'd ever longed for.

Then she thought again of Ma's letter.

'Come on,' she said, scrambling to her feet inside the storage hatch, bumping her head on the tarpaulin. 'Quickly, before we lose sight of them.'

Max leapt back, and Jarndyce missed him by an inch. He looked around wildly, panic beating like a small bat trapped in his chest. There was no escape. The door of the closet was blocked by a gathering of Reapers in black cloaks. It was hopeless.

Then he saw it from the corner of his eye – the small round window he'd been looking out of before, elbow-height, only three feet away. Its panes were blackened with dirt and soot, but it looked like the catch might open, if only he could reach it.

Barely more than a second had passed since Jarndyce had lunged, and he was gathering himself for a second attack. Max breathed in, and then he dived for the window; no time to fiddle with the rusted catch. Instead, he fisted his jumper around his hand and *punched* his way through the glass. It smashed with an almighty shattering *CRASH* and fell away in bright black splinters.

And then Max dived, with a speed and force he didn't know he had, straight through the jagged hole and into the open air.

Daisy, Indigo, Acorn and the Prof climbed down the ship's ladder so fast they almost fell onto the dock, and then they were sprinting through the market in pursuit of the colourful group, Napoleon at their heels. Daisy could just see the scarlet turban of the Russian woman bobbing through the crowds ahead of them.

'That way,' she said, pointing, and they hurried on, through boats selling edible chocolate butterflies and enchanted spades and unbreakable rope. It was lucky the group was so conspicuous, thought Daisy – the turbaned woman, talking ceaselessly in throaty Russian-accented bursts; the bear-like man so tall that his head knocked against the roof of every boat they passed through; and the woman with the elegant waistcoat and curling black hair. The market became shabbier and darker the further they went from the centre, until Daisy shivered and wrapped her arms about her waist for comfort. The group seemed to be slowing down now, bearing towards a small flotilla of four canal boats painted in blue and green and gold. There were bright flowers growing on their cabin roofs, but their paint was peeling, and they looked like they had seen better days.

'Here we are,' said the turbaned woman, delighted.

'And not before time,' said the woman in the waistcoat. 'It's only five minutes to moonset.'

'Yes, darlink,' said the woman. '*Lots* of time.'

The moon had almost reached the horizon and its light was sweeping across the river in a pathway as bright as a melted silver penny.

After that, several things happened at once.

Daisy heard screams coming from across the market, high and full of terror. She saw people running across the decks, scattering like tennis balls, sending stalls and spades and wheels of cheese careening into the water. She saw cloaked figures streaming like rats from one of the black ships, weapons held aloft, setting fire to barges and shops as they charged into the heart of the market.

Grim Reapers, she thought, dazed. *Grim Reapers here at Moonmarket.* Then from the corner of her eye she saw a window smash in the lower deck of a nearby ship, and a dark shape come plummeting out of it.

It was a boy.

Within three seconds, he was in the water. Within ten, he was drowning.

Chapter 19

Max felt a shard of glass slice his arm as he plunged from the ship towards the icy river below. He hit the water with an almighty splash and immediately went under. It was so cold that he gasped, and the skin tightened around his flesh until it hurt.

Also, he'd forgotten one tiny detail.

He couldn't swim.

Two years spent in hospitals and hooked up to blood pressure monitors wasn't exactly ideal for learning how to do the breaststroke. Even before he'd got sick, his mother hadn't been keen on swimming lessons, and she'd avoided the sea like the plague. ('It's far too dangerous,' she said, whenever Max had begged.)

The force of his fall pushed him down in a great plume of dark bubbles. He bobbed like a cork to the top, but immediately gulped an enormous mouthful of water and went under again. The river was suddenly inside his lungs. It felt like he'd swallowed a bucket of ice cubes. He couldn't breathe, he couldn't think, he didn't know which way was up or down or how to find the surface. He flailed around, every movement sapping the air from his chest. He saw a stream of silver bubbles rising from his mouth as it gave up the last of his oxygen.

Max's chest was burning now, and for a moment everything went ink black. His brain flickered as he sank. It was very cold, and he knew, deep in his bones, that he was going to die.

Then something astonishing happened.

He heard his mother's voice in his head, saw her grey eyes wide and insistent. 'No,' she said. 'You're going to live, Max. You are going to LIVE.'

With a strength he didn't know existed in his body, Max found the riverbed with his feet and *pushed* himself upwards with all the force of his twelve years. The effort sent him shooting up like a porpoise and he broke the surface with a great gasping gulp of air. Water was pouring out of his nose and mouth, and it burned so badly that his eyes streamed, and he could barely see further than his own desperately paddling hands. Then he was sinking under again and this time he was really going to drown; he had no strength left in his arms, no air left in his lungs.

He heard a splash near his head and felt a pair of arms wrap around his chest and begin pulling him through the water. He flailed and hit

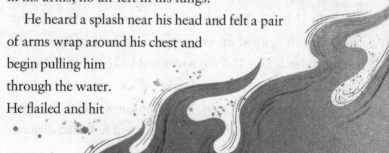

something behind him. The person spluttered and for a moment they both went under. 'That was my nose,' gasped the person – a girl, thought Max. Whoever it was, they were small but strong and determined – and very good at swimming.

They surfaced near a group of four canal boats with shabby paint. Max coughed and began to believe that he might not die after all.

Then he saw what was happening above the water and swiftly revised his opinion. Arrows flew through the air, their tips aflame, setting the river ablaze. The fire was racing towards them across the surface, and in its flickering light Max saw the pale, pinched face of the girl who had saved him. Her long dark hair was plastered to her head and neck, and there was a deeply unhappy kitten clinging for dear life to her shoulder. Max barely had time to take this in before he saw, flooding across the docks like a dark tide, the men from the black ship.

The girl was determinedly dragging him towards the shabby canal boats. Their sides were painted with peeling patterns of blue, gold and green. 'Come *on*,' she said. 'I'm not letting you ruin this.' She reached the nearest boat just as it began to shimmer bright and then more brightly, until it was white as a star and blinded his eyes.

The girl cried out, 'Indigo, Prof, Acorn, quick—'

But there was no time for anything else. The edge of the painted boat shivered violently, like a horse at the start of a race. Then the moon vanished and the whole world was set spinning like an old carousel.

Chapter 20

This time Daisy felt the sensation in the pit of her stomach, as if she'd touched a live wire and it was sending dazzles of electricity along every nerve of her body. Through the blaze of it she saw the boy beside her, and Indigo and the Prof clutching onto the rudder of the painted boat. Acorn was nowhere to be seen.

Already they were being whirled through the air, past darkness and light, hanging grimly onto the edge of the boat. Her fingers weren't strong enough; she was going to let go. The world swung round in a medley of colours and scenes. The boy she'd rescued was barely holding on. Daisy's own grip loosened just before the fleet of boats shimmered into place on the surface of a new sea, and she fell ten feet, landed hard in water – warm and salty as a pasta pot – and plunged beneath the surface.

For a moment all sound was muffled, and the water seethed around her in a mass of foam and bubbles. When she came up for air, she found that the boy was gripping onto her leg in desperation and pulling her back under. He seemed to be trying to climb on top of her. 'Stop it,' she shouted, 'or we'll both drown!' The four canal boats were already puttering steadily away, leaving them far behind in the water. But the boy was beyond listening, trapped in a place where nothing existed except water and fear.

Daisy raised her eyes to the heavens. Then she took a deep breath and plunged below the surface, diving out from under the boy. She came up a couple feet away and trod water for a moment, thinking desperately. She remembered a long summer she'd spent with Ma on the beach in California, and what she'd heard the lifeguards saying. 'Rescue a drowning person from behind,' she muttered to herself. '*From behind.*'

The boy was sinking again, his thrashing starting to give out. She didn't think he would be able to overpower her now or pull her under. She took a deep breath, circled around until she was behind him, and looped one arm around his chest so that they were both floating with their faces turned up to the star-bright sky.

The boy had gone very still, and Daisy looked around desperately for help.

Then she heard voices.

'Daisy,' they called. 'DAISY!' It was Indigo coming up behind her, and the sight was astonishing, because he was holding onto the fin of a sleek creature with a dark grey back and a playful blunt snout. 'Grab on,' he called, and then Daisy found herself on the creature's back, pulling the drowning boy up behind her.

She looked around and saw the Prof on the back of another sleek, grey creature. 'Porpoises,' called the Prof. '*Phocoenoides dalli*. Indigo sort of *called* to them, and they came. I think we're somewhere in the Aegean Sea.'

'Where's Acorn?' Daisy asked, looking around for the younger girl's bright red pigtails.

'We saw Artemis pulling her away from the battle,' said the Prof, sounding strained. 'She must have seen us leaving the boat.'

'Oh,' said Daisy, suddenly weak with relief. 'So, Acorn's safe. She got away.'

'Yes,' said the Prof. 'She did.'

Daisy closed her eyes, feeling the supple twist of the porpoise beneath her, its skin smooth and rubbery. Then she blinked and looked around at the waves. She could see the four canal boats in the distance, all of them low on the water with blue and gold sides that flashed in the starlight. 'Those are the boats we came with,' she said. 'The ones heading to Iffenwild.'

The Prof lifted her chin. 'We have to catch up with them.'

She looked at Indigo and he nodded, and then the whole pod of porpoises was in motion and Daisy felt herself soaring and diving with a sensation that was a bit like flying and a bit like dreaming and a lot like joy. She laughed despite herself and had to concentrate to keep her grip on the boy slung in front of her as the salt water splashed in her face and the speed blew the hair back from her neck and the stars shone like silver sequins on the dark water.

Then the boats came close and, too late, Daisy remembered Sheldrake calling the Iffenwilders a 'murderous nation'. One of the boats seemed to slow down and hang back. Daisy saw a face in the window of the rear cabin.

And then the first spear came soaring out over the water.

Chapter 21

'No,' shouted Daisy. 'We're not Grim Reapers. We mean no harm!' The boy in front of her was still unconscious, and she was beginning to shake with the effort of keeping him from slipping into the water.

Another spear whizzed past her ear, narrowly missing Napoleon, who was perched on her shoulder with his fur fluffed up in outrage at the wetness and indignity of the situation. Daisy felt despair grip her insides – and then the boy slipped from her grasp, limp and heavy as he toppled into the water. Shoving Napoleon into Indigo's arms, she dived in after him.

Moments later, one of the painted boats came cutting through the waves, and she heard voices. 'Stop!' said one, deep and amazed, from high above. It was the bear-like man with the baby strapped across his chest. 'They're children.' Then ladders were thrown down and arms lifted her up, pulling her and the boy onto the deck of the nearest boat. She looked around and saw Indigo and the Prof, and felt Napoleon licking and licking her cheek.

'Good,' she said tiredly. Her eyelids felt suddenly very heavy, and within minutes, she was fast asleep.

*

When Daisy woke, the sky was full of light and Napoleon was curled up on her chest, snoring gently. She was tucked into a soft white bed in a small bright cabin. The room had three round windows with red painted sills, and she could see waves through them, rising and falling and impossibly blue. She looked around and saw there were two bunk beds, and that she was in one of the bottom bunks. The strange boy was in the bottom of the opposite bunk, his face slack with exhaustion, and she noticed details that she hadn't seen before. He had very long, dark eyelashes and high cheekbones, and his dark hair – still crusted with sea salt – was thick and grew back from his forehead to reveal a strawberry birthmark beneath his right eye.

She sighed and turned her head to see Indigo's hand hanging down from the bunk above hers, and the dark halo of the Prof's hair poking out from a nest of blankets on the other top bunk. They were all asleep. Moving carefully so as not to wake Napoleon, she slid out of bed. She felt a terrible pang of guilt for his still-damp fur. He hated water, and he was snuffling in a deeply aggrieved manner.

Daisy crossed to the door and tried the handle.

It opened right into the face of the woman who had bought the apples. She had changed since the market and was now wrapped in a flamboyant silk dressing gown. She held a tape measure in one hand and a Russian tea glass in the other, and a dozen pink feathers were sticking out from her elaborate chignon. It was hard to tell how old she was, but her hair was a beautiful snow white above her pale face, and she had expressive lines around her eyes as if she'd spent a lot of time laughing and crying and singing.

Daisy watched as the woman took in her tangled hair, her still-damp trousers and her torn shirt. 'Oh, my dear,' she said, blowing a stylish white curl of hair off her forehead. Her voice was deep and throaty and Russian, almost a drawl. 'We will *have* to do something about your clothes.'

'Um,' said Daisy. 'It's nice to meet you?'

'Rozaliya Volkova,' said the woman. 'Wardrobe mistress.'

'Wardrobe?' said Daisy faintly. 'You're not from Iffenwild?' She sensed someone stirring behind her, then heard the Prof's voice carry loud and clear across the cabin:

'Who are you? And where on earth are we?'

Chapter 22

Daisy looked at the woman, waiting for an answer, but she only threw her head back and laughed, creasing the deep lines around her eyes.

'Tak,' she said. 'The children wish to know where we are!' She looked around as if they were all sharing a great joke. Indigo was sitting up now and rubbing his eyes. Jethro, his parakeet, was perching sleepily on his shoulder. Napoleon too was awake and had come to stand by Daisy's feet, his fur prickling, as though ready to defend her from harm.

Only the strange boy slept on, exhausted and oblivious.

'Well,' said Daisy. 'Are you going to let us out of the cabin?'

'Da,' said the woman. 'That is what I am coming down for – to bring you upstairs to meet the captain. Now you have slept, we will talk, and decide what we do with you. Maybe we throw you overboard to feed the fishes?' She laughed again uproariously, and several pink feathers fell out of her hair and floated to the floor. One of them landed on Napoleon's nose and he sneezed.

The woman – Rozaliya – clapped her hands in delight. 'A menagerie we have here, children and pets. Come. Come with me, upstairs.'

Leaving the strange boy still asleep, Daisy, Indigo and the Prof followed Rozaliya out of the cabin and up a small spiralling staircase onto the deck of the boat. It must, thought Daisy, be much larger inside than it looked from the outside, or there was no way the cabin they had slept in could have fitted below deck.

The wind was fresh, and the sky was blue and crossed with fresh white clouds like crisp pillowcases hung out to dry. Their boat was at the head of the three others they'd seen the night before, all of them as shabby as Daisy remembered, with peeling gold paint around their portholes. They looked like canal boats, except that they also had beautiful sails that snapped in the wind. 'Willow-silk,' whispered the Prof, eyes wide with wonder. '*The Compleat Botanist*, page four hundred and ninety-three. It's the strongest substance in the Greenwild, and it changes colour to predict the weather.' The three billowing sails on their barge were currently sunshine yellow and criss-crossed with tiny scudding clouds.

Like on the *Great Mallow*, the rigging was controlled by green vines that seemed to move of their own accord, which told Daisy that the people on the boat were users of green magic. There was a flat, open deck area at the back of the boat, where sailors sat sipping coffee and repairing a tangle of fishing nets. Beyond this was a wooden cabin where a tall man stood, slightly stooping to handle the ship's wheel. He had his back to them, and he was using one hand to steer and the other to stroke an enormous ginger cat that lay on the rail beside him, soaking up sunshine like a fat orange tiger.

Napoleon hissed and arched his back. The ginger cat opened a single pale eye, yawned and went back to sleep.

'Ah,' said the man, turning towards them. 'Don't mind Boris. He's been mousing all night and is having a nap.' It was the bear-like man

they had seen in the market the previous day and, as before, he held a sleeping baby in a sling across his chest. He was younger than Daisy had thought – not yet thirty – with dark hair and white skin tanned deeply by the sun. His keen, intelligent face was alert and poised, and his gestures were grand and dramatic, as if he was eternally centre stage in a performance where he was the hero.

'I'm Captain Alexei Speedwell,' he said briskly. 'Have a carrot.'

'Sorry, what?' said Daisy. The man gestured to a row of tufty stems that seemed to be growing straight from the decks of the ship. 'They're particularly tasty at the moment,' he said, bending down and pulling one out. He dusted it off on his trousers and took a large bite. 'Ah! Wonderfully sweet. Do try.'

'Er, no thanks,' said Daisy politely.

'As you wish, as you wish, dear child,' said the man. He flicked a hand, casually adjusting the vines of the rigging with green magic. Daisy found it hard to look away from him. Every movement was magnetic, from the way he tossed his carrot stalk overboard to the way he made the wheel spin under his hand. His charisma seemed to fill the whole boat and half of the sky.

'So, what can I do for you, now that you have, ah . . . graced us with your presence aboard the *Nautilus*?' He looked keenly at Daisy, waiting for her reply.

'Oh,' she said, glancing around. This was a mistake,

because the decks of the surrounding barges were crowded with people, all craning their necks to catch a glimpse of them.

'Lovely day, Captain,' called one of the sailors, clearly eager for an update on the new arrivals.

'Nice kiddies, are they?' asked another, casting a doubtful eye over their bedraggled outfits.

'All right, Bob,' answered Captain Speedwell. 'I'll deal with this.' He turned back to Daisy, Indigo and the Prof and held out an enormous hand to shake. 'I'm the captain of this theatre. This is my first mate, Marie-Claude.' He gestured to a sailor lounging on the opposite side of the deck, who Daisy recognized as the woman with curling black hair, warm brown skin and elegant waistcoat who had been so impatient at the market the previous night. 'And this,' said Captain Speedwell, crinkling his eyes and smiling down at the baby slung across his chest, 'is my daughter, Annika.' The blue cotton of her sling was patterned with little turtles, and the baby turned in it and yawned contentedly. Then she reached out a tiny, starfish-like hand, clutched one of his rough fingers and fell instantly asleep.

'Um – you said something about a theatre?' Daisy asked, tearing her gaze away from the baby and looking back up at the captain.

The man swept his arm in a dramatic arc, gesturing to the canal boats. All four of them, Daisy now saw, had the same symbol painted above the waterline: a theatre stage (the curtain was unmistakeable), with a dolphin leaping across the middle of it. Below it, in peeling gold letters, were the words *Nautilus Theatre*.

'Welcome to the Greenwild's premier theatrical seafaring company,' said Alexei Speedwell with a flourish. One of the sailors on the foredeck burped loudly.

'A travelling theatre?' asked Daisy. 'You mean, you travel . . . by boat?'

The captain's lip twitched. 'Indeed we do.'

'And you're going to Iffenwild,' she said eagerly.

He looked down at her, eyes suddenly sharp. 'What makes you think that?' She shrank back and Napoleon leapt onto her shoulder, teeth bared protectively.

The Prof piped up. 'We heard you in the market.'

'Ah,' said the captain. He glared at Rozaliya. 'Did you indeed?'

'You have to let us come!' said Daisy. 'We have to get to Iffenwild and ask for their help.'

'Iffenwild doesn't give help,' said Captain Speedwell, brushing his enormous hands on his trousers. 'And in any case, it doesn't exist.'

'But it does,' came a voice from behind them. 'We're heading straight for it.'

Chapter 23

Max had woken suddenly, feeling hot and confused. Every bone and muscle in his body ached as if it had been in a fight. He groaned as he sat up. There were two bunk beds in the room – the other bunks were empty, their sheets creased and pushed back – and the floor appeared to be rolling about. Beams of sunshine poured through three round windows onto the floor, and outside the windows Max saw foaming waves and seabirds joyriding on the wind. He was, he realized, on a boat. A *boat*! But how?

Then the events of the previous day came pouring back. He remembered Jarndyce, and the girl who had saved him from drowning. He remembered the canal boats, and drowning again. Was he dead? Was this some sort of afterlife? Max staggered upright and immediately stubbed his toe on a nail-head sticking out from the floor. *No*, he thought. Toe-stubbing wasn't something that seemed likely to happen in heaven.

Frowning slightly, he tucked in his salt-crusted shirt, checked his face in the low mirror beside the door, and hurried out into the corridor. He looked around, resisting the smell of bacon and fresh bread drifting from the deck. The more he could find out about where he was, the better it would be. *Always have a plan*, he heard his mother's voice say in his mind.

He ducked under a low beam and followed the corridor down to its end. There were a couple more cabins, he thought – and then, down at the end, a heavy oak door. It was locked, but that didn't matter. Max took out Jarndyce's pin badge and had it open in thirty seconds.

The room looked empty. He took a breath and stepped over the threshold.

Inside, he saw a low-ceilinged space with a large window that looked out over the stern of the boat. In the centre was a table scattered with maps and star charts, and there were more maps pinned to all four walls. The low roof beams were twined with hundreds of luminous flowers, each one casting a glittering coin of light. Max crossed quickly to the table and saw a huge map weighted down with a cutlass on one end and a dried sea-urchin on the other. There was a shining white seed on the map's surface, and it seemed to be moving very slightly. It was, he realized, a locus seed – a simple bit of green magic he'd seen his mother use. When placed on a map, it marked the user's position – and this one was telling him that they were somewhere in the middle of the Adriatic Sea. Their course was plotted minutely in blue pen, and it was leading to a city inside a small lagoon. Its name was labelled in curling red script, and Max squinted to read the words. *Iffenwild: capital of the Marindeep.*

He frowned slightly. Wasn't the Marindeep a made-up place? A story, like Atlantis, or El Dorado? And yet – he looked again at the map –

here it was, marked down in paper and ink. He heard a floorboard creak above his head and jumped. It was time to go.

Back out in the corridor, the smell of bacon was as strong as ever and Max realized he was hungry enough to eat a small elephant. He felt lightheaded as he climbed the small spiral staircase and emerged onto the deck to see a curious group of people: three children – including the girl with the cat who had rescued him – all looking at a tall, dark-haired man with a sleeping baby slung across his chest. He was clearly in charge – and he was talking about Iffenwild.

'And in any case,' he said, brushing his hands on his trousers, 'it doesn't exist.'

'But it does,' said Max, stepping from the shadows. 'We're heading straight for it.'

Daisy whipped around and saw the boy she had rescued standing at the top of the stairs. The whole crew turned to look at him. Captain Speedwell was staring with an unreadable expression.

'So,' said Daisy. 'It's true? We're going to Iffenwild?' She felt her heart skip. She had been right. This was their chance!

Captain Speedwell was still staring at Max, eyes roving over his face. He spoke slowly. 'How did you get here?'

'With them,' said the boy, gesturing. 'Well, I was locked

up in a cellar, but then I escaped, and I ended up coming with them by accident.'

The captain frowned, as if this wasn't enough. 'And how, might I ask, did you end up locked in a cellar?'

'It wasn't on purpose,' said the boy hotly. 'I was kidnapped. I don't know why, and I don't know what they wanted with me. All I want is to get to my mother. So, why won't you tell us where we're going?'

'Ah,' said the captain, his eyes bright with something Daisy couldn't quite place. 'Where we are going is, as I mentioned, none of your concern. It is a place where outsiders cannot enter. I would very much like to bring you with us' – for some reason, Daisy thought, this sounded true – 'but it is simply not safe.' He sighed. 'We'll put you down off the coast of Croatia, and we'll arrange an escort back to Mallowmarsh from there. That's where you came from, isn't it?' He gestured at Daisy's overalls, which were marked with the Mallowmarsh coat of arms. 'We usually visit Mallowmarsh at Christmas – so we can check on you in December, after we've finished touring for the year.'

Daisy heard the boy she'd rescued give a cry. 'Mallowmarsh,' he said. 'That's where I want to go. That's where my mother is.'

Daisy ignored him. 'We can't go back now.' She looked straight at the captain. 'We have to come with you!'

'Enough,' said Rozaliya, interrupting. 'We will speak more later. Now, it is time for lunch.' She swept into the cabin and a few minutes later returned with a pile of buttered toast and sausages, along with fresh bacon and piping hot fried eggs. Daisy, Indigo, the Prof and the strange boy sat on the deck and fell on the meal like wolves. It was hot and good, and it seemed to bring strength back to Daisy's arms and legs with each bite. Then there were sweet, sugared pancakes that they ate one by one from the pan with their fingers, and blackberries that were slightly salty from the sea air. Daisy licked her fingers and pushed her hair from her cheeks with the back of her hand.

No matter what Captain Speedwell said, she was going to stay on this ship. She glanced at Indigo and the Prof and Napoleon, who had just finished devouring a sausage and was licking his paws with satisfaction. She felt sure that between them, they could find a way.

Chapter 24

Max felt strength returning to him with every mouthful. Somewhere around his eighth pancake, he let out a deep sigh and felt himself become grounded in his body again.

The girl with the cat was staring at him with a hungry sort of look in her eyes.

'Iffenwild,' she said, pushing dark hair away from her pale face. 'How do you know that's where we're going? Tell me.'

Max shrugged. 'I saw a map downstairs. The boat is sailing a course for it, clear as day.'

'Okay,' she said, and looked around at her two companions: a boy with amber skin, wild curls and a parakeet perched on his shoulder; and a brown-skinned girl with a halo of dark hair and the careless poise of a dancer. 'Are you thinking what I'm thinking?' They both grinned back at her.

'Yep,' said the boy. 'We did it. We actually did it!'

'That's right,' said the girl. 'Now we just have to persuade them to keep us on board.'

'Exactly.' The first girl, the one with the cat, turned to

Max. 'I'm Daisy, by the way. Daisy Thistledown. This is Indigo,' she said, gesturing towards the boy with the parakeet. 'And this is the Prof.' The second girl grinned at him. She had long dark eyelashes that bumped against the rims of her spectacles, and her smile was extraordinary, like a flashbulb. 'So,' said Daisy. 'What's your name?'

'Max,' he said. 'Max Brightly.' He cleared his throat. 'Did you really come from Mallowmarsh? I've been trying to get there because it's where my mother is. She's called Marigold Brightly. Have you met her?'

But all three of the children were staring at him in shock, as if he'd sprouted an extra head.

'*You're* Max Brightly?' said Daisy, her voice thin. 'Artemis – she's the head of Mallowmarsh – has had people out searching the streets of London for you – for days! Where on earth have you *been*?'

Max flushed. 'I've been hiding. After I escaped from the cellar, there were people after me, trying to catch me.'

'Well obviously,' said the Prof, rolling her eyes. 'Half the British Greenwild has been looking for you. They're trying to keep you safe.'

Max shrugged slightly. 'Maybe. But the men who kidnapped me in the first place – they've been trying to catch me again, and they're not nice people, trust me.' He took out Jarndyce's pin badge. 'Here,' he said. 'This is their symbol.'

Daisy drew in a deep, shocked breath. 'Grim Reapers,' she said.

'Yes, maybe.' Max looked around at them, feeling impatient. 'But what about my mother? Has she been looking for me too?' The three children said nothing, and he felt a sudden chill run down his neck. 'She's all right, isn't she?'

Daisy glanced at the Prof, and Indigo cleared his throat.

'You have to tell me,' said Max forcefully. 'I have to know.'

Daisy looked at him, and he saw her throat bob as she swallowed. 'Marigold Brightly . . .' she said, and stopped. 'Marigold Brightly is dead.'

'What?' Max blinked. He felt suddenly very angry. 'No. No, you're wrong.' How dare this girl come out with such a terrible bare-faced lie? 'It's not true,' he said. He was overwhelmed, suddenly, by a memory of his mother's grey eyes; the coolness of her hands smoothing his forehead when he was feverish; the strength of her voice making him feel that she was ready to go into battle for him, even when the doctors had given up hope. It was impossible that those things no longer existed. But when he looked at Daisy's face, he saw that her eyes were bright with tears, and even as she blinked they brimmed over and began spilling down her cheeks, leaving streaks in the sea salt that had dried on her skin.

'I'm sorry,' she said. 'I wish it wasn't true.'

'What happened?' he asked, furious. How dare this girl be upset when she hadn't even *known* his mother? 'Tell me what happened. Tell me everything.'

She swallowed again and looked down. 'Um.' She paused, and she seemed to be picking her words very carefully. 'There was a big battle at Mallowmarsh. A battle against the Grim Reapers – the people who kidnapped you. And Marigold Brightly was hurt. She was . . . killed.'

'Oh,' said Max. His mind was suddenly blank. *No. Surely there was something he could do to make this thing not true. I'll be good*, he promised, not knowing who or what he was praying to. *I'll be so good. I'll never skip my medicine again. I'll do everything the doctors say. If only you make this not true.*

Then Max looked at Daisy's face, and with a terrible, falling plunge of realization, he knew she was telling the truth. Despair entered him like a dark fog and clouded his eyes. It was as if a wild creature was thrusting its claws through his chest, and he gasped with the pain of it.

But there was something else – the way Daisy was biting her lip.

'What aren't you telling me?' he demanded. 'There's more, isn't there?'

'No,' said Daisy, looking back at him. 'That's it. That's what happened.'

'Tell me,' he said, his voice low.

'There's nothing else,' she said, her voice shaking slightly. 'Really.'

Max felt a wave of exhaustion rise up over him, and for

a moment it was as if he was once more drowning in the cold dark water. Somehow, he managed to stagger to his feet and find the stairs. When he reached the cabin, he found the key and locked the door behind him.

Chapter 25

'Well, that went well,' said Indigo, looking after Max.

Daisy buried her face in her hands. She knew exactly how Max was feeling: the pain of it, unendurable, like a knife in the back that went on and on – because for several terrible days, only a few weeks ago, she too had thought her mother was dead, before Ma's first letter had arrived and changed everything. But for Max it was all true, and there was no coming back from it. She brushed away her tears with the stiff, salty ends of her braid and let out a shaky sigh.

The Prof was looking at her shrewdly. 'He was right, though, wasn't he? There *is* something you're not saying.'

Daisy opened her mouth to answer, but at that moment a cry went up from the deck. 'Wind ho!' came the captain's shout, and the canal boat began to swerve like a fat otter on the current as a stiff breeze rose on the port side. Daisy stood up and shaded her face with one hand, taking in the sight. The other three boats were all curving at the same angle, one after the other, the vines of their rigging dancing back and forth to trim the sails.

The boat she was on had a carved wooden balustrade, she noticed, while the one next to it was painted with gold stars. A third was carved with violins and cellos, and the fourth was swathed in lengths of red velvet spread out to dry in the sun.

'That's the boat that carries the stage set and the curtains,' said a drawling Russian voice in Daisy's ear. 'We have come through a terrible storm somewhere around the Strait of Gibraltar. My dear, everything was soaked. *Vot* a commotion! Now, we let the sun make everything dry again before we arrive in—' Rozaliya paused.

'In Iffenwild?' said Daisy eagerly. 'That's right, isn't it?'

The wardrobe mistress shrugged. 'Me, I say nothing.' She turned back to the balustrade. 'I tell you more about the boats instead. Over there,' she said, pointing to the boat carved with violins, 'is the orchestra barge.' Its deck was crowded with a small group of musicians tuning their instruments. 'And over there,' said Rozaliya grandly, 'is the wardrobe barge.' She nodded towards the boat painted with gold stars. Its every railing was decked out in ribbons and silks and masks, and there were people scuttling in and out of the cabin with boxes of buttons and sequins. 'That is mine, of course. I come only to look at you children.'

'And this boat?' asked Daisy, casting an eye over the deck, which was glistening with the first flecks of rain from the wind.

'This is the captain's boat,' said Rozaliya shortly, and folded her arms.

'Ri-ight,' said Daisy. She looked up and saw that the sunshiny yellow of the weather-forecasting sails had shifted to a dull gun-metal grey that was beginning to swirl with ominous storm light.

'Er,' she said. 'Should someone be doing something about—'

But Captain Speedwell was already ahead of her. 'Stations, everyone!' he called. 'Prepare for a storm.' Daisy saw the velvet stage curtains being hastily yanked below deck, while the tailors on the deck of the wardrobe barge hurried downstairs.

Scribbles of lightning flashed in the sky, flickering like silver pitchforks and sizzling across the water. Thunder drum-rolled through the air and the waves surged like horses with foaming white manes. Then – oh! Daisy stared. There *were* horses: a herd of great green-blue creatures coursing towards them, their bodies submerged while their powerful necks and heads rose above the water.

The herd swept past in a thundering cascade of foaming manes and wide green eyes, sending the canal boats buffeting on the waves. Then they were gone.

Or almost gone. There in the water was a small horse – a foal – its mane foaming weakly. It had been injured somehow, and it was barely keeping its head above the water.

'Oh no,' she heard Rozaliya mutter, dismayed. 'They should not be on this side of the door. How has this happened?'

Lightning flashed again and Daisy saw the whole scene frozen for a moment in the white light. The foal screamed in pain, and Daisy saw the crew on the wardrobe boat trying to get close enough to help. The creature lashed out with a silver hoof and knocked a hole in the side of the boat under the waterline. It was clearly impossible to get anywhere near without risking more damage. The foal was small but very strong, and most of the sailors were now rushing to plug the hole below the deck while the others danced around ineffectually, unable to help the injured horse.

Daisy looked around, feeling desperate. Then she met Indigo's eyes from across the deck and knew they were thinking the same thing. He nodded slightly, and she nodded back. Daisy knew her own magic wouldn't be precise or controlled enough for what they needed, but—

'Prof,' she shouted. 'We need a raft; something to get us out there.'

The Prof hardly blinked before calling down every vine from the rigging and weaving them together neatly into a mat of living green. For a split second, Daisy envied the ease and precision of her magic – then together they were casting it down onto the surging water like a raft, with the end of each vine still looped to the boat.

Daisy braced one hand against the side and looked

at Indigo, who had sprinted to join her. She grasped his hand. 'Ready?' she said.

Indigo clenched his jaw and tightened his own free hand on the side of the boat. Daisy closed her eyes.

'One,' she said.

'Two,' said Indigo.

'Three!' And together they launched themselves into the storm-tossed water.

Chapter 26

Max charged below deck and stood in the corridor, chest heaving. He felt hot and itchy, with a dull fury that throbbed in him like the beat of a drum. Dimly, he noticed that a storm was howling around the boat, tossing it up and down on the waves, and he staggered where he stood. He wanted to smash something to pieces; he wanted to destroy things and tear them apart.

He stormed straight past his cabin, half blind with rage. The thought of having to share the room with Daisy and the others made him even more furious. Lightning flashed outside. He spotted a door at the end of the corridor. He kicked it savagely, just for something to do. The pain in his toes felt good. He tried the handle. It was locked, but that didn't matter. A few moments with Jarndyce's pin and it sprang open.

The space inside was shadowy and the air smelled spicy and rich. It was full of crates of old bits of theatre set, jumbled up together so that moth-eaten wigs sat on top of old satin dresses and crates of glass eyes. It seemed to be a lost property room, with old botanical specimens piled here and there, some of them with hastily scrawled labels that said things like: 'left behind at theatre in Spiderwise', and 'gift from a fan in New Oakly'. The thought of this made him savage with anger: the idea of people going around calmly watching plays and giving stupid presents when his mother was—

He yanked open one of the crates and began smashing things to the ground. Pots shattered, fan mail became confetti, and ancient bottles of scent broke on the floor. Thunder cracked above the deck, as if the storm was part of Max's mood. He spotted a blue glass orb in the nearest crate and with a fierce sort of joy he hurled it against the floor. It smashed spectacularly, the broken shards glittering like furious tears. Then sparks flared up and Max saw a blue seed embed itself between the planks of the ship. It must have been inside the blue glass orb. Even as he watched, the seed put down roots and began sending up a small blue shoot. It rose up and up towards him, until it was as high as his knee, with a single leaf unfurling from the stem.

He moved closer and saw that the leaf was almost black with silver veins that glittered with light, as if tiny living fireflies were caught in its sap. The leaf's surface was very smooth and shiny, and it seemed to swirl with shapes and patterns. Max frowned and bent closer. The shapes were resolving into images – into people and things that he knew.

There, small but precise on the surface of the leaf, was his mother, sitting at the foot of a hospital bed. She was holding the hand of a pale, thin child, perhaps ten years old, who had the bedclothes tucked up to his chin. Her face was grey and exhausted, her golden hair flat and lifeless. It was, Max realized, a memory – for that child on the bed was him.

Even as he watched, the child blinked open his eyes, and his mother switched on her smile. All trace of the greyness and tiredness was gone, and there she was: the mother he knew.

'Good greenness!' she said, raising her hands in mock despair. 'What a sleepyhead! You've been asleep for hours.' Max's ten-year-old self giggled and sat up. 'Luckily,' his mother said conspiratorially, 'I have a plan for what we're going to do this afternoon, and it's rather good – if I do say so myself.' She whispered the last bit behind one hand, and the small Max laughed again.

Max remembered what happened next, and he watched it unfold, entranced. Somehow, his mother had wheeled him up to the roof of the hospital, which had a view over the whole of New York. He had been missing Bolderdash and all the magical plants he had grown up with – but his mother had sat beside him and made flowers burst up through the cracks in the concrete until the whole roof had turned into a fantastic roof-garden, looped with wild white roses and flecked with bright-blue cornflowers and yellow goldenrod.

The sun was setting, and it felt as if all the warmth of its honeyed light was caught in the flowers on that concrete rooftop in the middle of a big city, as Max held his mother's hand and laughed.

Slowly, the vision faded from the leaf, and Max – the Max of now – looked up, blinking. He felt exhausted, but also as if he'd been given something precious, like an unhatched robin's egg that he mustn't break. Moving slowly, he shifted the toppled crates so that they formed a sort of protective wall around the seedling and its leaf, hiding it from view.

Then he locked the door behind him and went back to the empty cabin, trying very hard to think of nothing.

Chapter 27

Rain lashed their faces, lightning flickered, wind howled in their ears – and then – *WHUMP!* With a great bone-bruising impact Daisy and Indigo landed on the mat of vines.

Up close, the whites of the foal's eyes were wide and glittering with fear, and its long pale mane frothed white and green like sea foam. It was the most beautiful thing Daisy had ever seen, like water given surge and muscle. It tossed its head, a wild thing with sharp hooves, lost and raging in the storm.

'Okay, Indigo,' shouted Daisy above the wind. She began moving their makeshift raft closer to the creature, and he leaned forward slowly with his hands open in front of him as if to show that he was harmless. He was whispering under his breath and even though Daisy guessed he was scared, his whole being seemed to her as calm and still as a summer pond. 'It's all right,' he was saying. Still standing on the raft, Indigo ducked under the creature's flailing head and caught its foaming mane in one hand – simple and clean as that. 'It's all right,' he repeated. 'You're safe.'

Miraculously, the horse quieted, and its movements

slowed. Daisy waved to the Prof and Rozaliya on the deck, and wide-eyed, the wardrobe mistress directed a gang of sailors to begin pulling in the vines, so that their little raft moved back towards the ship. Indigo held onto the foal's mane the whole time, and it swam alongside them, too exhausted to protest. Its white-blue flanks were rising and falling very fast, but its eyes were calmer now and had lost their edges of panicked white. At last, they reached the boat and someone lowered a part of the balustrade. Indigo stroked a hand along the creature's flank, and then, timing his movements with the next surging wave, he positioned the horse so that it was swept onto the deck.

Indigo and Daisy scrambled up after it. Moments later, Indigo was kneeling beside the foal, running his hands along its foreleg. 'Here's where he's injured,' he said. 'Does anyone have some chamomillion cream?' One of the crew rushed below deck and returned with a large pot, which Indigo tipped wholesale over the terrible laceration. It was weeping a watery green-blue substance that Daisy thought was probably the foal's blood. Slowly, the healing cream began to work. The foal shuddered and the wound began to knit together. Indigo was pressing his forehead against the foal's forehead, eyes closed. After a minute, he sighed and looked up.

'He'll be okay now,' he said. 'Can he stay for a while, until he's properly better? His name is Muir, by the way.'

Captain Speedwell nodded, speechless. Now Indigo was

pulling an apple from his pocket and feeding it to the horse, murmuring all the while.

'So,' said a voice beside Daisy, and she looked around to see Rozaliya at her elbow. 'Your friend is a Whisperer.'

'A what?'

'A Whisperer. One who can speak to the animals of the earth.'

'A Whisperer,' repeated Daisy. She watched as Indigo led the foal, both of them limping, to a sheltered corner of the deck, his hair a tangle of salt spray and horse spit. Jethro, his parakeet, landed atop his head and began pecking lovingly at his ear, while Boris the ship's cat curled around his feet, begging to be fussed over.

'Yes,' she said, as the foal closed its eyes and sank into sleep. 'I suppose that's what he is.'

A few minutes later, Indigo arrived at their side, beaming and breathless.

'Well done, lad,' boomed a nearby sailor, clapping him on the back so hard that his legs almost buckled under him. 'Jolly good show.'

Captain Speedwell, with baby Annika still fast asleep in the sling against his chest, was speaking softly to Marie-Claude, the first mate. Daisy thought she heard Max's name, but the captain's next words distracted her.

'Water horses are sacred to Travellers,' he said, turning to Indigo. 'We are bound to protect them. So, until the foal is better, it will stay on the boat – and you will stay with it.'

He sighed. 'You – and your friends, I suppose – will have to come with us.'

'To Iffenwild,' said Daisy eagerly.

The captain sighed in defeat. 'Yes,' he said. 'To Iffenwild.'

Daisy sucked in a breath. Her whole body tingled, like a bottle of sparkling water with the bubbles racing towards the top.

'You'll have to make yourselves useful,' said Captain Speedwell warningly. 'We're down two stagehands, as it happens, so we could do with the extra help.'

'Of course,' said Daisy, nodding so hard that her braid smacked her cheek. 'We can do that. We can do anything.'

She grinned. They were on their way.

A few minutes after Max got back to the cabin, he heard a knock on the door.

'Max?' It was Captain Speedwell's voice, firm and full of authority.

Max was silent. He heard the captain shift. 'Daisy told me about your mother,' he said. 'If you need anything, if you want to talk – I am here.'

Max didn't reply, and eventually, the footsteps went away. A few minutes later, there was another knock at the door, this one much more hesitant.

'Max?' It was Daisy this time, and he scowled at her small, tentative voice. 'Are you okay? Can I bring you anything?'

'No.' The word came out as a croak. He cleared his

throat and tried again. 'No, you can't. Go away.' The storm outside seemed to have calmed, but he felt as if an enormous python was coiled around his chest, making it hard to breathe.

'Okay,' said Daisy. 'I – um – I wanted to let you know that they're letting us stay on the *Nautilus*. We're going to Iffenwild – you were right about that. I'm sorry, though. I know you wanted to go to Mallowmarsh.'

Max said nothing. It didn't matter anymore whether they went to Mallowmarsh or not, because his mother was not there. She wasn't anywhere in the whole world and this single monumental fact suddenly seemed too huge and terrible to comprehend.

He closed his eyes and turned his face to the wall.

Chapter 28

'Oi, Indigo!'

Daisy tried to get his attention for the third time and failed. He was staring out across the water from the captain's barge towards the wardrobe ship, where Muir was stabled – which was pretty much his default state whenever he wasn't actually on board and checking on the foal's progress. 'I think he'll need about two weeks to heal,' he'd said the previous night.

Daisy picked up a bread roll and tossed it at his head.

'Ow! What?' Indigo picked the roll off the floor and took a large bite. 'Mmm. Rosemary bread.'

'Earth to Indigo,' said Daisy. 'Has the crew on the other boat told you anything about Iffenwild?'

He shook his head, distracted by a couple of ravens flying alongside the boat. 'No. But I have found out more about the water horses. They're a breed so rare that most Greenwilders think they don't exist. Some people call them kelpies, but they're not malicious – just wild and a bit misunderstood. Last night we saw them sort of swimming through the sea, but apparently when the moon shines on the water, they can actually gallop on the surface of the waves. And their hair is magical, you know. People pay thousands for a single strand at Darkmarket.'

A day had passed since the storm, and they were sailing steadily along the coast of what Daisy thought might be Croatia. No one would tell them where exactly the door into Iffenwild was located – though not for lack of trying on Daisy's part. Instead, she and the Prof had been busy finding out all they could about the Nautilus Theatre and its fleet.

The most unusual thing about the four boats was their size – or rather their lack of it. Although there were dozens of rooms inside the captain's ship alone, including multiple cabins, a kitchen and a cavernous storeroom, it looked no bigger than a canal boat on the outside. 'Flexilis wood,' explained the Prof. 'It's a cousin of the rubber tree, native to Brazil and Venezuela. The interior grows or shrinks itself to whatever size is needed, while the exterior stays the same.'

The boats shifted in other ways too: growing new porthole windows whenever a passing sailor needed to look out from one of the cabins, or sending out a fresh masthead when someone wanted to hang a new sail. Daisy had been taken aback the previous evening when she'd reached for a place to put her book, and a leafy wooden shelf had sprouted from the wall beside her bed. Best of all, her bunk had grown a sort of canopy: a branch of willow fronds that cascaded down to the floor, so that the bed was shaded by a leafy curtain that turned the morning sunlight into diamonds on the soft white bedspread.

Daisy soon discovered another benefit of travelling with the Nautilus Theatre. Rozaliya had taken a despairing look at her clothes the previous evening and seemed to reach breaking point. She had breathed deeply and pinched the bridge of her nose, and then whipped out a flexible green vine that was marked with centimetres like a tape measure. She flicked her fingers to send it looping around Daisy's waist, and then to measure every inch of her, from the length of her fingers to the distance between her shocked eyebrows. 'Leave it with me, darlink,' she said – and the next morning there was a pile of clothes waiting outside her cabin door: cropped trousers in shades of jade green and pale blue, and thin white shirts with tiny gold buttons shaped like dolphins, and a jacket the colour of the ocean at midsummer, embroidered with bursts of silver stars.

'Thank you,' she said to Rozaliya as she came onto the deck for breakfast. Today the wardrobe mistress was dressed in a black velvet jumpsuit with a jaunty yellow cape, and there was a large yellow turban wrapped around her head. She waved a hand dismissively so that a ring the size of a quail's egg caught the light. 'Now I don't have to look at your terrible old clothes anymore. *Vot* a relief!' Then she paused and smiled. 'Life is a theatre, child. It is important to dress for the show.'

Indigo and the Prof had new clothes too – although Indigo's were mostly for working with horses, and within twenty-four hours the Prof had contrived to make holes in the elbows of her new shirts.

Max, though, refused to speak to anyone, and stayed alone in the cabin all day, staring at the wall.

For Daisy and the others, that first day was when they met the rest of the crew. '*Crew* is a useful word,' said Rozaliya. 'We are a boat crew and a theatre crew, both. And we all have our roles to play.'

There was Marie-Claude, for example, who was the captain's first mate and also one of the leading actresses. She was a master navigator and could often be found beside Captain Speedwell at the wheel of the main boat, alternately practising lines and plotting their course by the stars.

Marie-Claude was married to the ship's carpenter and theatrical prop-master, a Scandinavian woman called Ingrid, who was almost as tall as Alexei, with long red hair that made her look like a magnificent ginger mountain. She moved gently and precisely, her large hands handling every object they touched with the delicacy and care of an antique collector.

'Theatre is storytelling,' she said to Daisy the next morning, as she finished painting one of the backdrops. 'The right prop can make a story fall into place.' Ingrid and Marie-Claude had a small, solemn-looking toddler called Archibald, who wobbled around the deck reciting snatches of Shakespeare and telling anyone who would listen that he intended to play Hamlet as soon as he was old enough.

Then there was the so-called leading man, the actor Gabriel Rose, who wore iridescent green capes and was, Daisy suspected, more than a little bit in love with his own reflection. Unfortunately, several of the younger crew members were in love with it too, and Daisy soon began rolling her eyes every time he walked past, preening his outfits and smoothing his shining cap of blond hair.

Captain Speedwell oversaw all of it with theatrical panache, piloting the small fleet, watching the angle of the sails and the course of the wind, and directing the plays they put on. He was the brains of the operation, but also, Daisy realized, its heart: laughing with the tailors and wigmakers, reviewing the work of the scene-painters, snatching bites of bread in between feeding Annika and plotting out a solution for a tricky scene.

'"Captain Speedwell" makes me feel old,' he told the children. 'Call me Alexei.' And so, they did.

Chapter 29

Daisy spent most of that afternoon worrying about Ma and calculating how long it would take them to get to Iffenwild.

'It takes how long it takes,' said Rozaliya, shrugging. 'Okay, okay,' she said, catching Daisy's glare. 'Two more days, I think, before we reach the door.'

In calm moments, as the barges glided through the water, the crew gathered on the deck of Alexei's boat to rehearse the play they would be performing when they reached Iffenwild. It was called *A Midsummer Night's Dream*, and everyone was very excited about it.

'Shakespeare,' said Rozaliya, with a fanatical gleam in her eye. 'Such genius! Such power! Such insight into the human condition!'

The captain winked at Daisy. 'Let's not forget that this is a play about a fairy king and queen who get into a fight – or that it involves a character called Nick Bottom who ends up being turned into a donkey.'

Daisy laughed. She had seen the play with Ma one summer in London, and she had loved the silliness of it. There was also a fairy called Puck who went around causing mischief with love potions, and a group of hopeless actors (including the unfortunate Bottom), who were trying to put on a play to celebrate the wedding of King Theseus (played by Alexei) and Queen Hippolyta (Marie-Claude).

After rehearsals, the whole crew gathered on the decks of the four ships for dinner – and that was when Daisy worked up the courage to ask them more about Iffenwild.

'Iffenwild,' said the captain – Alexei – quietly, and his eyes looked distant. 'I suppose you'd better hear something about it before we arrive.' Daisy, Indigo and the Prof sat forward slightly, as if this would help them catch every word. 'Iffenwild is the capital of the Marindeep – that's what we call the federation of maritime pockets across the world. Iffenwild is an old and wild city that belongs to the water more than the land. After the Great Divide – when the Marindeep cut itself off from the Greenwild – the ocean pockets ringed themselves around with protections and wards. Only Marindeepers know where the doorways into their realms can be found. Marindeepers know it . . . and Moon Travellers like us.'

'So you *are* Moon Travellers?' said Daisy. 'I wondered . . .'

'Yes,' said Alexei, taking a sip of wine from his glass. 'We belong to an ancient people who travel between the pockets of the Greenwild and the Marindeep, welcome in all and belonging to none.'

'Is that why you didn't have to hitch yourself to another boat to get here?' asked the Prof shrewdly, looking at the dazzling expanse of Aegean water around them.

'Mm,' said Alexei with a half-smile. 'Let's just say that Travellers have rights of way that circumvent the normal rules. What most Greenwilders don't know is that we still visit the Marindeep. That is a secret that we are sworn to keep.'

'But how come you're allowed to go back and forth, when no one else can?' asked Daisy.

'Ah,' said Alexei, with a glint of mischief in his eye. 'That is because of one small and interesting fact. The people of Iffenwild love theatre. The Nautilus Theatre Company has existed in one form or another for centuries – and our people have been visiting the Marindeep for over two hundred years. Not even the Great Divide could stop us being invited back.'

Daisy frowned and took another piece of the hot fresh bread that was on the table. There were seagulls wheeling high in the sky above the boat, and a pair of ravens pecking at the rail. 'Did the Marindeep really have to cut itself off?'

Alexei sighed, looking suddenly older. 'The whole world is under attack from human greed and negligence, Daisy. The oceans have suffered greatly, even though the damage there is often easier to overlook than on land.'

Daisy thought of the news stories that Ma had covered, about bleached coral reefs and plastic inside the bellies of whales, and oil pumped into the sea. She swallowed, and Alexei went on speaking. 'Well, the Marindeep cut itself off, thinking it would protect them from all of this. It's a delusion, as far as I can tell. The two worlds are linked. If one fails, so does the other.'

Then he rubbed his nose thoughtfully. 'Either way, when we get there, it might be wise if you don't mention to anyone that you're Greenwilders. As far as they're concerned, you'll be young members of our crew, excited about your first theatre season. All right?'

Daisy lay sleepless for a long time in her leaf-canopied bunk that night, with Napoleon curled up in a ball on top of her chest. She had lost control of her magic again while helping mend some fishing nets after dinner, and had almost sent a deckhand overboard in the chaos. Her cheeks burned at the memory.

Napoleon meowed sleepily. 'I know,' she said. 'I should think about something else.'

She closed her eyes and tried to remember nights with Ma, driving back late from her many research trips. She remembered Ma telling her Persian fairy tales as they drove: stories about brave princesses and magical birds and enchanted pearls.

She remembered falling asleep in the car with the lights of the dashboard shining against the dark windows, as if the wheels had lifted off the ground and they were floating along the edge of the world. She remembered being lifted sleepily in Ma's arms and tucked into a bed that was as soft as a cloud envelope, folded up in a sense of safety that seemed to stretch for ever in all directions.

Very little had seemed safe or certain to Daisy since Ma's disappearance. She watched Napoleon breathing in and out, snoring with a feline steadiness that rumbled through the mattress. But even this couldn't stop the feeling that spread through her veins. It was the bone-deep feeling of missing one person; and the sense that everything was wrong, and that she didn't know how to fix it. How on earth would she persuade the Iffenwilders to come with her to the Amazon? And how was she supposed to find Ma when she couldn't even control her own magic?

Chapter 30

The next morning, Max got up from his bed for the first time in three days.

Without saying a word, he appeared above deck and took a bread roll at breakfast. The three other children stared at him, astonished.

Max stared back at them. He took in Indigo's scuffed riding boots, the Prof's sparkling gold-rimmed spectacles, and Daisy's wide-set dark eyes.

Her cat climbed onto the table and bared its teeth at him.

Max was assailed by the familiar hot, itchy feeling he had when he was around other people.

'What are you looking at?' His right cheek burned, and he glared at them.

'Nothing,' said the Prof quietly, and the parakeet on Indigo's shoulder cheeped.

'Good,' he said, and he snatched his bread roll and left the table.

He stormed downstairs and headed straight to the storage room. He unlocked the door, moved the crates aside, and breathed an unexpected sigh of relief. The sapling was still there. It had grown as high as his knees and put out a second leaf. Without thinking, he bent his head towards it. The colours sparked and swirled on its polished surface, and then he was inside the memory.

He could see his younger self – perhaps six years old – running through banks of sparkling white snow. It had been coming down all day and all night, and the whole of Bolderdash was outside having a snow fight. Cries of laughter and outrage floated through the garden as snowballs hurtled through the air, exploding in powdery white puffs.

'Stop! Come here, Max,' said his mother. This was four years before he'd become sick, but he had always been small for his age and prone to colds. She was running behind him, blonde hair flying out like a flag. 'At least put on a scarf.' He shook his head but allowed himself to be caught, the hated object wound around his neck. It itched horribly.

Then he was off again. 'Wait for me!' he cried to the other children. 'Wait for me!'

They laughed and he heard one of them say, 'We'll never get rid of him at this rate. Come on, let's go this way – maybe he won't follow us.'

Max watched his younger self drop back as if he'd been slapped. He remembered how his eyes had stung, and how his throat had closed up so tightly he couldn't speak. He had begged so hard to be allowed out to play in the snow, but it had made no difference. He would always be the one left behind.

A great gust of snow swirled across the surface of the leaf, and the memory faded. Max stood up, blinking. Then he rearranged the crates to hide the sapling and left the storage room.

'So,' came a voice from behind him, as Max walked blindly past his cabin. 'You are up.'

It was the wardrobe mistress he had seen briefly on his first night on the ship. Her voice was loud, and he found her Russian accent very comforting, because this was the language that his best (and only) friend at Bolderdash had spoken. Ivan had turned up two years after that day in the snow, and he'd taught Max many useful Russian words (most of them rude), while their mothers talked downstairs and Max played Tchaikovsky on the record player.

'Da,' he said, without thinking, which meant 'Yes', and the old woman's face broke into a smile. 'Russkiy?' she asked delightedly, and he shook his head. 'No,' he said in Russian, and the woman cocked her head. 'But I speak a little.' Five minutes later he was sitting in her cabin with a slice of Russian honey cake and a steaming glass of sweet tea, while Rozaliya Volkova tried to persuade him to wear a gold cape (he declined, politely) and have another slice of cake (he accepted). The players came in and out of the wardrobe mistress's domain talking loudly and waving their hands, and she made them all cups of tea too, sometimes pouring in a tot of something that smelled like a cross between wood-smoke and lighter fluid.

Rozaliya was, thought Max, like the ship's cantankerous grandmother, scolding and dismissive in a way that the crew seemed to find soothing. Max sat watching quietly and discovered, rather to his surprise, that he was enjoying himself. He liked the way that the actors made big gestures and laughed from their bellies. He liked the way they wore whatever they wanted and gulped their tea and called each other 'darling' in loud voices. It was so different from the hushed corridors of the hospital, where the only disturbance was the doctors' ward round each morning. Some of the players took out their lutes and violins and began to play old Traveller melodies and sing along in their low, deep voices.

He found himself humming along without realizing. His mother had never encouraged his love of music ('it's not practical,' she had said, tucking her hair behind one ear) – but he couldn't help himself now. The melody was too beautiful.

He swallowed slightly, and a drop of water fell onto the deck by his feet. Then another, and another, and Max looked up. It wasn't his tears. It was spray blowing in through the open porthole. He raced onto the deck in time to see—

'A whale!' cried Indigo, who was leaning over the edge of the deck so eagerly he was in danger of falling in. Daisy was beside him, hanging onto the guard-rail for dear life, cheeks red from the wind. It was a whole pod of finback whales, long and sleek and slender, surging like flexing muscles beneath the skin of the sea. Then one broke the surface and rose like a volcano, spouting seawater that showered down all over the deck in a thousand million drops of light.

Max looked up and for a moment he locked eyes with Daisy and saw his own expression mirrored back at him: wide-eyed, wonderstruck. Then the whales surged onwards, dived deeper, and vanished.

Chapter 31

The wind rose before sunset, whistling through the rigging like a restless spirit, and the air swirled with cawing seabirds.

'We're getting close to the gate,' said Alexei from the prow. 'The birds are drawn to the frequency of the magic. It's somewhere very near here, although the exact location shifts around a bit . . . An extra defensive measure to stop people getting in.' He hummed low in his throat and adjusted his grip on the wheel. 'It may take us a few hours.'

Daisy looked around at the deep blue of the sea, and the sheer grey-white cliffs of a distant coast plunging into the water in great slices of basalt and limestone. She looked at the crushed clouds piled up in the sky, like mountains the colour of rose petals. Then she sensed something on the air.

She turned and was the first to see it. A black ship etched against the sunset, moving swiftly towards them, tacking against the wind.

'Look!' She pointed and the others massed at the railings to see what it was. Daisy squinted and was just able to make out the emblem on the black flag that flew from its mast. A silver scythe: the symbol of the Grim Reapers.

Already the ship was closing in on them. With a roar Alexei sprang into action. 'Stations, everyone. Ready the defences.' Ingrid and Marie-Claude's toddler was hurried below deck while the rest of the crew rushed to trim the sails. Daisy could see black-cloaked figures on the other ship now, and white foam peeling back from its prow as it surged through the water. At its head stood a man with lips drawn back to bare his yellow teeth. Daisy heard a sharp intake of breath beside her and glanced around to see Max, his face as white as paper.

'Jarndyce,' he whispered.

Daisy felt her heart pounding in every part of her body, all the way to her fingernails. The very air seemed to crackle.

Alexei had said it might take a few hours to search for the gate, but they needed to find it now. Staying to fight was not an option. The Reaper ship was bigger, and it was equipped with guns and cannons. The *Nautilus* fleet would not survive a conflict – but if they could find the gate, the black ship wouldn't be able to follow.

Pushing through the crew rushing about the deck, Daisy forced her way to the wheel, where Alexei was steering with every inch of his skill. He seemed to anticipate the movements of the sea before they happened, cutting a course through the waves while the other *Nautilus* boats followed behind. Their flat-bottomed shapes weren't built for speed and the black ship was gaining fast.

She pulled the dandelight from her pocket as she reached

Alexei. Its light shone out from the glass, moon-bright and blinding.

'What are you doing?' the captain roared over the wind. 'Get below deck.'

'No,' said Daisy. 'I can get us to the gate – fast. This is a dandelight. It's like a compass that points to magical places. I'm hoping it will work for the Marindeep too.'

Alexei looked from her to the dandelight, his eyes wide. Then he seized the wheel. 'Hold that thing steady,' he said, nodding to the dandelight. Daisy saw that, as she had hoped, its beam of light had narrowed like a compass needle and was pointing slightly to the right. 'STARBOARD HO!' Alexei bellowed, spinning the wheel. The boat heeled about, surging along the line of the dandelight beam, and the three other boats turned behind it.

Moments later, Daisy saw a sort of shimmering in the air between two great spires of rock. It was dusk now, and the beam of the dandelight was cutting through dark air spattered with sideways rain that fell in huge, heavy teardrops into the inky sea. Daisy glimpsed a great, shining gateway through the downpour, bright as the silver mist that rises from the bottom of a waterfall.

For a moment, she thought they were saved. Then the air darkened and the gate vanished behind a fresh squall of rain. The black ship was bearing down on them, close enough to see the guns in the hands of the men on deck. Bullets whined through the air like hornets. Alexei swore an oath.

Napoleon meowed from Daisy's shoulder, soaked and shivering. Daisy glanced at the beam of the dandelight and strained her eyes through the gloom.

'There!' she cried. There it was again, between the two great spires of rock – bright silver now, arched like a pale mirror rising up from the water. It was taller than the ship's tallest mast, with a coat of arms above it forged in glittering green water.

The four little canal boats surged towards it. Then they were upon it, passing through it, and the whole fleet seemed to groan with the pressure, as if they were coming out of an airlock. Any moment the Reaper ship would catch up, Daisy thought desperately. Any moment—

And then they burst out into the air of another world: air that was clear and blue and honey-bright. The sideways rain, the bullets, the roaring wind and shouting noise vanished, and they floated forwards across the rippling waters of a vast green lagoon.

In the distance, at the edge of the lagoon, was the shape of a city such as you see only once in a lifetime, and then perhaps only in dreams. A city of spires and domes that shone like stars over the water.

It was the city of Iffenwild.

Chapter 32

Max gazed at the horizon and gasped. It was as if all the oxygen in a ten-mile radius had rushed into his lungs.

He saw a city of spiralling shell towers – purple and midnight blue and sea green – rising up from the edge of the water. The air was full of birds – parakeets and doves and kingfishers – and shoals of fish swimming and flickering through the air as if through water, scudding past buildings and leaping over clouds. All along the skyline were mother-of-pearl domes and turrets topped by fluttering flags and pennants, all reflected in the shining surface of the green lagoon.

Before them lay the shadows of a vast coral reef, with spires reaching up from the depths in complex patterns that reminded Max of a maze. Even as they floated on its margins, a trio of sentry boats sailed out to meet them, flags fluttering.

'Halt!' came a cry from the lead boat. 'Who goes there?'

'The *Nautilus* fleet,' called Alexei. 'Here for our annual performance at the Iffenwild Opera House.'

There was a brief consultation, and then the closest sentry boat peeled away from the others and navigated through the coral maze towards them.

'You are expected,' called a uniformed woman through a loudhailer. 'Please follow our lead. Do not deviate from our course.'

'The Great Barrier Reef of Iffenwild,' said Rozaliya. 'It is designed to keep intruders out.'

The sentry boat sailed out in front and the four *Nautilus* boats followed with meticulous care. Alexei navigated them through the great coral peaks and razor-like outcrops with tiny, specific movements, calling out instructions to the three boats behind him.

'Hundreds of ships have been wrecked here,' whispered Rozaliya. 'The coral feeds on the bones of drowned sailors.'

Max shuddered and tried not to look down. It seemed like a long time before they emerged from the coral, and then they were out into the main lagoon. The water was clear as glass and Max saw starfish the size of wagon wheels sunning themselves in the depths, while giant rainbow jellyfish pulsed through the shallows and flicked lazy tentacles at each other.

They entered the city through a bustling, boat-filled harbour and sailed onto a broad canal lined with weeping willows and houses painted in ice-cream colours. There were masses and masses of fruit trees with little ripe pears growing on them, and glamorous parakeets and rainbow fish soaring across the sparkling air.

'Iffenwild is a pocket of the old Austro-Hungarian empire,' said Rozaliya. 'Some people call it Vienna-on-the-water.' The houses had an elegant Austrian feel to them, and

Max noticed that many were actually houseboats, looking like floating cupcakes on the surface of the canals. Their walls were made from old, lustrous shell, with cascades of vines tumbling from their window boxes and sparkling glasshouses sitting on their roofs. From open windows drifted the beautiful, mournful sound of violins and cellos, along with the mouth-watering smell of apple pastry.

The water was still and calm. Alexei lowered his sails and gave orders for the crew of all four boats to propel themselves forward with oars. Sculling gently, they floated deeper into the network of winding canals, beneath old, crumbling stone bridges, and around bends that smelled strongly of leather and perfume and damp. Max saw wooded hills rising steeply on either side, and children running barefoot beside the canals, shouting and laughing. He saw old men sitting on the doorsteps of small houses shelling oysters, and boats filled with fruit and vegetables being poled along beneath brightly striped awnings. Bottlenose dolphins were leaping through the water ahead of Alexei's boat, and strange greeny-blue ferns trailed rubbery ribbons around the prow. People sat beside the water on arcaded streets, eating slices of *sachertorte* and chatting away in happy, voluble German.

It was, Max realized, warmer here – warmer than should have been possible for a day in March. The light was richer than any he'd seen before, extravagant as gold silk.

'So,' said Rozaliya, standing beside him. 'Welcome to the Lost Pocket of Iffenwild.'

Chapter 33

Daisy watched two high-flying swordfish chase each other across the brilliant blue of the sky. Her mouth was hanging open and she nearly swallowed a bug.

Sheldrake had called Iffenwild a murderous nation – but that didn't seem right at all. The city around her was certainly strange, with its houseboats and flying fish and gold-freckled anemones clinging to the sides of its canals – and yet she saw similarities with the Greenwild everywhere she looked. She saw people crossing canals on giant, flowering lily pads, just like the lilypaddles that scudded across the lake at Mallowmarsh. She saw people stringing up laundry on ribbons of seaweed, calling up great banks of bulrushes to cushion their houseboats from the swell of passing water traffic, and summoning fronds of kelp to act like curtains around their front porches. The only difference to the Greenwild was that these were clearly marine Botanists, and their love was for water plants.

Daisy touched her necklace, suddenly filled with longing for Ma. She remembered a day at the beach with Ma, and the hours they'd spent staring down into a rockpool as though it was its own entire world – with hairy whelks and funny crabs walking sideways. There were anemones fluttering their tiny tentacles, and lazy pink starfish and winkles like little ivory buttons. That pool had been in the Greyside, but it had cast its own spell of enchantment. 'Magic is everywhere,' Ma said, trailing her hand in the water; 'if only you look closely.'

Daisy looked up now and felt that same head-rush of amazement she'd felt at the rockpool: as if she was looking at something wild and rare and full of possibility.

Then Napoleon coughed up a hairball on her shoe.

A moment later, the captain's boat shuddered, and Daisy felt the mast lurch and sway above her. They had reached what looked like the main square of the city, lined with magnificent shell buildings, and something was strung across the canal just beneath the water. 'Ah, yes,' said Alexei. 'The palace chain. It's drawn across the mouth of the royal canal to stop boats getting too close.' He gestured towards a great, pompous wedding cake of a building with the tallest and most spiralling shell tower in the city.

'These Iffenwilders,' said Rozaliya, adjusting her cape. 'They have no faith in people. All so *paranoid*.'

The square, Daisy saw, was shaped liked a horseshoe – lined on three sides with buildings and trees, but open on the fourth side to the other half of the lagoon, so that the pink-marbled palace faced out across the water.

There was a call from the sentry boat up ahead and an

answering cry from the square. A moment later, a troop of guards in blue uniform marched across to the ramshackle little fleet. Each of them was holding a gleaming trident.

'Yes,' said Alexei in his most winning and theatrical tones. 'It's true. We have arrived – the finest theatre troupe in the magical world, here to grace your fine city with our spectacular talents.'

One of the guards grunted, unimpressed. Then he beckoned to the others and over the next half hour they searched the four *Nautilus* boats from top to bottom.

'Any contraband items from the Greyside will be removed and destroyed,' called the leader, pulling books from the shelf in the main cabin. 'We cannot allow the taint of the outer world within our city.'

Rozaliya sighed deeply and began filing her nails.

Shouts came from the captain's boat, as a pair of guards congregated around Max. 'Remove your shoes, please,' said one of them.

'What? These?' Max looked down at his black Doc Martens, baffled. 'But they're just ordinary—'

'They are Greyside items,' said the guard implacably. 'Remove them, please.'

Slowly, hands shaking, Max unpicked the laces and slid the shoes off. One of the guards snapped on a pair of gloves and deposited the shoes in a special sealed bag. Then he handed them to a constable who built a small bonfire on the shore and torched the lot. Within minutes, the air was full of the acrid scent of burning rubber. Max looked on the verge of tears. It was a good thing, thought Daisy, that Rozaliya had given him a new set of clothes, or he might have had to hand those over too. The shoes had been the only thing left from his life in the Greyside.

Finally, when the search was finished, the guards nodded. 'Very well. You may proceed. Remember, curfew in the city is at ten p.m. You must be back at your boats by that time every night. Failure to comply will result in the expulsion of the whole company from the city.'

Rozaliya looked at Daisy, Indigo and the Prof. 'That means you too,' she said quietly. 'The city has changed in the last couple of years. It's dangerous at night. And the Reef is strictly out of bounds.'

The palace chain was lowered as she spoke, and the four boats were able to continue into the canal. They navigated past the palace and turned into a quiet backwater, where they moored beside a pear tree with several angelfish roosting in its branches.

Down the end of the street, Daisy made out a building with a domed roof and a facade of marble arches. It was decorated with mosaics of leaping dolphins, and a shoal of rainbow fish darted in and out of the solemn sculptures of men and women that lined the balconies.

'Those are famous singers and actors,' said Alexei, pointing. 'And that is the Iffenwild Opera House, where the Nautilus Theatre performs each spring.'

'We are the event of the season,' said Rozaliya, with more than a hint of pride in her voice. 'Like every year. We have fans that come from all across the Marindeep to see us. It is not easy being so beloved, no.' She sighed deeply. 'But somehow, we must bear this burden.'

Daisy heard a small, stifled noise from Max that sounded suspiciously like a laugh.

'Sorry,' he said, voice shaky. 'Just a sneeze. Terrible hay fever.'

A crowd had gathered on the bank to greet the four *Nautilus* boats. The players were soon overwhelmed with greetings from fans and old friends alike, and Daisy remembered what Alexei had said about the Iffenwilders being lovers of theatre.

'Will you be doing the *Tale of the Wandering Botanist*?' asked one bluff old gentleman. 'That bit where his glass eye falls out – never laughed so much in my life! I came back to watch it six times.'

'Oh no, it's *The Glasshouse in the Air* that's my favourite,' said a little old lady with a shopping trolley attached to her wrist with vines. 'The way all the panes of glass smashed at the end – it made me want to do a dance with my walking stick.' She waved the stick in the air to demonstrate, cackling gleefully. Others chimed in, and Daisy's eyes wandered over the crowd. Her eyes snagged on a boy just as he extracted a pastry from the old lady's shopping trolley and took a large bite. He had a thin, clever face with bright hazel eyes, and a scruffy black dog clutched in his arms. When he caught her looking, he winked.

'Well, I hope it's *The Tempest*,' said the formal-looking man standing beside the boy. 'Nothing like a bit of Shakespeare!'

'But of course,' came a low, delighted voice. 'The play will be a surprise, like every year.' The crowd parted and Daisy looked up to see a woman coming towards them from the direction of the palace. She was tall and very beautiful – more beautiful than anyone Daisy had ever seen. She was wearing a dress the colour of a pearl, and her coils of dark hair were threaded with tiny beads of coral. Giant pearls hung from her ears and a magnificent pearl tiara sat on her head. Her skin was very white and her eyes were like green glass polished by the sea. There was a small retinue of guards behind her and a short, squat man at her elbow juggling a pile of papers.

'The Duchess of Iffenwild,' whispered Rozaliya, her breath hot in Daisy's ear. 'The regent of the city.'

Chapter 34

Daisy looked up and saw that Alexei was taking two glasses from inside his waistcoat and filling them with amber-coloured liquid from a flask he drew from another pocket. 'To arrivals,' he said dramatically. 'And to theatre – the stuff of life itself!'

The Duchess looked charmed. 'Indeed,' she said, raising her glass towards the captain and then the crew. 'Welcome, all of you.' She smiled and looked around at the boats. Then she caught sight of Muir, munching on fish guts (his preferred lunch) on the deck of the wardrobe boat, and her eyes widened in delight. 'A water horse!' she cried. Indigo, holding onto Muir's mane, only just managed to keep him from rearing up in alarm. 'What a beauty!'

Indigo beamed.

'You must make yourselves at home here in Iffenwild,' said the Duchess. 'Our city loves theatre. We have several acting companies of our own, of course. But nothing can match the magic and artistry of the Nautilus players.'

'You flatter us,' said Alexei gallantly.

'Not at all, Captain.' The Duchess smiled and took a

final sip of her drink before turning to leave. 'I look forward to the first performance.'

'Wait!' Daisy ran down the gangplank to the street that ran alongside the canal. This was her chance to speak to the leader of Iffenwild, to persuade her that the Greenwild needed help. From the corner of her eye, Daisy saw the boy who'd stolen the pastry restraining his scruffy dog, which was leaping up and down.

There was a shocked hush as everyone looked around, catching sight of the girl with the bedraggled braid and the cat on her shoulder as she ran after the Duchess. The ruler of Iffenwild turned, her eyebrows arched. Daisy rested her hands on her waist, panting.

'Please,' she said. 'I know you don't usually talk to anyone outside the Marindeep, but we need your help. The Greenwild is in danger. A group called the Grim Reapers has declared war and people are going missing – or being killed. We need to rescue the missing Botanists – they're being kept in the Amazon rainforest – but we need reinforcements. We need you.'

The Duchess looked at Daisy as if she was an adorable puppet, or a dancing dachshund. 'Why, aren't you charming! Are you going to be in the play too? You would make an excellent character in one of the dramatic scenes. Don't you think, Pompey?' She glanced around at the short, bustling man who was carrying her papers.

'Undoubtedly, my lady,' he said, sounding bored.

'Wonderful!' she cried. 'There is so much dramatic talent on board the *Nautilus*.'

'But,' said Daisy, feeling sick, 'my mother is missing and we need help to rescue her. People are dying. The Greenwild needs you.'

Daisy's words finally seemed to register. The Duchess opened her mouth to speak, eyes warm with sympathy, but her bustling little assistant, Pompey, stepped forward and cleared his throat.

'Ahem! If I may?' He went on without waiting for a reply, looking down his nose at Daisy. He had a moustache that looked a bit like a caterpillar had died on his upper lip. 'The Federation of Maritime Pockets – of which Iffenwild is the capital – closed our borders for good reason. We did it for our own protection, and for the safety of our citizens.'

The Duchess looked at Daisy hopelessly. 'I'm sorry,' she said. 'I have to listen to my advisors in these matters. Perhaps the situation in the outer world is not as bad as you think?'

Daisy opened her mouth to speak, but Pompey snapped his fingers and three blue-uniformed guards stepped forward slightly. She shut it again. The Duchess smiled at everyone and stepped quickly towards a hot-air balloon that was waiting on the edge of the dock. She climbed into the basket, while Pompey clambered on behind her and gestured to an attendant to fire it up.

'That man,' said Rozaliya, narrowing her eyes. 'Every

year he seems to have more influence.' A moment later, the balloon was rising into the air, floating over the glittering tangle of waterways until it vanished behind one of the shell towers of the palace.

'What's with the hot-air balloon?' asked the Prof, raising an eyebrow.

'Ah,' said Rozaliya, shrugging. 'The Duchess has always preferred to travel by air rather than water. You have to admit, it's very theatrical.'

Shortly after that, the crowd began to disperse, and Daisy saw the clever-faced boy carried along with it, his scruffy little dog trotting along in his wake.

'So, that's that,' said Indigo glumly.

'No,' said the Prof, standing at Daisy's other side. 'We're the Five O'Clock Club. Giving up is not what we do. We keep trying. We find another way to convince her.'

'Like what?' asked Daisy. Her cheeks were still smarting with humiliation.

'I don't know,' said the Prof, her eyes fierce. 'But there will be a way. There has to be.'

Daisy lay awake in her bunk that night, staring out at the angelfish roosting in the trees and the stars shining like huge fireflies over the dark canals. Images moved through her mind like trails of light in a cloud chamber. A dead woman with bleached white eyes. The smudged black lines of Ma's last letter. Flames spreading like red flowers across the water at Moonmarket.

Had the Mallowmarsh boat escaped? Had they reached Amazeria? Or had they gone somewhere else? She wished, desperately, that she could find out.

Then she sat up. Napoleon fell off her chest with an indignant hiss. 'Indigo,' Daisy whispered. 'Wake up!'

'Wha?' Indigo sat up sleepily, his hair a bird's nest of curls. 'What's wrong?'

'Can we send a parakeet to the Mallowmarsh boat?' she asked, still whispering. 'Could Jethro find it?'

Indigo rubbed his eyes. 'This couldn't wait until morning?'

'Yes, or no?'

'All right, all right. Yes, I think so. The *Great Mallow* is made of wood from Mallowmarsh, so it'll work like a sort of homing beacon. He should be able to find it, wherever it's ended up.'

Daisy shook the Prof's shoulder, and ten minutes later they had devised a message, scrawled it on a torn-off sheet of paper and watched Indigo launch his parakeet out of the porthole window of their cabin while Max snored on, oblivious. She didn't tell Artemis where they were – better, she thought, to wait and see how things turned out – but she said that they were safe.

Five minutes later, Indigo and the Prof were once again fast asleep. But Daisy lay awake a little longer, thinking. Ma had been alive when she'd written her last letter, but that had been over a week ago. Anything might have happened since then. With every passing beat, Daisy's heart was tugging her towards the rainforest and towards Ma. What was she doing here, so far from everything she longed for?

She thought of Ma's letter: *Come with help, or not at all.*

Napoleon meowed and stuck a paw into her hair. 'Yes, I know,' said Daisy. 'We're doing what she said. But it's going to be much harder than I thought.' Alexei had told her that the *Nautilus* would be staying in Iffenwild for nine days – two days for setting up, one for the dress rehearsal, and then six days of performances. That gave them nine days to persuade the Duchess and her people to join them in the fight against the Grim Reapers. The sooner she did that, the sooner they could be on their way towards the place she was needed most: at Ma's side.

Chapter 35

Daisy spent the next morning feeling bleary-eyed and distracted as the players began to unpack the four boats and shift great boxes of props and materials into the theatre. Rozaliya was in her element, shouting at wigmakers and tailors as they staggered back and forth with bolts of cloth and enormous trunks full of costumes.

'Come on, Daisy,' said the Prof, expertly directing a series of vine-pulleys to carry trunks across the stage and into the wings. 'It's good practice.' But when Daisy tried, her vine exploded into a giant beanstalk and almost crushed one of the stagehands.

'Ah!' cried Rozaliya, rushing into its path. She took control of the rampant vine and used her own magic to shrink it back to a manageable size. 'Child! This is the second time! Has no one taught you how to—'

'Control my magic?' asked Daisy glumly. 'They've tried, but I can't seem to manage it. I'm pretty sure that I'm a lost cause.'

Daisy saw Max staring at her curiously and she coloured, furious at being caught in such an embarrassing position.

'Lost cause?' cried Rozaliya, flaring her nostrils. 'Vot is this! Don't let me hear you say such words, child. There is no such thing. I will teach you myself.'

She was as good as her word, and at the next tea break she sat Daisy down in the dressing room with a piece of cloth and a giant darning needle. In her pocket was a coil of vine as thin and flexible as yarn.

'Like this,' she said, making the vine coil into the air before threading itself through the needle and then through the cloth. 'Watch – the preciseness is everything.' In five minutes flat, she had made a simple jacket and the green thread had bloomed with fat white roses in place of buttons. 'Now you try. Just a simple stitch to start with. Pay attention to the vine. Listen to it. Most of all, *don't let it get too excited.*'

Daisy closed her eyes and felt the sly green whisper of the vine in her mind. She tried to grab hold of it, but it was like trying to thread a needle while wearing boxing gloves. In frustration, she sent out a surge of energy and the vine exploded out into a thicket of knife-like thorns, impaling the piece of cloth like a harpoon. Napoleon hissed and leapt onto Daisy's head. Rozaliya jumped back hastily and removed a thorn from her turban. 'Is okay,' she said, breathing hard. 'Is OKAY. We will practise. In theatre, practice is everything.'

Daisy wasn't so sure. She felt, more than ever, a failure. If she couldn't even manage to control a tiny vine, what use would she be in a rescue mission?

*

Max had watched Daisy's accident at the theatre with amusement, but it wasn't enough to take his mind off the pain in his chest. *Mom, Mom, Mom*, went the beat of his heart. Rozaliya's words to Daisy echoed in his head. *Lost cause? Don't let me hear you say such words, child. There is no such thing.*

Max shook his head and brushed at his cheeks angrily. He missed his mother so badly it was like a fever. He even missed her telling him not to do things. '*Don't go near the water, Max. Stay away from the edge, Max. Don't get out of bed, Max. Don't use that word, Max. Don't tire yourself out by listening to all that music.*' He had longed for freedom, but now that he had it, he felt cast adrift.

He had observed Daisy's talk with the Duchess outside the theatre with a feeling of blankness. So what if Botanists were dying? What did it matter when the only person who really mattered was gone?

'Wake up, boy!' It was Rozaliya, and as usual she had little apparent sympathy for his feelings or anyone else's. Somehow, thought Max, this was a relief. 'You look like you are sucking on a very sad lemon,' she said. 'Come with me and be helpful.'

Back inside the opera house the air was rich and dim, and the red velvet seats curved around the stage in a rising semi-circle.

'Aha! MAX!' said Alexei, leaping up to greet them

as they came in. He looked inexplicably delighted. 'It's marvellous to see you up and about! What can I get you? A carrot? Some tea?' Max refused, and five minutes later he was put to work raising one of the curtains with Daisy. Not for the first time, he felt his back prickle with dislike. It was more than that, though. It was a sort of visceral, silent howl of *not fair* that rose up inside him every time he was near her. Daisy's mother was still alive. Daisy's mother sent her letters – he had seen her reading one of them. And perhaps worst of all, Daisy had spent time with Max's own mother at Mallowmarsh – while *he* had been trapped in a cellar eating rat-nibbled bread. What right did Daisy have to go around demanding that duchesses answer her questions? She was unbearable.

'Here you go,' she said quietly, handing him the end of the vine that would string up the curtain. 'I don't – I can't control—' She swallowed. 'What I mean is, you might have to help me put it up by hand.' Max gritted his teeth. *Everything* about her annoyed him. Her clear, low voice. Her thick braid. Her snooty cat! And the conviction she had that she was somehow *owed* help. He snorted. Didn't she know that no one was owed anything? Not family, not happiness, not aid of any kind.

The sooner she learned that, the better it would be.

Chapter 36

Jethro returned that afternoon, feathers slightly rumpled but otherwise no worse for wear. In his beak, he held a message on paper headed with the Mallowmarsh crest.

Daisy, it began, in Artemis's precise writing. *Thank greenness you are safe.*

Artemis was writing from an Italian pocket near Rome, where the *Great Mallow* had escaped after the battle of Moonmarket. The ship had been too damaged in the attack for the original plan to go ahead, and needed serious repairs before it would be ready to sail again.

The whole market was laid waste, wrote Artemis. *The Grim Reapers control it now. We were lucky to escape with our lives: Acorn especially. How could you put her – and yourself – in such danger? Where are you now?*

Daisy stood in the opera house with the letter in her hand, feeling sick at the idea of the Reapers lording it over Moonmarket; sick with guilt at what could have happened to Acorn; sick with relief that Acorn and the other Mallowmarshers were all right.

She swallowed and turned just in time to see the curtain rise. Very little could have distracted her in that moment, but the stage was beautiful, like a wild forest inside a theatre. Thanks to the genius of Ingrid and her team, banks of thyme and violets were flowering near the footlights, foxgloves were springing up to stage left, and the willow-silk curtain shone in the light of the many lanterns that glittered from the theatre's grand circle. The dress rehearsal was in two days' time, and the crew was nearly ready.

Daisy, on the other hand, felt as if she was still at sea. The *Great Mallow* was safe – well and good – but getting the support of the Iffenwilders seemed impossibly daunting. To make matters worse, she could feel Max standing nearby, glaring as if she'd done him some sort of personal injury. Daisy seethed inwardly. All she'd done was save his life – twice! And instead of thanks, what did she get? Silence and glaring and – yes, she was sure of it – an attempt to trip her up with the curtain vine while they carted props across the stage. She'd only just managed to catch herself in time.

She scowled and rubbed her palms against her trousers. Napoleon had picked up on her mood and sat perched on her shoulder, glaring at Max with every strand of fur on his body bristling.

Daisy knew she should be kinder. The worst thing in the world had happened to him. He had lost his mother. For some reason, though, this seemed to make it harder to talk to him properly. It was like looking her own greatest fear straight in the face. It made her feel dizzy, like standing on the edge of a cliff.

Instead, she went back out to the boat and helped Alexei with the last of the boxes. As she returned, a boy darted into the chaos of the theatre entrance and handed her a folded note. Half of his face was hidden by a black muffler, and beside him was a scruffy dog that looked familiar. Inside, the note read:

> *If you want to find out more about Iffenwild and the Duchess, come to the Jolly Fishhook in the Old Harbour tonight. I'll tell you what you want to know.*
> *– A friend*

Daisy frowned and looked around for the boy, but he and the dog were already gone. She passed the Prof on her way back to the captain's boat to collect the next box of props, and murmured, 'Five O'Clock Club meeting after this, in the cabin. Tell Indigo. And leave Max out of it.'

'I say we go,' said Daisy, striding up and down the cabin and clutching the mysterious note. Indigo was lounging on a moss-covered armchair that had grown from the wooden floor during the night, while the Prof sat cross-legged on her top bunk, glasses glinting and hair almost touching the ceiling. 'We need to talk to some Iffenwilders,' Daisy went on; 'find out what it's like here, whether any of *them* have gone missing. Whoever this is,' she said, holding up the note, 'they want to help.'

'How do we know it's not a trap?' said the Prof, wrinkling her nose.

'I think Daisy's right,' said Indigo suddenly. 'I saw the boy as he left – he had a dog, right? Well, that dog was happy. I could feel it. I think we should trust him.'

'Oh, great,' said the Prof, rolling her eyes. 'The scientific method. Now we're judging people by their dogs. What next? Trust someone because they have a contented pet dormouse?'

'Um,' said Indigo. 'Is that a trick question?'

That was how Daisy, Indigo and the Prof found themselves walking through the city of Iffenwild on an afternoon so full of silver light that the whole sky seemed to shine. The light glittered in pale dashes off the canals and the round windows of the houseboats and shop-boats that lined the banks. Daisy watched a glasshouse-boat drift past, with hundreds of bright flowers and leaves pressed up against its sparkling walls.

But she mustn't be distracted. They were looking for something in particular – a place called the Jolly Fishhook. And an anonymous note-writer who might be able to help them.

Luckily, the Prof was fluent in German – she spoke twelve languages, not counting Latin and Ancient Greek – and she wasn't afraid to ask for directions. Half an hour later they found themselves in a peaceful little square lined with whispering linden trees, where groups of loud fishermen sat at wooden tables beneath a red-and-white-striped awning emblazoned with the words *Der Lustige Angelhaken*. Below it was the English translation for merchants and travellers: *The Jolly Fishhook*. For a moment, Daisy thought she heard a rustle behind her, and she glanced back. But it was only the trees swaying in the spring wind.

To one side of the tavern door was a small gang of kids, and in the window was the boy Daisy had seen in the crowd yesterday – and who had delivered the note. He looked up as they approached, and his dog barked.

The boy was thin and tanned, with a snub nose and hazel eyes that shone with mischief. His tufts of spiky brown hair reminded Daisy of a hedgehog.

'It's you,' he said, darting outside to meet them. 'The children from the theatre. You got my note?'

'Yes,' said Daisy. She cleared her throat. 'Er . . . you said you could help?'

The boy glanced around. Then he beckoned them around the back of the building and pulled them inside.

Chapter 37

Max had thought that he knew all about feeling left out. But the sting he'd felt in the theatre when Daisy had whispered to the others, and they had hurried back to their cabin, was unexpectedly painful, like sitting on a hornet.

Perhaps that was why he'd followed them and listened through the cabin door – and then trailed them through the streets of Iffenwild to a sun-washed square and a tavern with a ridiculous name. Honestly, what was so jolly about a fishing hook?

He wasn't sure at first how he would follow them inside. Perhaps he would simply sit in the square and enjoy the sunshine.

But then he thought of Daisy's words – *Leave Max out of it* – and he slipped through the door behind them.

It was cool and dark inside the back room of the tavern, and it took Daisy's eyes a moment to adjust. Through the slats in a pair of wooden swing doors, she saw a bustling front room full of fishermen and fisherwomen sitting at big wooden tables, mending nets and reading enormous newspapers, and taking huge bites from plates of steaming Austrian dumplings. The air was raucous with noise and chatter, and rich with the smell of good coffee and the tiny crescent-shaped vanilla pastries that lay in trays on the counter ('Kipferl,' said the boy, catching her hungry glance).

In the main room, light streamed in through large round windows set in the white plastered walls, hung with displays of glinting fishhooks in every possible size – some curled smaller than Daisy's smallest fingernail, others the size of harpoons. But in the back storeroom, the light was blue and dim. The walls were stacked with shadowy crates of flour and barrels of smoked mackerel and brandy-wine.

'So,' said the boy, sitting down on a wicker basket full of tablecloths and looking hard at them. He was about thirteen, Daisy thought, and his thin, intent face creased into interesting lines when he spoke. 'My name is Emil. My father is coming back in ten minutes, so we have to talk fast.' His voice was low, Austrian. 'You want the Marindeep to bring down its walls, to help the Greenwild, yes?'

They nodded, surprised. 'How do you know that?' asked Daisy.

The boy ignored this. 'That is what we want too – me and . . . lots of other people in Iffenwild.' He waved a hand vaguely. 'We cannot be, how do you say, *isolated*, anymore.'

'So, how come the Duchess doesn't agree?'

Emil scowled. 'The Duchess is a regent. She is controlled by her advisors. You saw this already. And her advisors do

not let her talk to the people – the fishermen, the divers, the net-makers.' He gestured to the people in the main room of the tavern. 'She does not know what we know.'

'And what's that?'

'Iffenwild is dying,' said Emil. He paused, and Daisy felt something icy slip down her spine like a hailstone. 'Our coral reef protects us from the outside, and holds all the magic of the city. Now it is dying, piece by piece. When the coral wall falls, then Iffenwild falls too, into the water.'

Daisy leaned forward, feeling Napoleon's claws squeeze her shoulder.

'The people know this,' said Emil. 'But the Duchess, she stays in her palace, and no one can get close enough to tell her. Already, there are things that come through the defences; things that the coral used to keep out. Siren reeds and sea snakes and poisonous bindweed. They creep through the canals at night. So, her advisors make a curfew to keep us off the streets after dark. They keep us away from the Reef. Only the pearl divers are allowed to visit it now. The black market is full of pearls, the old fishermen say. And people are disappearing.'

'Wait. What do you mean, the coral is dying?' asked the Prof.

'It is going white,' said Emil, 'white like bone. Bleached. The divers say that the seaweed goes white, and the water goes grey. Everything, rotting.'

Daisy drew in a sharp breath, thinking of the white

branch of the Heart Oak, the bleached soil in the Sump-Rose Garden. 'The same thing is happening where we come from too: trees and earth going white, like something is sucking out all the colour.' She looked at Emil's face and hesitated; then decided to trust him. 'We're not Travellers, you see. We're Greenwilders, and we come from a pocket called Mallowmarsh.'

'Ah!' said Emil, leaning forward excitedly. 'Real Greenwilders! But you don't have green hair.'

'Sorry?'

'In the stories, Greenwilders always have green hair.'

'Afraid not,' said Daisy, tucking a stray piece of braid back into place.

'Okay,' said Emil, clearly readjusting. 'You see, we are forbidden to talk about the Greenwild. We are supposed to pretend that it doesn't exist. But we need to know. We need to talk to each other.'

'Yes.' Daisy leaned forward eagerly. 'Most Greenwilders think that the Marindeep is a myth. They've never even heard of its capital city.'

Emil nodded. 'My father, he says that after the Great Divide, the king sent scouts out into the Greenwild. They destroyed every map of the Marindeep they could find, and they spread rumours about a land of violent bandits – all to keep people from coming to look for us.' Daisy thought of *The Wild Atlas*. Had it survived only because it had lain hidden inside another book?

She glanced at Indigo and the Prof, then turned back to Emil.

'You said that people are . . . disappearing? Well, the same thing is happening where we come from too. Botanists have been vanishing for months – and a group called the Grim Reapers is behind it. They attacked Mallowmarsh last month.'

'Yes,' said Emil. 'I heard you tell this to the Duchess, about these Grim Reapers. But how did they get inside?' He looked puzzled. 'Your pockets are like ours, no? Closed to people without magic?'

'That's right,' said Daisy, nodding. 'But the Reapers were blackmailing someone inside Mallowmarsh; a woman called Marigold Brightly. She helped them get in.'

She heard a sudden creaking noise and looked around uneasily. 'What was that?'

Emil waved his hand. 'The storerooms are old and full of mice.' Then he leaned forward, eyes very bright and anxious. 'People are going missing all the time,' he said. 'Yes, even though we are cut off. Even though we are supposed to be safe. My uncle Matteo is gone, and a girl who was at my school. The people vanish from the streets – on their way to dinner, you understand, or on their way home. Into thin air. Pompey himself has sent his family to a different city, to be safe. They left Iffenwild three years ago.'

Daisy glanced at the Prof and saw that they were both thinking the same thing.

'It sounds a lot like the Reapers,' she said slowly. 'But how would they be getting into Iffenwild?'

Emil looked ferocious. 'This, we need to find out.'

The Prof nodded. 'Yes. And if it's true, that means Iffenwild has no excuse not to join the fight against the Grim Reapers. It means we're on the same side. If only we can get the Duchess away from Pompey – and persuade her to listen.'

Chapter 38

They were all very quiet at dinner that evening on the boat, thinking about what Emil had told them. The entire crew of the *Nautilus* had been invited to a special welcome dinner at the palace, where they were, said Alexei, expected to be entertaining and provide the Duchess with tales of their theatrical triumphs and misadventures. 'She loves the story of when I was playing Hamlet and accidentally fell off the stage,' he said, rolling his eyes. 'Makes her laugh every time.' ('Well, darlink,' said Rozaliya, adjusting her mink eyelashes, 'it was rather funny.')

Daisy, Indigo and the Prof had been left behind on the *Nautilus* with a pot of warm, spiced stew and Rozaliya's special Russian honey cake. Indigo had spent the afternoon with Muir, who was getting better rapidly. He was testing the foal's strength by riding on his back – something which made Alexei whistle in amazement. 'That,' he said, 'is something I've never seen, in all my years of sailing.'

Even so, Muir was a wild water horse, and Indigo had taken his fair share of tumbles. He sat rubbing at various bruises on his legs, while Daisy and the Prof took second helpings of stew. Napoleon was cleaning salt off his whiskers and looking even grumpier than usual. He was not happy about the amount of water in Iffenwild, and one of his ears was crooked from a recent run-in with Boris, the ship's enormous ginger cat, who took great pleasure in swatting at him with a weighty paw whenever he came too close.

Max didn't come out of the cabin to eat, but no one remarked on it. They were all exhausted and thinking hard about what they'd learned at the Jolly Fishhook.

'What did Emil mean when he said the Duchess is a regent?' asked Indigo, polishing off a plate of dumplings.

'It means,' said the Prof, 'that she was appointed to look after the throne as a sort of caretaker, after the king and queen were assassinated. Apparently –' she patted a pile of weighty German history books beside her – 'they were killed in some sort of plot about twelve years ago. The queen was pregnant with their second child. It was terribly sad.'

'So the Duchess is the ruler, then?' asked Indigo.

'Well,' said the Prof, 'according to what I've read, on the same day that the king and queen died, their thirteen-year-old son vanished. The Duchess was the king's sister, and she stepped in to take care of things until the boy could be found. So, he's the true heir, but until he turns up, yes, the Duchess runs the show.'

'It's just like a play,' said Indigo dreamily. 'Kings and queens, lost children, wicked relatives . . .'

'Sort of,' said the Prof, adjusting her spectacles. 'Except

the Duchess isn't wicked. I mean, okay, maybe she's a bit too fond of pearls. But it sounds like she's a kind ruler – and she's doing everything she can to find the missing heir. She wants to restore the true king as much as anyone. Without him, you see, the power of Iffenwild is only a fraction of what it could be. They used to have great water magic here,' she explained, flipping through a volume called *Time and Tide: A Recent History of Iffenwild*. 'There used to be people with the power to move the seas and change the course of rivers. It wasn't very common, but when it appeared, it was strong. And whether they were born in a grand house or a fisherman's shack, these Iffenwilders were given the honorary title "Marina", meaning "of the sea".' The Prof frowned. 'I don't approve of monarchy as a rule, but in this case, it seems to have been useful. The king or queen was always someone with water magic – someone chosen by the sea itself. The sea's power was channelled through them to the rest of the city. So without a monarch, the people are limited to small magic: canal drainage, preventing minor floods, that kind of thing.'

'Oh,' said Daisy, remembering what she'd overheard Artemis saying in the kitchen of the Roost. *Their power could turn the tide. Quite literally.* It suddenly made sense. 'So the Duchess doesn't have water magic?' she asked.

'I don't think so,' said the Prof, turning back to *Time and Tide*. 'That's why she's regent, not queen. According to this book, the lost prince had it in buckets, though.

He accidentally flooded the city when he was two years old and had a bad tantrum. The Iffenwilders believe that restoring the rightful heir would restore water magic to its full strength. For now, though . . .' She shrugged, and Daisy thought of Ma's letter: *Bring help.* She hadn't considered that the Iffenwilders might not be able to give help, even if they wanted to.

When at last they became too sleepy for more talking, they gathered up their empty plates and headed down to their cabin. There was a light under the door, and Daisy felt a knot in her stomach. She needed to apologize to Max for leaving him at the theatre that morning. She knocked quietly at the door, and when there was no answer, she opened it.

The cabin was empty.

Chapter 39

Max was up to his neck in a canal, and he had never felt so happy in his life. There was music everywhere, the sweetest music he had ever heard – a music that was soft and yearning and which seemed to fold him in its arms. There was no space for sadness with this music, which rose up like silver streamers through the air and towards the stars that shone so bright above the sleeping city of Iffenwild.

Dimly, he was aware that vines were coiling around his ankles underneath the water, winding softly up his legs and towards his wrists. Above the water, the vines were shaped like beautiful green birds, and they opened their silver beaks in a song so beautiful that Max felt every part of him tingle.

He'd had to wait a little while to slip out of the Jolly Fishhook, and he had been sure he knew his way back to where the *Nautilus* fleet was moored. But he had been furious, distracted by what Daisy had said about his mother. *She had been blackmailed. She had let the Grim Reapers into Mallowmarsh*. It couldn't be true. Daisy was lying, he was sure of it.

He must have taken a wrong turn because he'd ended up

here, at the edge of this canal, and it was the best mistake he'd ever made because otherwise he would never have heard this music and stepped into the water to get closer to it. The music smoothed out his anger and his hurt and his grief, like cool sweet water poured over a burn. And indeed, the water in the canal was cool and full of moonlight, and Max felt nothing but a sort of drunken exaltation as the vines pulled him deeper. The music was showing him his mother, her grey eyes bright and her golden hair swaying. He stepped into her arms and felt a pure, shining relief. She wasn't dead! He had known it all along. His chin vanished beneath the water, and then his mouth, and Max smiled because, finally, everything was right.

A moment later, there was nothing on the surface of the canal except a small stream of rising silver bubbles.

Daisy looked at the empty room and immediately she *knew*. The rustling noise behind them on their way to the Jolly Fishhook. The soft sound in the storeroom when she'd mentioned Marigold Brightly's name.

'Max followed us,' she said, looking with horror at Indigo and the Prof, who were behind her in the corridor. 'He followed us to the tavern. He must have got lost on the way back.' If Max had heard her talking about his mother, there was a good chance that he'd been angry enough to storm off into the city – alone.

The Prof was staring at her, horrified, and Napoleon's fur was prickling with dismay. 'But –' Indigo swallowed, his eyes wide – 'the city's dangerous after dark. And it's after curfew. If he's caught, the whole *Nautilus* crew could be thrown out of Iffenwild.'

The Prof nodded. 'We should tell Alexei, or . . .'

But it was no use. The players were out at their welcome dinner, and the three of them were quite alone.

'We have to find him,' said Daisy. 'This is my fault. If we hadn't left Max out, he wouldn't have tried to follow us. He wouldn't be out alone at night.'

Indigo nodded and shrugged on his coat. The Prof polished her glasses and resettled them on her nose.

'Okay,' said Daisy. Napoleon leapt onto her shoulder as they stepped off the gangplank onto the empty street that ran alongside the canal. 'We have to retrace our steps.'

The streets were dark and eerily silent, and the sound of their heels echoed off the shuttered houses and boats. The temperature had dropped, and fog swirled around their feet like milk.

'Where do you think he is?' whispered Indigo, glancing around nervously.

'He could be anywhere,' said Daisy. 'That's the problem.'

The Prof gave a soft cry and smacked her forehead. 'I'm an idiot. Indigo, could you get Jethro to look – fly over the streets and see if he can see anything?'

Within moments, Indigo had sent the little parakeet into the air, and the emerald streak of his feathers surged over the nearest canal and out of sight. For several minutes they stood tightly huddled beneath a streetlamp that shone with ghostly swamp-fire – a sort of phosphorescent seaweed that was used as street lighting throughout the city. 'I wish they'd use oil lamps instead,' said the Prof, glancing uneasily at the pale lanterns.

Indigo had his eyes closed in concentration and his lips moved silently. Daisy knew that he could speak to animals and hear their thoughts in answer. 'But it's more than that,' he had told her once. 'I can see through their eyes too.'

Daisy watched him now and wondered if he was seeing what Jethro saw. What did the world look like to a bird? The minutes passed, first two, then three, then five. Daisy was about to give up hope when Indigo gave a little cry and opened his eyes. 'I think we've found him,' he said. 'But oh, if it is him, we have to hurry.' He began to run, leading them through the maze of dark canals and down a narrow alleyway where the water shone black as an oil slick under the night sky. Jethro was circling desperately above a point in the canal where bubbles were swirling up from below. Music rose through the air, glorious music, and Daisy saw a mass of plants that looked like birds, all plunging cruel silver beaks into the water until ribbons of blood rose from the body below the surface.

'Siren reeds,' said the Prof, horrified. 'They shouldn't be in the city; they should only exist on the edge of islands and lagoons. They lure sailors who get too close to land.' She looked around and began pulling wads of moss from the wall of the alleyway. 'Daisy, Indigo, stuff this in your ears. Now!' But Daisy didn't wait to do as she was told.

She dived into the canal.

For a moment there was only confusion, a chaos of darkness and cold water – and then the music was everywhere. Daisy felt it filling her up like gold honey rising from the soles of her feet to the tips of her hair. She could see her father there beneath the water, with his kind eyes and the scar through his eyebrow. He smiled at her and stretched out his hand.

Then Daisy heard a yowl and felt something tiny but fierce land on her head in the canal. It was Napoleon, and it must have taken every bit of his resolution to brave the water. His claws raked the back of her scalp and the dream snapped. The magic, she now saw, was coming in great waves from the reeds that were binding themselves around her ankles. 'No,' she told them. 'NO!' And she pushed out with all the force of her green magic. For once, her lack of control was exactly what she needed. Her power exploded outwards with a force that sent the water up in a great rocketing plume, and the plants cringed back as if they'd been scalded. Daisy felt her ankles and wrists become free, and the shape in the water that was Max sagged as the vines released him. She lunged forward, grasped him around the waist, and half pushed, half pulled him to the edge of the canal. 'This is the THIRD time I've saved you from drowning,' she muttered. 'We have *got* to stop meeting like this.'

Chapter 40

Max landed hard on the flagstones beside the canal. For a moment he was still, blood and water streaming off his body. Then he gasped and water poured out of his mouth in great, coughing, blackish-green gouts.

'No,' he said, struggling. The face of his mother was slipping away, and he grasped at it desperately. 'No! Let me go back!'

Someone slapped him across the face, and he opened his eyes. It was the Prof, glasses glinting in the swamp-fire of the streetlamp. He pushed himself onto one elbow and looked around, dazed. 'You almost got eaten by a flock of siren reeds,' said the Prof, gesturing to the group of silver-beaked plants that were now skulking on the far side of the canal. He glanced up and saw Daisy, soaking wet and shivering beside him. Her cat was glaring at him balefully, water dripping from the tip of his tail.

'Feel free to say thank you,' said Daisy, wringing a stream of water from her braid.

'For what?' Max heard the sharpness in his own voice, but he couldn't help it. The way she'd spoken – so superior

– had set his teeth on edge, and he was still aching from the loss of his mother's face; the plunge back into a reality where she was gone, gone, gone.

'Oh, forget it,' Daisy muttered, and turned away.

Voices approached from the end of the canal. The four of them ducked – Max crawled – into the shadow of a doorway. He peered out from behind a water butt and saw two figures silhouetted at the end of the alley, one tall, one short.

'Everything's fixed for next Sunday,' said the short one. The tall figure said nothing but inclined his head. 'And here's the item you asked for,' the shorter man continued, pressing something into the other's hands. 'Don't waste it.' His voice was low and urgent, and he spoke with the now-familiar cadence of an Iffenwilder. Max tried to get a better look, but the short man was already gone. The tall man lingered for a moment at the mouth of the alley, and then he too turned away, leaving it empty once again.

'What was *that*?' hissed Daisy.

Indigo shrugged. 'Some kind of black-market trading, it looked like.'

'Emil mentioned a black market,' said Max.

Daisy glared at him. 'Oh yes, because you were eaves-dropping on us.'

'What?' he said defensively. 'I just happened to hear what he said.'

'So, you *just happened* to follow us?' said Daisy, voice

dripping with sarcasm. 'By accident?'

'Whatever,' said Max, clearly fuming. 'Let's get back to the boat.'

'Good idea,' said the Prof sharply. 'Let's go before anything *else* decides to eat us for a midnight snack.'

The walk back to the barge was silent except for the squelching of Daisy's and Max's wet shoes. They were both scowling.

Everyone was relieved when, at last, the four *Nautilus* boats came into view, their round windows blazing with warm light.

'I can't stand him,' said Daisy crossly. 'Why is he so – so . . . Ugh!'

It was the next morning, and she, Indigo and the Prof were gathered in the cabin with a stack of hot buttered toast and three large mugs of hot chocolate. The players hadn't returned from their party until at least an hour after the children had got back, two of them dripping wet and all of them exhausted. By the time Rozaliya had peeked into their cabin to check on them, they were tucked innocently into their bunks, pretending to snore.

Max had got up early and left the cabin at dawn. He was clearly avoiding them.

The Prof looked at Daisy with something like sympathy. 'Sometimes it's hard to get along with people who are very similar to you. It's like looking in a mirror, and sometimes you don't like what you see.'

'What?' said Daisy, outraged. 'I'm *nothing* like him! We aren't similar AT ALL.'

'Okay,' said the Prof, and shrugged an elegant shoulder.

Chapter 41

'That's it,' called Alexei excitedly. 'Move your arms and legs slowly through the water.'

It was very early the day after Max's brush with the siren reeds, and he was, once again, up to his neck in a canal. This time, though, the experience was voluntary.

He had crept out of the cabin at dawn and sat on the deck to watch the sunrise, picking ruthlessly at a loose nail in one of the planks. Alexei had found him there an hour later.

'Max?' he said. 'Are you all right?'

Max nodded, but his throat was tight.

'Ah,' said Alexei, sitting down next to him at the edge of the deck. He slopped a large cup of coffee as he settled himself, and checked on baby Annika, tucked up in her sling against his chest. She was fast asleep, one tiny thumb plugging her pursed mouth.

'She might look peaceful now,' said Alexei grimly, taking a large gulp of coffee, 'but she's been awake *all night*.' He paused and added, 'I came back early from the welcome dinner to look after her. And of course, when you're up in the small hours, you hear all sorts of interesting things. Voices, footsteps . . .' He glanced at Max and raised an eyebrow. 'Is there anything you want to tell me about yesterday?'

'Er,' said Max, stalling for time. If he told Alexei that they'd broken curfew, he'd land Daisy, Indigo and the Prof in a pile of trouble taller than the Duchess's palace. For a moment, this was a tempting prospect, but . . . no. What was the point of making them hate him more than they already did?

'Nothing happened,' he said, keeping his face blank. He was good at this. His mother had often told him he had the makings of an all-star poker champion.

Alexei looked politely incredulous. 'Really,' said Max. 'I'm fine.'

He glanced at Annika, who was making faces in her sleep.

'Her mother died when she was born,' said Alexei, answering Max's unspoken question. He looked, suddenly, very sad and very tired. Max remembered that Alexei was an actor and wondered if, here, for the first time, he was seeing the real man.

'It's okay not to be fine, Max. In fact, it's normal.'

Max nodded, a little jerk of his head. 'Okay,' he said quietly.

Then he looked at Annika's fat cheek pressed against Alexei's shirt. Her skin looked as soft as an apricot.

'Can you,' he said, 'teach me to swim?'

*

That first lesson was chaotic, and Max swallowed more of the canal than was probably good for him. But by the end of it, he could doggy paddle his way from the edge of the wardrobe boat to the bank, and stay afloat in the water for almost a minute.

'Yes!' said Alexei. 'You're a natural!'

Max's muscles were still weak, but it felt good to use them like this. The water felt kind on his arms and shins, like a greeting from an old friend. It shifted around him in gentle ripples and coils that lifted him weightlessly. But then baby Annika woke up with a wail, and Max, distracted, flailed in the water and almost swallowed a goldfish.

'Tomorrow morning,' said Alexei, hauling him dripping from the canal. 'And the day after. We'll keep going until you're the best swimmer Iffenwild has ever seen.'

Chapter 42

More and more, Daisy found herself consumed by two thoughts, like twin alarm bells ringing in her head. First, her desperation to leave Iffenwild and find Ma in the Amazon. Second, the urgent need to convince the Duchess and the Iffenwilders to come with them.

'We'll find a way,' said the Prof, again and again. 'We just have to be patient and make a plan.' But this was easier said than done.

'Less chit-chattering,' said Rozaliya when she found them discussing ideas in the dressing room that morning. 'Tomorrow is the dress rehearsal, and we need all hands on deck.' Guiltily, Daisy remembered her promise to Alexei to help with things at the theatre. It was time to make good on the deal.

The players were on stage from dawn to dusk, stopping only to grab cups of tea and scribble on their scripts. Rozaliya worked double-time on fitting their costumes, a brace of pins caught between her lips as she pinned and tucked. Daisy, Indigo and the Prof dashed back and forth for hours with spare ribbons, stage paint and make-up –

though Daisy was so busy thinking of Ma and the rescue mission that she tripped over Boris's tail and dropped a box of sequins all over the footlights.

She also discovered some of the more interesting plants that the Nautilus players used to help them on stage. For example, there was a special type of powdered seed they threw into the air to create a total blackout between scenes. 'Testing, testing,' said Marie-Claire, tossing a pinch above her head. The seeds hung suspended before billowing out into a pocket of darkness that engulfed them and turned the theatre suddenly to night.

'Black velvet seed powder,' said the Prof, sounding impressed.

Daisy sneaked a twist of it into her pocket. It might come in useful, she thought.

In breaks between rehearsals, Rozaliya took it upon herself to continue the children's education in green magic. 'So that you keep practising,' she said. Daisy suspected this was mostly for her benefit, given the previous day's disaster with the sewing vine, but the Prof was thrilled. 'It's essential that we stay in training,' she said, before the start of their first lesson. 'I, for one, have no intention of getting rusty.'

Daisy knew that the Prof was right. Any plan – and any Amazon rescue mission – would involve green magic. Still, she was less than pleased to find that Max would also be attending classes. Even though he was twelve and should have started learning a year ago, he was a complete beginner. Annoyingly, Rozaliya had partnered him with Daisy because they were 'on a similar level', which made Daisy bristle furiously.

All the same, by the end of their first hour, Max had managed to make his water pansy bloom calmly under the surface of the canal, while Daisy's had blossomed so fast that it had exploded, sending shredded pink petals everywhere and splashing her in the face.

It wasn't until after dinner that evening that Daisy, Indigo and the Prof finally had the chance to speak alone again. Max had disappeared somewhere, and Daisy barely waited for the cabin door to close before she began.

'I've been thinking about what we saw last night; and what Emil said about a black market here in Iffenwild. It sounds like something the Reapers would be involved in. Darkmarket was the heart of their operations in the Greenwild, remember?'

'I've been thinking the same thing,' said the Prof. The three of them were sitting cross-legged on the cabin's worn planks, sharing a plate of Rozaliya's famous *pryaniki* – Russian spice biscuits – to which they'd become mildly addicted. The Prof bit neatly into one before continuing. 'I think we should get a note to Emil, ask him if he knows anything more about it.' Daisy nodded and the Prof dashed off a few lines that Indigo attached to Jethro's leg. The little bird flew out of the cabin window, gleeful at the chance to stretch his wings.

'Right,' said the Prof. 'So, what if the Reapers *are* getting in somehow?'

'But how?' asked Indigo, taking four biscuits and shoving them into his mouth. 'Growun boes . . .' He swallowed and tried again. 'No one goes in or out of the Marindeep, apart from the—'

'Nautilus Theatre,' finished Daisy slowly. 'What if that's how black-market goods are being smuggled in and out of Iffenwild? What if there's someone in the *Nautilus* crew who's a – a traitor?'

'Oh!' The Prof sat up. 'That would explain how the Reapers were able to find us – you know, when the fleet was getting close to the Iffenwild gate. We were in the middle of the ocean; we should have been untraceable. How could they have known where we were unless someone on board signalled to them? They could have used a Greyside telephonic device before we passed into the Marindeep.'

'They're called phones,' said Daisy, hiding a smile.

'I don't know,' said Indigo, sounding doubtful. 'It makes sense in theory. But I mean . . . who are we talking about? Rozaliya? *Alexei?* They hate the Reapers. Marie-Claude's twin sister went missing three months ago – just like your Ma, Daisy. We're all on the same side here.'

Daisy slumped back onto her bunk.

'Well, there is one thing we *can* do. We can find out more about the coral – whether it's dying, like Emil said. If it's the same as what's happening in the Greenwild, then maybe we can use it to show the Duchess that the two places are the same. That being cut off isn't the answer.'

'Yes,' said the Prof. 'Ordinary Iffenwilders know that it's dying, but the Duchess's advisors don't let anyone get close enough to talk to her. Whereas we . . . we're part of the Nautilus Theatre. Which means that we might actually have a chance to convince her.'

'Exactly,' said Daisy. 'So we need to get out to the Reef. We need to bring back some proof – something she won't be able to ignore, no matter what her advisors say.'

'I don't know,' said the Prof reluctantly. 'Rozaliya said the coral was dangerous, out of bounds. We'd get in so much trouble.'

'Yes,' said Indigo, leaning forward. 'But only if we're caught.'

Chapter 43

Max had spent the afternoon in the storeroom. His tree had grown another memory for him, and it was a happy one. He crouched beside the new leaf and watched himself – eight years old – following his mother around one of the Bolderdash glasshouses. It contained a magical ice garden, full of Alaskan frostflowers and Artic snow-foxes, and Max enjoyed the feeling of being bundled up in his anorak as his mother told him about Canadian snow-weeds and the rare bandersnipe flower that grew only on the tallest glaciers.

'These plants,' she said quietly, 'no longer exist in the Greyside. And they're dying out in the Greenwild too. It's up to us to protect what we can. There is more wildness and wonder in both our worlds than you or I can possibly imagine – and it's up to us to fight for it with all our might and breath.' She glanced at him. 'Never forget that, Max. Promise me.'

'Yes,' said Max. 'I promise.'

But he'd never had a chance to learn green magic; never had a chance to gain the skills he'd need to really make a difference.

That was why the lesson with Rozaliya had been so exciting. For years he had longed to go to school, but his mother had always told him, 'Not yet, Max. After you're better.' He didn't know if he was 'better' now. The pain was gone for good, he hoped, and he was getting stronger every day, but he still felt breathless when he ran, exhausted when he climbed into bed at night. That hadn't stopped him joining that morning's lesson, though. He remembered the warmth in his fingers when he had made his water pansy bloom underwater – the ripple of currents around it and the wardrobe mistress's cry of delight. 'Bravo!' she had said. 'We have a natural!' Daisy had scowled, and he had felt a sense of deep satisfaction.

Max spent that evening in the dressing room of the opera house, watching the players preen in front of the mirrors and practise their lines for the following day's dress rehearsal. He watched Gabriel Rose, the leading actor, applying a pair of false eyelashes, and tried not to laugh when Rozaliya winked at him in one of the mirrors. He was already looking forward to the next day's lessons.

The following morning found him up on deck, where it was turning into a brisk day with clouds racing across the sky like a film on fast forward. Alexei was waiting, nursing a pint of coffee. That morning's lesson was a good one. Annika was sleeping in her cot below deck, so Alexei joined Max in the water for the first time. He swam better than anyone Max had ever seen, and surfaced with showers of spray that dripped joyfully from his hair and eyelashes.

'That's it,' he called encouragingly. 'Let the water lift you.'

Max approached Alexei's instructions with a furious sort of focus, as if he could fix the world by perfecting his breaststroke.

'Good,' said Alexei, raising an eyebrow as Max pulled himself out of the water after swimming for five minutes – four more than yesterday.

By the time the lesson was over, Rozaliya had appeared on deck and begun repairing a hole in the corner of a costume cape. She glanced up as Max came over, unsurprised at the water dripping from his hair.

'Here,' she said, handing him a spare piece of cloth, which he used to towel himself semi-dry. 'Toast is over there,' she added, nodding towards a plate balanced on a nearby barrel. It was piled high with tiny, sweet figs and hot buttered apricot bread, and it smelled heavenly. Max took a bite, and then another, and licked butter and apricot jam off his wrist. He was so hungry after the swimming that the food tasted technicolour, and by the time he'd finished eating, he was feeling like the world might not be such a terrible place after all.

Rozaliya managed to squeeze in a second lesson that afternoon during a break between rehearsals. While the players wandered around muttering their lines and Gabriel

Rose admired his reflection in the canal, the four children walked the five minutes down to the edge of the lagoon, where they would be trying to tame a small outcrop of what looked like underwater Venus flytraps – except that instead of eating flies, the fanged plants feasted on fish.

'Neptune fish-traps,' whispered the Prof, half fascinated, half horrified.

'They're partial to sardines,' said Rozaliya, opening a tin and scattering it over the plants. The fish-traps went wild, lunging after the fish with their razor-toothed jaws and sending up wild explosions of bubbles. 'Now, darlinks,' said the wardrobe mistress. 'Concentrate. See if you can rein them in. It is about control.'

But despite her best efforts, Daisy's attempts to control the fish-traps only sent them into a further frenzy, and several of the plants almost uprooted themselves in the resulting chaos. Indigo managed to soothe them slightly, but Max, once again, surprised them all by calming the whole crop with a single gesture. The Prof scowled at him. Her efforts hadn't been much better than Indigo's. For perhaps the first time, the Prof was struggling with green magic.

'It's all this dratted water,' she said, wringing out her jumper and then darting out of the way of a hungry fish-trap. 'It's so – so – wet!'

Chapter 44

Daisy was on edge all evening, her mind going over and over their plan to visit the Reef. 'Tonight,' said the Prof quietly, as they sat backstage. 'After everyone's asleep.'

That night's dress rehearsal finally began at ten p.m., two hours behind schedule. It wasn't, thought Daisy, exactly the Nautilus Theatre Company's most glorious moment. One of the backdrops collapsed, two of the French actresses sprained their ankles on the same bit of sticking-out root, and Alexei's trousers fell down when someone accidentally cut through his belt with a rapier in one of the fight scenes.

'Oh dear,' said Daisy, watching through her fingers as the curtain came down, snagging several times on the way.

But Rozaliya was cheerful. 'This is a good sign,' she said. 'Always, the dress rehearsal is *terrible*. We have all the disasters tonight – and everything will be fine tomorrow.'

Some of the actors, staggering offstage after the final collapse of the curtain, didn't look so sure. Daisy knew that Ingrid and the stagehands would be up half the night trying to repair the damage in time for curtain up in less than twenty-four hours. 'Come on,' said the Prof, looking queasy. 'I think I ate a bad oyster at dinner, and I want to get back to the cabin.'

They went to bed late, but Daisy hadn't been asleep for more than an hour before she was woken by Indigo shaking her shoulder.

'Get up,' he whispered. 'It's time to go. Now or never.'

Napoleon meowed and suddenly Daisy was wide awake.

'Prof,' she said, swinging herself quietly out of bed and reaching up to her bunk. 'Come on, we're going.'

But the Prof groaned. 'I can't,' she said. 'I *knew* that oyster was a bad idea. I don't think I can move. I'm sorry, Daisy. I know you needed me for the plan.'

'Don't worry,' said Daisy. The Prof *did* look rather green in the moonlight shining through the cabin window. 'We'll manage. Will you be okay, though?'

The Prof nodded and pulled a slop bucket nearer to her pillow. 'Yes. Just promise me you'll find that proof and bring it back safely.'

'I promise,' said Daisy. 'Napoleon will stay and look after you.' The cat glowered at her, but curled himself on the end of the Prof's bunk.

Indigo was already at the door, barefoot and waiting. Daisy took a last look at the Prof, whose eyes were closed like a medieval martyr's, and at Max, who was fast asleep in the bunk below her, breathing heavily. For a moment, Daisy hesitated.

Then she turned away and stepped out into the corridor.

Whispers. Voices. Dimly, Max realized that the others were moving around the cabin. Then suddenly he was fully awake, listening to the click of the door being shut. Daisy and Indigo were gone.

Sixty seconds later, he was up on deck. He saw the two of them standing beside Muir on the far side of the deck. The foal had grown dramatically in the week since he'd been rescued, and he now stood twice as tall as Indigo, alert and pawing at the ground. His silver eyes were as bright as the moonlight that laid a path over the surface of the sea. 'Ready?' Indigo said quietly to Daisy. 'I'll boost you up, then I'll get on behind.'

Max stepped forward and had the satisfaction of seeing them both jump about a foot in the air. 'Where are you going? You can't go riding off on your own again. Look what happened last time.'

'Oh yes,' said Daisy, recovering. She put a finger to her chin. 'You mean when you followed us and nearly ruined everything?'

'That doesn't matter,' said Max, his ears burning. 'What matters is that you shouldn't leave the boat again or go wandering off alone after curfew. It's dangerous.'

'Is that a threat?' said Indigo. 'Are you planning to tell on us?'

'Maybe I will,' said Max.

'Look,' said Daisy impatiently. 'The coral is dying. We need to get hold of some to convince the Duchess it's really happening and stop it getting worse.'

Max heard his mother's voice in his head. *It's up to us to protect what we can. Never forget that, Max. Promise me.*

There was movement from above – a crewmember on the foredeck – and Max ducked down in order to avoid being seen.

'All right,' he whispered. 'I'm coming. But only to make sure you don't get into trouble.'

'Oh right,' said Daisy sarcastically. 'Because *we're* the ones who always need to be rescued.'

Indigo cleared his throat. 'It might be a good thing. The original plan had three of us, remember? In case something goes wrong.'

'Goes wrong?' said Max, suddenly nervous. 'Is this going to be dangerous?'

'Probably,' said Daisy. 'You should have thought of that before you invited yourself along.'

Indigo made a stirrup with his hands and tossed Daisy onto Muir's back, before vaulting on after her.

'Will he manage with three people?' asked Max nervously. He had never ridden a horse before.

'Yep,' said Indigo. 'We tested it out earlier today with

the Prof. Muir's strong – remember how he kicked a hole in the wardrobe boat? – and he's been fully healed for a few days now. He's a foal, but he's already bigger than most land horses.' He stretched out a hand and yanked Max up behind him.

Max landed with a grunt, feeling the ripple of the water horse's muscles beneath his legs, the soft-coarse texture of its silver-green coat, the flow of its pale mane the colour of sea foam. Muir snorted but was still. 'He likes you,' said Indigo, raising an eyebrow.

Then Indigo murmured something softly, and the horse moved forward, stepping off the deck and onto the surface of the water, where he stood, pawing impatiently at the moonlit waves.

Max's mouth fell open. Muir was a kelpie, he reminded himself. He could gallop over the surface of the water when the moon shone upon it. Max looked down and saw the bottom of the canal deep below the foal's hooves, glinting with fish scales and black pebbles and river weed.

There was a whisper from Indigo and then they were moving, first at a trot, then at a canter that took them racing over the surface of the canal. The rushing air was cold against Max's cheeks, and he gripped onto the horse's mane with white-knuckled hands. The houses and boats on either side of the bank began to blur with the speed of their movement, and spray rose up from pounding silver hooves as they galloped through the waterways of the city.

The houses began to thin and the canal to widen, and then they gained the freedom of the great lagoon, which shimmered darkly in the moonlight with all the glittering domes and shell spires of Iffenwild reflected on its surface.

For a moment, they paused and looked back across the shining water. All around them were drifts of pale white lilies, thick as snow on the surface of the lagoon. In the distance Max saw floating trees the size of small islands, gliding past with strange lights flickering in their branches. And deep below the glass-clear surface, even by night, Max could make out a vast kelp forest, its green ribbons hung with fat seedpods like gold coins.

For a long, suspended moment, the only sound was the swell of the waves and the snort of Muir's breath. Then, with a cry from Indigo, the horse wheeled and turned to gallop across the vastness of the open sea.

Max felt the wind in his hair, and he gave a whoop of joy. This feeling was extraordinary, electric – the power of the horse flexing beneath him, its silver hooves sending up great arcs of spray that shimmered around them in prisms of light. Pink dolphins rose up from the depths and soared and dived beside them as the water horse galloped onward along the path of silver towards the moon. Max felt his whole body soaked with salt water and spray. The sea was vast and wild and unknowable, and for the first time this thought filled him not with fear but with a fierce, overwhelming joy.

At last, Indigo raised an arm and Muir slowed. He stood

in place, pawing at the moonlight on the surface of the waves.

'This is it,' said Daisy.

Max looked around at the far reaches of the lagoon and saw spires of coral rising up below them. An icy wind whipped across the open water, and he shivered.

What on earth had he got himself into?

Chapter 45

'So . . .' came Max's uncertain voice in the dark. 'How exactly are we going to do this?'

'Right,' said Daisy. She hoped Max wasn't going to chicken out on them. 'The plan is for two of us to go into the water and swim down as far as we can. I think that'll need to be me and Indigo, since you can't swim.' She didn't give Max time to contradict her. 'We need a third person up here to stay with Muir. I'll be tethered to him with this rope –' she fastened it around the kelpie's harness with a sailor's knot – 'and I'll use it to pull myself back up when we're finished. We shouldn't be more than about ten minutes.'

'Er . . .' Max's voice sounded very distant and far away. 'How are you planning to breathe underwater for TEN MINUTES?'

'Iffenweed,' said Indigo, tethering his own rope to Muir's harness. 'Stol— ahem, borrowed, from one of the glasshouse-boats this morning.' Daisy watched as he fished in his pocket and pulled out a ball of sticky sea moss about the size of his fist. It was fluorescent green, and it made a slight sucking sound as he divided it in two and handed one half to her.

'Um – how does it work?' said Max.

'Like this,' said Indigo, sticking a wad of the moss into each of his nostrils. It made a nasty squelching sound as it went in, and his voice became indistinct. 'The Prob says that when you breab through it ubderwater, it filters the oxygeb into your lungs but keebs the liquib out. You just have to rembember not to breab through your mouth.'

Daisy glanced across at Max. 'Do you think you can do this? All you need to do is hold Muir steady. Okay?'

She watched Max nod, wishing that the Prof was here instead. Then she stuck her own moss into her nostrils. It had an unpleasant spongy texture and it smelled like a mixture of oysters and soap. She turned to Indigo.

'Reaby?' she asked. He was looking slightly sick, though whether at the taste of the iffenweed or the foolhardiness of what they were about to do, it was impossible to say.

'Okay,' said Indigo at last, double-checking his rope. He turned on the headtorch he'd fastened around his head, and Daisy did the same. Their white lights blazed out into the night, making everything seem very big and very cold. 'I'm reaby. On my count.' He looked around at them.

'One.' Daisy and Indigo clambered off Muir's back.

'Two.' They slipped into the black water, icy as the grave.

'Three.' And then they dived beneath it.

*

Daisy felt the shock of the water like a hundred frozen needles all over her skin. She felt the surge of the sea, criss-crossed with a hundred living currents, as their headtorches blazed beams of pale light through the murk. Tiny red fish flickered away from the beams as they swam down. Daisy was still holding her breath, not quite trusting that the iffenweed would work. Finally, clenching her mouth tight shut, she breathed in through her nose. Pure air filled her lungs, cool and fresh, streaming out into her grateful bloodstream. It gave her a great surge of energy in her fingers and toes, and she swam deeper. Indigo was a dark shape beside her, and their torch beams bisected as they swept their gazes back and forth.

Then something astonishing began to happen.

The deeper they swam, the lighter and warmer the water became. They were in a level now where the water was like twilight, and great phosphorescent jellyfish the size of small cars propelled themselves through the dimness with ghostly streamers sparkling behind them. A minute later, the water had lightened to a luminous and dappled blue. The fish here were yellow and orange and turquoise and hot pink, moving in great swirling shoals that shivered and rippled in murmurations and whirlpools of motion.

Here, finally, was the bulk of the coral – rising up in towers and cathedrals of colour, reefs and outcrops like palaces rising level upon level in every imaginable shade – shelves of orange and bright blue, delicate fans of crimson and swathes of pale pink that looked like living shaggy carpets with tiny fluorescent fish darting between them. The coral rose up above them endlessly, all the way to the surface of the water. The light, Daisy realized, was coming from the pure white sand on the ocean floor – rich with magic and radiant as the summer sky at noon.

Daisy stopped and swam in place. She looked sideways and saw that Indigo was looking back at her with the same wonder she felt on her own face.

They signalled to each other and swam deeper, until the lightness of the water dazzled them with diamonds of light, and among the coral on the shining sand they saw giant pearls in oyster shells, each one the size of a fist. No wonder, thought Daisy, people risked their lives for such pearls. Each one would be worth a king's ransom. Many shells, she saw, were empty.

Slowly, she and Indigo swam the length of the Reef, and this was where they saw it begin – the great bleaching. The coral in these places was bone-white and devoid of life. No anemones opened and closed their petals here; no starfish clung like pinky-red ornaments to the side of the cliffs. There was only silence and death, on and on into the distance.

Daisy stopped swimming. It was the saddest thing she had ever seen. Silently, she broke off a large piece of dead coral. Beside her, Indigo did the same, his mouth set in a flat line. Without needing to signal, they began to swim upwards, rising through levels of water that darkened and cooled as they rose.

Daisy's lungs worked harder as she propelled herself up, and she pulled in great lungfuls of air through the iffenweed in her nose. Then she saw a vast shape move towards her in the light of her headtorch. It was an enormous stingray, as wide and long as a truck, with a great whip of a tail that sparked with electricity. She darted out of the way just in time, but the tail caught her headtorch and she felt it crack against her forehead. When her vision cleared, the stingray was gone, but so had everything else.

The sea was dark.

Indigo had vanished.

Daisy gasped in panic and a flood of water poured in through her mouth and into her lungs. She tried to clamp her mouth shut but it was too late. She gasped again and spluttered, swallowing more water. Her legs and arms suddenly felt heavy and poisonous. The ocean spread out around her in all directions, invisible and black in its immensity. She yanked at the rope around her waist, but with a sick swoop to her stomach, she felt it hang slack in her hand. The stingray must have sliced through it as it swam off, or else it had been cut by a bladed edge of coral.

Daisy felt herself panicking, her lungs burning. Spots appeared in front of her eyes and her fingers began to feel numb – she wouldn't be able to last much longer.

Then something yanked at her hair, her wrist. She was being pulled upwards, dragged through the black water with strong strokes, until suddenly, with a great wrench, she was above it, and she surfaced, gasping, to see Max beside her, swimming in place.

Then there were arms pulling her up – Indigo's arms – and she landed like a hooked trout across Muir's broad back, the piece of coral still clenched in her fist.

Max, she thought, dizzy. 'But you can't swim.'

Her voice wasn't working, but he looked up at her, and she thought, for a moment, that he smiled.

Then she vomited onto Indigo's legs.

Daisy barely remembered the journey back into the city – only an indistinct sense of jolting and broken moonlight as the tired horse trotted back across the expanse of the lagoon. They reached Iffenwild just as dawn was breaking and the moonlight vanished; and as it did so, Muir's silver hooves began to sink beneath the water until he was swimming through it, waves surging against his sinewy chest. Daisy felt her legs pulled and buffeted, and gave silent thanks to whoever had lashed her broken rope around Muir's middle. Her grip on his mane was weak, and without it she would have been swept away into the sea and lost.

They arrived back on the deck of the captain's boat just after sunrise, each of them wetter than a thunderstorm.

There was no one awake yet. All was silent as Indigo tethered Muir to the mast and began to rub him down with wisps of hay and feed him buckets of the raw fish guts that he loved.

Then a voice came from the shadows beneath the mast.

'What on earth,' it said grimly, 'do you think you're doing?'

Chapter 46

Max turned around slowly. If he hadn't already been shivering from head to toe as water poured from his trousers and pooled around him on the deck, he would have quaked at the expression on Rozaliya's face.

'So,' she said. She spoke in short, clipped sentences, as if she was biting small chunks out of the vastness of her anger. 'You have been out. All night. On the horse. And –' her gaze fell to the shards of bleached coral in their hands – 'to the Reef. The *one* place I told you not to go. Don't you understand? The whole Nautilus Theatre could be thrown out of Iffenwild for this.'

They were all silent, staring back at her in dismay. She was wearing a gold lamé cape and she looked like a furious Russian film star.

'I—' began Daisy, but Rozaliya cut her off with a sharp motion of the wrist.

'I don't want to hear about it. You have all been very, very foolish.' She turned to Max. 'You, child, especially. I thought you, at least, had some sense.'

'But,' he said, 'it's important. What we found proves

that Iffenwild is in danger too. It's not just the Greenwild; the Marindeep isn't safe either.'

Rozaliya made an impatient gesture and tossed her cape over one shoulder. She was wearing an elegant black dress beneath it, trimmed with beads in the shape of lobsters. 'Do you think we don't know?' she asked. 'The Travellers have felt it in the sea for months. This dying. But the Duchess – her advisors do not let anyone get close enough to tell her.'

'But –' Max held up one of the bleached pieces of coral – 'this *proves* it. This is a piece of the dead wall of the barrier reef.'

Rozaliya waved a hand. 'Her advisors will say it is fake. Anyone who is speaking about it – the fishermen and the divers – they go missing. Oh yes,' she said, seeing their surprised expressions. 'I see things and hear things too.'

Daisy looked up, draggle-haired and soaking from beside Muir. 'Wait. Does that mean that someone *wants* Iffenwild to fall?'

Rozaliya shrugged. 'That is none of our business. The Nautilus Theatre Company comes to entertain the people of Iffenwild, nothing more. We do not get involved in politics. That is how we have survived for so long, and why we are still allowed to come here.' She gazed around at them all, her blue eyes sharp as fishhooks. 'Is this clear? No more interfering around. No more find-outing. What Iffenwild does is its own business – and we must stay out of it.'

There was a long silence.

'Yes,' said Max at last. But he crossed his fingers behind his back. And when he glanced sideways, he saw that Daisy was doing the same. He felt sure that if they could only *talk* to the Duchess, they would make her understand.

'Now what?' said Daisy later that morning, and immediately sneezed three times in a row. Despite being fed a bowl of hot broth and tucked into her bunk with a hot-water bottle, she had woken with a sore throat and streaming eyes, and currently had about six scarves wrapped around her neck. Napoleon was sitting on her lap like her own personal and very grumpy radiator. He had not been happy about being left behind the previous night and had spent the first ten minutes after their return licking Daisy's cheek, as if to reassure himself that she was really back.

Daisy looked around at the others. They were sitting on the edge of the canal opposite the *Nautilus* fleet, swinging their legs above the water and tackling giant ice-cream cones. An ice-cream boat had moored nearby during the night, and immediately attracted a long queue of overexcited neighbourhood kids. They had all sorts of special local flavours, including seaweed ('it tastes sort of . . . green,' said Indigo, sampling it) and sea salt (which made you so thirsty that it came with its own glass of water). The speciality of the day was sardine, but none of them felt quite brave enough to try it.

Daisy took a large lick of her chocolate ice-cream and

hoped it would help her sore throat. 'So. What's our plan of action?'

'It's obvious,' said Indigo, licking a cone of raspberry ripple. 'We have to find a way of getting the Duchess away from her advisors and showing that they're lying to her. The Iffenwilders know it, but no one has the power to *do* anything about it because she hardly ever leaves her palace.'

'Except for on the opening and closing nights of the annual performance of the Nautilus Theatre,' finished the Prof, who was looking better this morning. 'We've been over this. It's our one chance to talk to her.'

'But how will we get close enough?' asked Indigo.

The Prof frowned and rubbed a hand across her forehead. 'What if we send her a special invitation to "Celebrate with the actors" after the first-night performance in one of the dressing rooms tonight? Alexei said she loves hearing their stories. Maybe then we could speak to her, face to face. It's more than any ordinary Iffenwilder can do. She has her own entrance and private box at the opera house – but her advisors can't stop her from coming backstage.'

'It's a good idea,' said Daisy, warming to it immediately. 'We'd have to make the invitation look official. But Indigo, do you think you could get it to her by parapost?'

Indigo grinned. 'Jethro needs some exercise,' he said, glancing at the little jade-coloured bird perched on the lamppost above them. 'And I think this might be just the thing.'

Chapter 47

'This one, I think,' said Max, holding up a feather boa to Daisy's face. 'Or maybe this one?' He selected another that was almost as ostentatious.

'Stop!' she said, laughing, and fished a moustache out of the box of props in the corner of the dressing room, which she pressed onto her upper lip. 'How do I look?'

'Very dashing,' said Max, nodding seriously.

They were supposed to be finding a replacement tiara for the actress who played Queen Titania. Her original crown had been sat on by one of the stagehands during morning break and crushed into sparkling dust.

'Aha!' Daisy dug a promising-looking tiara from the depths of the chaos. 'Here we go. Will this do?' Indigo was already at the theatre, and the Prof had been coerced into helping Ingrid put the finishing touches to the lighting design.

Max nodded, and together they headed across the street that lay between the canal boats and the opera house. The two of them had reached a sort of truce after the events at the coral reef. It had something to do, thought Max, with the way he had saved Daisy last night. Still, it wasn't *quite* enough for him to point out that she'd forgotten to remove her moustache.

Suddenly he saw a flicker at the edge of his sight; a dark shape that sent a familiar coldness shivering down his neck. 'Look out!' he cried, and rolled to the ground, pushing Daisy over as he went. The throwing knife lodged in the wall behind them, quivering. It had missed Max's head by inches. Daisy was looking around wildly, but Max had already spotted his attacker, crouched on the rooftop of a nearby house.

Jarndyce.

In the seconds it took Max to get back to his feet, Jarndyce had swung down from the rooftop and landed heavily on the cobbled street in front of them. He was holding a knife.

'Finally,' he said, breathing hard.

And then he lunged.

There was a great noise of metal against metal and Max realized that he had raised the tiara into the space between them to defend himself. It fell apart in his hands, and he darted away as Jarndyce swung again, roaring. Max had nothing left to shield himself with, and a wall at his back.

No way out.

He closed his eyes – and then heard an almighty shout. Daisy, crouching forgotten on the pavement, had wrapped her arms around Jarndyce's leg and sent him crashing him to the ground.

Blood flowed from a cut across Daisy's arm.

'*Run!*' she said.

Max didn't know how long they darted through the streets in the heat of the midday sun. Long enough for him to feel that his chest was burning up. Long enough to feel that without water, he might faint.

'Okay,' said Daisy, panting. 'We've doubled back at least six times, so I don't think he could have followed us.' She paused. 'That was him, wasn't it? The Grim Reaper who was chasing you in the Greyside?'

Max nodded, dry-throated and breathless. 'Jarndyce. He was one of my guards.'

'What does he want with you?'

Max swallowed. 'I don't know. I don't know how he got into Iffenwild either. He shouldn't have been able to get through the door into the pocket. I'm pretty sure he doesn't have magic, or I would have seen him use it by now.'

Daisy nodded, and they began taking a long route through the backstreets towards the theatre. 'Someone must have let him in,' she said quietly, as their steps echoed off the cobbles. 'Either that, or they've somehow got hold of another dandelight.'

Max had seen the paperweight Daisy carried around with her everywhere, and watched her use it to guide them to the entrance to Iffenwild. It had been round and shining, just like—

'Daisy,' he said, putting a hand on her arm. 'I never told you how I got into Moonmarket. I came in from Greyside London, not through a pocket. It should have been impossible, but Jarndyce drew a sort of doorway in the air using this glowing white rock. I didn't know what it was, but maybe it was—'

'Another dandelight,' said Daisy, shocked. 'I've only heard of them being used to find and open doorways, not to make new ones. But I suppose it's possible.'

The Prof came out of the theatre as they approached, and her eyes went wide. Max glanced down and saw that Daisy's arm was covered in a sleeve of red from her cut.

'What happened?' asked the Prof, leading them inside. 'And Daisy – why are you wearing a moustache?'

'We were attacked,' said Daisy, snatching it from her upper lip. Then, speaking in a low voice, she began to explain.

The Prof frowned, listening intently. 'Okay,' she said, finally. 'So, the Reapers are getting into Iffenwild. And they want Max dead. But *why*?'

'We don't know,' said Daisy, and Max didn't have the energy to feel annoyed that she was speaking for him. 'But I think one thing's pretty clear. They're not going to stop.'

'So,' said Max, hearing his mother's voice in his head, and speaking her words. 'We need to come up with a plan.'

Chapter 48

Daisy peered out from backstage and nodded. 'We're all set.'

Max's head was swathed in a curly blond wig, his body was buttoned into an elaborate waistcoat, and he looked as if he was trying not to sneeze, or laugh, or cry.

As soon as they'd made their plan, they had gone straight to Alexei and explained what they needed.

'Yes,' he said immediately. 'If this man is after you, then you need a disguise. And you need a guard with you at all times – including when we're on stage for the performance each night. The solution is obvious, isn't it?'

Daisy nodded. 'Max needs a part in the play.'

After that, they went and found Rozaliya in her workroom and brought her in on the plan. The wardrobe mistress sprang into action at once. Daisy watched in awe as she outfitted Max with the most convincing costume that she could concoct from the miracle of her theatre wardrobe.

'There is one character in the play who doesn't have a speaking part,' she said as she rummaged through trunks and costume rails, tossing stockings, ribbons and old garters behind her. 'Some productions of *A Midsummer Night's Dream* do not have him on stage. But this is the perfect part for you, Max. The changeling child. You will be hiding in plain sight, disguised on the stage.'

'Yes,' said Alexei, eyes gleaming. 'Rozaliya, you're a genius. This Jarndyce person won't think to look for you in the one place that's the centre of attention in the whole of Iffenwild. And if he does . . . well, the crew will be there.' He grinned at Max. 'The part is perfect for you. All the changeling has to do is stand around looking moody and mysterious, so it shouldn't be too difficult.'

Max rolled his eyes and Daisy stifled a laugh.

'Remember,' said Alexei, 'the changeling is a young prince. Oberon, the fairy king, wants him for his pageboy, but Titania won't give him up.' Max was inundated with acting advice as the cast rallied round, and he forgot himself in the rush of their attention. The actress playing Queen Titania, who had been in the dressing room doing her make-up, brushed powder onto his face until his birthmark vanished. Marie-Claude grew him a giant, yellow daisy to hold parasol-like above his head on stage ('Very charming,' she murmured, admiring the effect), and Alexei dug out the blond wig and helped Max put it on.

'Thinking about it,' said Alexei, 'you'd better wear this from now on, whether you're on stage or off. We can't be too careful.'

'It smells like a birdcage,' said Max, wrinkling his nose.

'And it itches.' He shoved his fingers under the edge of the wig and scratched his scalp. Rozaliya slapped his hand away. 'None of that. Do you want the assassin to find you?'

For a moment, Max worried about the possibility of a spy among the crew. But he refused to believe it. The Nautilus was like a family, and it looked after its own.

'Five minutes to places, please,' called Ingrid through a crackling backstage speaker. 'Five minutes to places.' There was a flurry as the cast moved to their starting positions for the opening night performance. Gabriel smoothed his hair in the backstage mirror and kissed his reflection.

Daisy stood beside Max, watching as the curtain rose and revealed the massed rows of the glittering Iffenwild audience. He was clutching his giant floral parasol and scowling.

'I look ridiculous,' he muttered out of the side of his mouth. The audience clapped, rings and headdresses sparkling, and the lights went down.

'No, you don't,' Daisy lied, trying not to grin. Then the orchestra began to play, and they were both swept up in the music.

Max was barely breathing, and Daisy strained for his cue, praying that nothing would go wrong. Finally, they reached the second act and she heard the words they were waiting for.

'. . . a lovely boy, stolen from an Indian king,' said the

mischievous fairy Puck, swinging down from the nearest tree. 'She never had so sweet a changeling.' Max hesitated for a moment too long and Daisy shoved him in the back. He stumbled out onto the stage, his giant flower parasol glittering in the golden footlights. Then he straightened, and something remarkable happened. His shoulders went back; his eyes turned mournful. Max *became* the lost prince. He never spoke, but the audience followed his every move.

Daisy watched the play unfold with seized-up breath, waiting for something to go wrong. Even as Oberon and Titania fought over the changeling boy, and Bottom was turned into a donkey, Daisy scanned the audience, searching for Jarndyce's face.

At last, the final line was spoken. There was a moment of perfect silence. Then the audience began to clap, to cheer, to whoop. The curtain fell with a velvety swoop as they stood and applauded. 'Bravo!' cried someone from the back of the theatre, and members of the audience began to conjure flowers from handfuls of seeds in their pockets, which they showered down upon the stage. The curtain rose and the players joined hands and bowed. Applause thundered down like a waterfall. Daisy closed her eyes and breathed a sigh of relief.

Chapter 49

Five minutes later, there was a knock on the dressing room door. There was a glittering, celebratory atmosphere backstage that had as much to do with Max's successful disguise as with their brilliant first-night performance. Barely anyone looked up from the glasses of champagne that Rozaliya had poured for the cast (Daisy, Indigo, Max and the Prof had been given fizzy pink lemonade). Annika was in a cherrywood cradle in the corner, being rocked by a group of adoring stagehands.

'Ahem!' There was a pompous throat-clearing from the doorway, and Pompey, the Duchess's chief advisor, poked his head around the door. 'Her grand Duchess, the Lady of Iffenwild, has come in response to your invitation. She wishes to bestow her favour.'

'What invitation?' muttered Marie-Claude.

Alexei was the first to remember his manners. He swept off the enormous hat that was part of his Theseus costume. 'Welcome, Duchess,' he said, flourishing the hat so dramatically that the feather touched the ceiling. 'What an honour!'

'And what a performance,' she said graciously. She was dressed in another pearl-coloured gown tonight, and she wore more pearls than ever. They were threaded through her dark hair, embroidered on her hems, and they hung, gleaming, from a necklace so elaborate that it was more like a breastplate. Behind her came Pompey, looking more officious than ever. Daisy nodded quietly to Indigo, and he nodded back. Then Jethro launched himself straight at Pompey's head, while Napoleon tangled himself around his feet, meowing.

'Dratted bird,' Pompey shrieked, batting ineffectually at the air around him. 'Wretched cat!' There was a large streak of parakeet poo all the way down the front of his jacket.

'Oh dear, how unfortunate,' said Indigo. 'Here, let me help you with that.' He led Pompey away to the other side of the room and began rubbing energetically at the stain, spreading it over the jacket's lapels.

Daisy moved closer to the Duchess amid the commotion and gathered her courage in both fists. It was now or never.

'Duchess,' she said, taking a deep breath. 'Can I talk to you?'

'Mmm?' said the regent of Iffenwild, adjusting her pearl necklace and smiling at Daisy. 'What is it, my dear?'

'There's something we think you should know about.' Daisy pulled the piece of bleached coral from her pocket, speaking quickly in case they were interrupted. 'You can't tell from the surface yet, but the Reef is bleaching from the bottom up. Soon it will all be dead, and it's the same kind of dying we've seen in the soil of the Greenwild. We think it's because magic is under attack by the Grim Reapers; whole ecosystems are failing, all across the magical world. Being cut off isn't doing the Marindeep any good. Don't you see?' she finished desperately. 'If you don't do anything, the Marindeep is going to die.'

She ran out of breath and glanced up to see the Duchess looking at her with deep concern. 'But this is terrible,' she said, eyes wide. 'Why, this is proof that—'

'That the coral that protects Iffenwild is dying,' said Daisy.

'But I don't understand it,' said the Duchess, her green eyes swimming with tears. 'Why has no one told me?'

'I think they've tried,' said Daisy. 'But people have to go through your advisors.'

'And my advisors,' said the Duchess bitterly, glancing towards Pompey, 'love to keep me in the dark. They tell me nothing, just as if I'm a spoilt child. But I am the regent of this city, and it is my duty to protect it.'

For the first time, Daisy imagined the Duchess as the young girl she must have been twelve years ago, thrust into power when her beloved brother was killed – and now having to deal with the kind of responsibility she'd never dreamed of.

She looked at Daisy. 'You say the bleaching is on the coral wall – and that it's spreading?'

Daisy nodded, hardly daring to hope that the Duchess was paying attention. But she was, her face tight with concentration and distress. 'I will speak to Pompey this evening,' she said, glancing again at the little man, who was now agitatedly stripping off his jacket. 'Will you let me take this coral as evidence, to help convince him and my other advisors?'

Daisy handed it over and the Duchess tucked it away carefully.

'I shouldn't say this without Pompey's agreement –' she looked around and lowered her voice – 'but I would like to send a fleet to the Amazon to stand against the Reapers.'

'Really?' Daisy's heart leapt. 'Do you really mean it?'

'Yes, I do.' The Duchess held her gaze. 'I cannot promise to succeed; but I will try.'

'Can't you do whatever you want?' Daisy asked. 'Isn't that the point of being a ruler?'

The Duchess gave an infinitesimal shake of her head, and looked round for Pompey, who, having escaped Indigo, had now been waylaid by Rozaliya. 'Let me show you my collection of glass eyes,' Daisy heard the wardrobe mistress say gleefully, shepherding him into the corner.

'It is not so simple,' murmured the Duchess, her voice barely above a whisper. 'I am the regent, not the queen; my advisors make the real decisions. I can't say more than that, but I am not – I am not a free agent.' She looked pale and agitated – almost, thought Daisy, as if she was scared.

'There's another thing,' said Daisy quietly. 'I've heard a rumour about a . . . black market in Iffenwild. Do you know anything about it? We think it might be connected to the Grim Reapers.'

'A black market?' said the Duchess, looking horrified. 'I have heard whispers, but I don't think such a thing can be true here on Iffenwild soil.' She smiled bravely. 'Thank you again, child, for finding a way to speak to me.'

Then Pompey looked up and caught Daisy staring. A shiver went down her spine. Even as he came over, the Duchess straightened and smiled at Daisy as if they'd been chatting about the weather and cucumber sandwiches. Then, with renewed congratulations and compliments to all the players, she swept from the dressing room in Pompey's wake.

Daisy exchanged a triumphant glance with the Prof. The Duchess was going to assemble a fleet for the Amazon – or at least, she was going to try. It was better than she could have hoped.

Chapter 50

That night, Max visited his tree in the storeroom, feeling that he had been away from it for far too long. To his delight, he saw it had grown three more memories for him. One from when he was five, and his mother had shouted at a girl who'd made fun of him for loving Mozart. One from when he was ten, just after he got sick, when she had bribed a doctor to get Max onto a more advanced medical trial. And one from last year, when she had caught him in the midst of a hospital escape attempt and shepherded him firmly back to bed. Max had been furious about the last one, and he returned to the cabin feeling restless. He couldn't stop thinking about the tree. What was it? Where had it come from? How did it work?

He felt sure that there was one person who would know the answer, and he hung back after their lesson the next morning to speak to her alone.

'Prof?'

She raised an elegant eyebrow. 'Yes, Max?'

He stuck his hands into his pockets and tried to sound casual. 'Have you ever heard of a tree that grows memories on its leaves?'

She looked at him thoughtfully. 'It sounds to me like a Feirg tree.'

'What's that?'

'It's essentially a parasite – though a benign one,' she added hurriedly, when she saw Max's face. 'You know how different plants thrive in different conditions, like moist air or acidic soil?'

He nodded.

'Well, a Feirg tree thrives in an atmosphere of intense grief and loss. It feeds on that emotion in the air. It's a very rare species, but according to *The Compleat Botanist*, the leaves display memories of the people or things that have been lost.' The Prof's gaze sharpened. 'Why? Have you seen one?'

'No, no,' said Max hastily. 'Just asking out of interest.' And he slunk away, more restless than ever. He needed to be outside, free to hold his thoughts up to the light.

Max straightened his wig and looked longingly across the canal. He felt sure that Alexei wouldn't approve of him wandering the streets – but his disguise had worked on stage in front of an audience of hundreds. Even if Jarndyce saw him, Max was confident he wouldn't be recognized.

Rozaliya had pressed a little round container of face powder into his hands after the play the previous night. 'You must never forget, Max,' she had said seriously. 'This is what will keep you safe.'

'But why does Jarndyce want me?' he had asked, for the hundredth time.

'I don't know,' said Rozaliya, yet again, her expression hard to read. 'But you can't be too careful.'

Max dusted the powder onto his cheek that morning before leaving the boat, and he was surprised by how sad it made him feel, covering up his birthmark. It felt like he was hiding away some essential piece of Max-ness, and it gave him an unexpected knot in his stomach.

He slipped away in the hour after dawn, when the sky was the colour of a peach. Even this early, the floating bakeries were busy selling loaves of bread, and the canals were filled with ferries that puttered to and fro, leaving behind white ribbons of water and sending the houseboats bobbing on their moorings.

For the next three days this became Max's routine. Before anyone else on the *Nautilus* was awake, he would slip out to wander the streets for a few hours, and come back in time for his swimming lesson with Alexei, just as the players surfaced for breakfast.

Max learned many interesting things in those hours of wandering. For one, he learned that Iffenwild was a city in love with music. Music poured from the houseboats, waltzes were played in every cafe and on every street corner, and large, tattooed fishermen sang their hearts out every morning at the grimy fish-spattered docks, carolling sea shanties as they brought in their nets. The music was part of the magic-making of the city: housewives sang vines into existence and strung up their laundry on them; children sang pansies out of their window boxes; and gardeners sang enormous blossoms onto the submarine orange trees that flowered just under the surface of the canals.

There was only one thing the city loved as much as its music, and that was its food. The Iffenwilders really loved to eat. Wonderful cooking smells wafted through the streets and canals – vanilla and cardamom, lemon and basil, fresh bread and smoked fish. Even potatoes, which in other places can smell sad and heavy, had a wonderfully crisp, salty scent in Iffenwild.

Wearing his wig and his powder, Max went everywhere and tried everything. He visited floating sweetshops where he bought tiny chocolate goldfish that wriggled as you ate them, and toffee shrimps curled snugly in caramel shells. He went to bakeries where he found braided sugar loaves in the shape of boats, and gingerbread pirate ships complete with sugar-drop cannonballs. He passed cake shops that sold ten different kinds of chocolate cake, along with tiny golden vanilla biscuits shaped like dolphins, and shiny opera cakes with layers and layers of almond sponge and coffee cream. And he sat beneath windows and listened to music for hour after hour.

Max also found himself drawn back to the Jolly Fishhook, which wasn't far from the docks. When he looked out of the front windows of the tavern, he saw a forest of masts and crowds of shrieking seagulls that swooped over everything like furious, beaky confetti.

'It's always busy,' said Emil, indicating the bustling main room, where fishermen sat repairing their nets by humming over the frayed knots. Meanwhile, guild members sat bickering and merchants from other marine pockets tucked into hearty bowls of plum dumplings. 'It's where most of the trade from the wider Marindeep comes in and out. Bespelled salt, giant pearls, coral seedlings – and probably some illegal things smuggled back and forth too.'

Max watched with interest as the dockside surged with tides of people haggling beside their great boats, bartering for passage and for goods.

'How do the Marindeep traders get in and out?' he asked, adjusting his wig. He'd had to tell Emil about Jarndyce's attack to explain why he was in disguise, and although Emil had been shocked, he also thought Max's blond curls were hilarious.

'My dear Goldilocks,' he said, 'they come by ship, of course. When the moon is full, boats can sail straight between marine pockets, but only if they're made from the wood of the Mondenbaum tree. The trees have to be planted by moonlight and they only grow in Iffenwild. They won't take root in any other pocket; people have tried. That's why the boats are so precious, and why Iffenwild is the capital of the Marindeep. We control the wood that people need to travel.'

Max loved roving around the city, and now that he knew about Mondenbaum trees he saw them growing everywhere – their trunks broad and silvery in the woodland slopes above the city, and in the floating forests that criss-crossed the vast lagoon. And yet, after a few hours of wandering, Max was always happy to return to the *Nautilus* fleet – to Rozaliya's Russian honey cake, and the musty, spicy smell of the costume wardrobe; to baby Annika's funny expressions, and Alexei's shout of welcome ('It's the magnificent MAX,' he'd cry, delighted) – and of course, to the memory tree's glittering black leaves. It was possible that he even looked forward to seeing Indigo, the Prof and Daisy. Not her cat, though. That would be a step too far.

The afternoons were taken up with rehearsals and chores and patch-ups to the set. There were mousetraps to empty and costumes to wash and snacks to be fetched – and, whenever there was time, lessons to be attended. Rozaliya was clearly enjoying herself, and there were classes in planting seagrass, taming horned bullrushes, and pruning sea-roses, which grew in splendid profusion in the canals behind the opera house. Max had told them about how the Iffenwilders used music in their magic-making, and Rozaliya had immediately approved of the idea. 'Decidedly, it helps,' she said. 'After all, music is one of the nine muses.' Max found that singing improved his magic, and he went around humming all afternoon.

Then, in the evening, the theatre would fill, the curtain

would rise with a sighing sort of swish, and another kind of magic would begin. Max would step out onto the stage and become someone else. Or perhaps it was that he became more himself than ever before: a child taken from his mother; a lost boy in a strange place.

'You are a sensation, darlink,' said Rozaliya after the second night's performance. 'So moody, you know. The audience *adores* it.'

Max slept deeply, and in the mornings the routine would begin again. Exploring the city, swimming with Alexei, visiting his tree, performing on stage. He took to having an early breakfast at the Jolly Fishhook, where Emil would be rushing around with plates of sprats for the dockworkers and fishermen. Max wrinkled his nose at the squirming mass of tiny fish. 'People really *like* this stuff?'

'Yep,' said Emil cheerfully. 'And a good thing too, or my family would be out of business. Watch out, your wig is getting in the mayonnaise.'

Max looked at the mass of traders and merchants and storytellers crowded into the main room of the tavern, dressed in the costumes of different nations. 'How many other marine pockets are there?'

'Oh, many,' said Emil, who was dunking dirty knives and forks into an enormous water barrel. 'Just like there are lots of land-based pockets in the Greenwild. There are Marindeep pockets in places like Venice and Madagascar and Hawaii, of course, but also the islands of Scotland and

French Polynesia and Greece. They are all over the world. Everywhere that blue magic exists.'

'Blue magic?' asked Max.

'Yah,' said Emil. 'Water magic.'

'Oh.' Max's eyes widened. 'How does it work?'

'I am not the right person to ask,' said Emil, wiping dishwater across his forehead. 'But I know that it is different from green magic. Green magic is about – how do you say? – interacting with plants, things that are alive. Blue magic is –' he searched for the word, wrinkling his forehead – 'it is *elemental*. It would be like someone in your Greenwild using magic to move the earth and rocks. Blue magic is about interacting with water itself.' He dropped a pile of dirty plates into the washing-up barrel, which slopped all over Max's shoes.

'Anyway,' Emil continued, 'they say blue magic belongs to people who feel the water in their blood.' He shrugged. 'Whatever that means. No one in my family has had blue magic since my mother's great uncle Ambrose, and he died forty years ago.'

'Blue magic,' said Max softly. The two words echoed in his head as he lay in bed that night, and they followed him into sleep.

Chapter 51

It was the night after the third performance and Daisy was lying in bed, feeling restless. Max was snoring in the opposite bunk, and she rolled her eyes. She liked him a lot better now, but even so, it wasn't *fair*. Max was clearly Rozaliya's favourite. And Alexei's too – all those special swimming lessons! She'd caught them laughing together as she'd come up onto the deck for breakfast that morning, Alexei slapping Max on the back like a brother. And even though Max had only just started learning green magic, it seemed to come to him effortlessly. He was so good that he made Daisy feel stupid every time a kelp frond or a water pansy surged out of her control and slapped her in the face. It didn't help that Boris the ginger cat had taken to watching their lessons from the deck rail, smirking every time she did something clumsy.

'All right, all right,' she said as Napoleon hissed at Boris from her shoulder. 'At least I'm trying.'

Max gave another trumpet-like snore, and she turned over fretfully. Her mind returned, like a compass pointing north, to the thing she was always thinking about: Ma in the Amazon, ten thousand miles away and waiting for help.

For a moment, she looked at Max's sleeping face and thought about his own loss. She tried to imagine how he must feel, and her imagination flinched, like skin from a flame.

At last, she sat up and set the dandelight on her pillow. It glowed at her touch like a firefly lantern, and she unfolded Ma's letter and read it for the hundredth time. Napoleon perched on her shoulder and read along with her, his tail brushing her cheek. *Come with help, or not at all.* The words were the only thing that were stopping Daisy from leaping out of bed and begging Alexei to take them to Peru *now*, immediately.

She kneaded her temples as questions chased each other around her head. How had Jarndyce got into Iffenwild? What were the Reapers doing in the city? What did they want?

She remembered standing in the kitchen of the Roost and Artemis saying: 'The Greenwild has almost unlimited resources, Daisy. It contains wonders that could make an unscrupulous person very rich indeed.'

Now Daisy flopped back onto her bunk and sighed. It was no use; sleep felt as distant as the bottom of the sea. Perhaps a glass of milk would help. Quietly, she scooped up Napoleon and padded barefoot to the door. The corridor was silent and empty. At the far end, the kitchen beckoned, door ajar.

Five minutes later, she was tiptoeing back to bed with

her milk and a biscuit when she saw a dark shape on the landing. Someone was heading up the stairs.

Daisy stood still for a moment. Then she darted into the shadows as the figure vanished onto the deck. She crept, mouse-like, halfway up the stairs, craned her head and heard low voices. Then the moon came out and she saw everything etched for a single moment in silver and black: the great pale sweep of the furled sail; a cloaked figure standing on the path beside the canal, like a bat with black wings; and another figure, leaning over the railing of the barge, handing over something that flashed in the moonlight. 'Yes,' he said quietly. 'At the carnival.' He shifted, and his hair caught the gleam of the streetlight and shone like spun gold.

It was Gabriel Rose – the self-obsessed leading man of the Iffenwild crew.

Chapter 52

The next morning everything felt normal, and Daisy wondered if she'd imagined the whole thing. But she looked at the empty glass of milk by her bunk – she'd drunk it in three gulps to steady herself – and knew that what she'd seen had been real.

What had Gabriel Rose been doing at that hour of the night? Who had he been talking to? And why had he done it in secret?

Speaking in an undertone, she summoned a meeting of the Five O'Clock Club immediately before breakfast, while Max was having his swimming lesson with Alexei. Daisy didn't have any appetite, but Indigo was busy wolfing down a plate of pickled oysters. The Prof watched him, looking queasy.

'Look,' said Daisy, and explained what she'd seen. 'I'm sure Gabriel wouldn't do anything against the Nautilus, but . . . I think we should be careful.'

The Prof shook her head. 'Gabriel is vain,' she said. 'And a bit of an idiot. But I don't think he'd betray us. The Nautilus is a *family*.'

Daisy shrugged, thinking of Marigold Brightly and everything she'd betrayed to keep her son, Max, safe. 'We don't know that,' she said quietly. 'Nothing and no one can be trusted.'

This thought made Daisy even more determined to get her magic under control. She needed to be self-reliant – and that meant not causing a minor disaster every time she tried to move a vine.

She frowned at the strand of giant purplish kelp she was supposed to be wrangling in that morning's lesson with Rozaliya. *Come on*, she coaxed. *Roll up.* The key was not to push. For a moment, nothing happened. And then, softly as a song, the kelp shivered beneath the surface of the canal and rolled itself into a pleasing cylinder.

'Bravo!' said Rozaliya. 'That's more like it!'

The Prof caught Daisy alone just as they were heading towards the theatre. She looked even more anxious than usual.

'What's wrong?' asked Daisy.

'Nothing, really,' said the Prof, adjusting her glasses tiredly. 'Or maybe everything. I'm so worried about Grandfather that I can't sleep. I can't concentrate on anything.'

Daisy nodded. She understood exactly. It kept her up too, the worry that felt like a snake coiling around her chest in the middle of the night. 'It's the not-knowing that's the hardest,' she said. 'I know Ma was alive when she wrote that letter, but now . . .'

'Exactly,' said the Prof. She closed her eyes, and when she opened them, they were bright with tears. 'Oh Daisy, I *know* we have to get the Iffenwilders to support us. But I want to be on our way to the Amazon already.'

'Yes,' said Daisy fiercely. 'Me too. And we will be – soon.' She hoped that it was true.

'I don't like the green magic here,' said the Prof. 'It's so . . . damp. All these marine plants – slimy seaweed and kelp and pesky water pansies! And those awful siren reeds.' She shuddered. 'And you have to *sing* all the time. Ugh!' Daisy looked at her friend sympathetically. The Prof wasn't used to not being the best. But Max continued to outstrip her effortlessly, lesson after lesson. After Daisy's modest success with the kelp that morning, Max had hummed a simple tune and the whole kelp forest had begun billowing through the shallows of the lagoon like a submerged jungle, while dozens and dozens of bright blue flowers sprang out of nowhere and sent bubbles of pure oxygen racing for the surface like champagne. After that, everyone else's efforts had looked rather feeble.

'It's not fair,' said the Prof huffily. 'I *know* all the theory. He doesn't know a thing, and he makes it look so *easy*!'

Daisy tried hard not to laugh. 'Now you know how the rest of us feel when we're with you.'

'Humph!' said the Prof. 'Well, I don't like it. Give me good, solid earth and nice, *dry* magic any day.'

*

Now that he knew about blue magic, Max looked for it everywhere and actually saw one or two Iffenwilders using it. He saw a man making water leap in small green bubbles from the canals, before juggling it into pails and kettles for washing and cooking. He saw an old woman creating miniature whirlpools that rose up and sluiced across the decks of her houseboat to clean the planks at the end of a hot day.

'But this is nothing compared to what we used to be able to do,' said Emil, 'when the king and queen were alive. If we ever find the lost heir – well, *then* you'll see what the water magic of Iffenwild really looks like.'

That evening, Max locked himself in the cabin with a glass of water. He stared at it hard. He stared at it so hard that his eyes burned, and the glass rattled. The water began sloshing about like a tiny tempest, splashing the table and dripping onto the floor. Max found himself humming without realizing it; an old tune his mother had sung to him when he was very small. The water rose high around the sides of the glass, which began to shake back and forth until finally it tipped over, and Max passed out.

When he came to, Alexei was shaking him gently on the shoulder.

'What happened?' asked the captain, looking about at the damp floor and the rolling water glass.

'Nothing,' said Max, sitting up shakily. His voice was a

croak. 'Maybe I forgot to eat lunch.'

'Hmm,' said Alexei, and helped him up.

After that, Max didn't stop practising – always in secret, while the others were out. It reminded him of the first days after he'd woken up in the cellar of Craven's house, training his weakened muscles to carry him across the room – first once, then ten times, then twenty. This blue magic – if that was what it was – was just like a muscle, and Max knew how to be patient with it. At the end of the first day, he was able to make a large glass of water tip over without blinking. On the second, he summoned a storm in a teacup. On the third, he made a whirlpool in a bowl of tomato soup. After that, he began stealing down to the canal at night and making the waves leap up to touch his hand like friendly dolphins. It left him exhausted, but Max was used to that too.

What mattered was this: it made him feel alive.

Emil came looking for them late on the night after the fourth performance, when the last players had finished playing their accordions in the starlight and gone to bed.

'Psst!' came the call outside their window. Daisy rolled over and saw a pale face outside the window. Emil looked more like a hedgehog than ever, his spiky hair sticking out all over his head. 'I got your note about the black market,' he said, when she, Indigo and the Prof tiptoed up onto the deck to speak to him. 'There are rumours everywhere, and more than rumours. Some people think they know where the market is. They say it's a bad place, very bad.'

Daisy and Indigo glanced at each other. 'What do you mean, "bad"?'

'I do not know,' said Emil uneasily. 'But the people I talked to, they looked scared.'

'Okay,' said the Prof cautiously, 'we understand.' She paused. 'Can you take us there?'

Emil glanced at them, assessing. 'How much?' he asked. 'This thing, it is dangerous. If my father knew I was thinking of it, he would lock me in my room.'

'We can pay,' said Daisy. She reached into her pocket and pulled out the little purse of gold moon pennies Artemis had given her when she'd decided to stay at Mallowmarsh. 'Six pennies,' she said. 'Half now, half later.'

'Okay,' said Emil. He held the three gold coins in his grimy palm, bit one of them, and then spat on the ground. 'It's good.' He glanced at them. 'I will take you to the entrance, but no further. Let's go.'

Chapter 53

'I'm coming too,' said Max, climbing up onto the deck. He'd heard them leave the cabin, just like the last time.

'Again?' asked Daisy. 'Haven't we been through this before?'

'Yes,' said Max. 'And last time you needed my help.'

'We'll be *fine*,' said Daisy.

Emil rolled his eyes. 'We don't have time for this. He's coming too.' And he grabbed Max by the wrist and began marching him away from the boat.

'Listen,' said Max, disentangling himself as the four of them stepped into the street beside the canal. 'These Reapers took my mother. I need to see them. I need to know what they're like.' It was the closest he'd ever come to asking Daisy for anything. He knew that seeking them out was reckless – even with the disguise of his wig and powdered cheek. But tonight, recklessness felt good, even necessary.

Daisy looked at him for a moment, and then, unexpectedly, she smiled. 'Okay,' she said. 'Just don't blame me if you end up falling into another canal.'

Max laughed, and then they were on their way.

*

Nobody spoke much as they walked into the gloom of the winding canals. Even if they had, thought Max, the fog would have swallowed their words.

This late at night it was very dark, and the colourful shoals of rainbow fish that filled the sky in the daytime were nowhere to be seen. Instead, the air was filled with sinister-looking lampreys with luminous fins and teeth like overlapping knives. Some of them had ghostly lanterns that arched up from their spiny backs and bobbed in front of their heads.

They walked for a long time through the maze of waterways – long enough for Max's feet to feel sore and for the first tinge of dawn to touch the horizon. The others walked with their heads down, concentrating, following Emil, occasionally exchanging whispers that Max couldn't hear.

Then he heard something on the breeze. A noise of murmuring and squawking and barking and screaming – the kind of noise you expect to hear only in your deepest nightmares. They turned a corner and came face to face with a wall of water weeds that coiled and twisted upwards like slimy, glistening ivy from the neighbouring canal.

'Duck!' hissed Emil, and they darted back around the corner as a tall, cloaked woman hurried along from the opposite direction. She glanced over her shoulder, slipped through a parting in the cascade of weeds, and vanished.

'This is where I stop,' said Emil. 'Are you sure you won't come back with me?'

'Yes,' said Daisy, looking at the others. 'We're going to investigate.'

Emil bit his lip. 'In that case, good luck. Be careful. And don't get caught.' He shook her hand solemnly, then turned and disappeared into the night.

There was a tense silence, and then Daisy's hushed voice in the dark: 'I think we just have to risk it.' Max could just make out Napoleon perched on her shoulder, tail raised with bravado. The sight gave him courage. Together, the four children hurried forward. Max felt the water weeds clammy and slick as tentacles against his face as he pushed through the stone archway they concealed. When he opened his eyes, they were standing at the shadowy edges of a hidden square. Before him was a sight that would stay etched in his memory for the rest of his life.

Daisy drew in a sharp breath and heard Indigo let out a choked sob beside her.

The square swarmed with figures hawking and haggling over captured animals. There were monkeys crouched in too-small cages, pulling out their own fur in distress. Magnificent toucans stuck their beaks out from between iron bars, chattering with horror. Great pink elephants curled their trunks around the mesh of cramped cages; and beside a dark canal at the square's edge, dolphins in enormous tanks banged their noses against reinforced glass.

Indigo gave a cry and Daisy spun to see a full-grown water horse with its silver-green mane matted and its eyes dulled with pain, its neck fastened to a halter pegged into the ground. Most of its long, priceless tail hairs had been plucked out.

'It'll die if it's not allowed back into the water,' said Indigo. He looked on the verge of tears. 'This is – this is evil. I can hear them all in my head. The pain . . . the pain is so huge.' He clenched his hands over his ears. 'We've got to do something.'

The Prof pulled them behind a half-furled awning so that they were hidden from view. Daisy felt Napoleon's claws digging into her shoulder in anger. 'You're right,' she said. 'This can't be allowed.' She turned to look at Max and saw that his eyes were blank and wide with horror.

'I know what it's like to be locked up,' he said quietly. 'No one and nothing should be imprisoned like that. Ever.'

'Let me at them,' said Indigo, suddenly furious, and the Prof grabbed his wrist to hold him back. He looked ready to pull out his penknife and do battle single-handedly with every person in the market.

'Stop,' said Daisy. 'Do you want to be killed? We need to think.' She turned to the Prof, who had so far been silent. 'Prof, what are you thinking?'

The Prof swallowed. She looked slightly sick. 'You're both right. We need to stop this. But first, we need a better place to hide.'

The four of them crawled into a nest of abandoned crates behind the awning. From between two rotten planks, Daisy watched as one of the stallholders yanked at the neck of the wounded water horse with a tight halter and the creature's fine silver-green legs buckled beneath it. It was being haggled over by a pair of women with dark cloaks and sharp expressions. Daisy drew in a breath. Their cloaks were pinned with badges just like the one Max had stolen from Jarndyce. Grim Reapers.

Money changed hands, and then the creature was hauled

away and loaded onto the deck of a black ship moored in the canal that ran alongside the market square. Daisy could just see the creature's wide, bloodshot eyes as the boat glided away into the dark.

'Lord Pompey ordered that one specially,' said the seller to his assistant. 'There's good business here.' He lowered his voice. 'Even the Great Reaper has placed an order.' Daisy and Indigo turned to each other, eyes wide.

So it was true. The market was tied up with Reapers – the Great Reaper was their leader, though no one knew his identity – and Pompey was in on it. Daisy felt bile rush up her throat so fast she thought she might faint, and she had to grip Indigo's arm to stay steady.

The market was filling up now, and the noise became deafening as deals were done and animals bellowed in pain. Plants were being sold too – priceless gold-leaf trees and silver-date palms and weeping willows that grew real green emeralds on their branches.

'A packet of fireweed from Tanzania,' called one trader, 'going for sixty gold moon pennies. A bargain! Burn your enemies with unstoppable fire. Perfect for arsonists.'

'A vial of Whipple seed powder,' murmured another to those who passed by his stall. 'From the finest Colombian trees. Imagine, my friends, if you could make yourself invisible . . .'

'A mortle,' whispered another, so quietly that Daisy barely heard him. 'Six thousand moon pennies. But for something this rare, what price is too high?'

For a moment, the word snagged on something in her mind. But then—

'Come on,' said Indigo, his whisper urgent. 'We need to make a plan.'

Chapter 54

'This is ridiculous,' said Max. 'This is impossible. This is four children trying to take down the most horrendous black-market operation in the world.'

'No,' said Daisy. 'It isn't impossible.' She was crouching with the others behind the fallen awning, and she knew her face was probably grey with fear. She forced herself to look around at them. 'Listen,' she said. '*We can do this*. We've got Indigo, who can talk to animals. We've got the Prof, who's so clever she can think her way out of any problem. And –' she paused, looking at Max – 'we've got you. One of the bravest people I've ever met.'

Max reddened. 'I'm not brave.'

'How many people would jump into the cold ocean in the dark to rescue someone they didn't even like?'

'That's not—' said Max.

Daisy ignored him. 'How many people would do it when they'd only just learned how to swim? I'd call that pretty brave.'

'Or pretty stupid,' muttered Indigo.

The Prof elbowed him. '*And*,' she said emphatically,

'we've got you, Daisy. Someone who's kind and determined, and who always, always has a plan.'

Just like his mother, thought Max, feeling a stab in his stomach. But it was accompanied by an unexpected warmth. He was part of this, as much as they were.

'Okay,' he said. 'Let's go over the plan, one more time.'

This was a performance where there could be no mistakes.

Daisy swallowed and tried not to feel sick. She was hiding under a stall, and she was no more than six feet away from a golden rhino. Its horn had been sawn off and the stump was weeping a clear, glistening fluid. To her other side were two tiny capuchin monkeys, their fur glimmering black and gold within their cage.

Control, she thought. *Precision*. That was what she needed. She thought of all her lessons with Rozaliya. Then she pressed her hand into the ground, where she'd planted a tiny vine seedling. She closed her eyes and reached for her green magic, sending it into the seed until it began to sprout. *Control*, she thought again. But it was hard. Another water horse was being yanked past her hiding place, its flowing silver mane matted and almost black against its bloody flank. She remembered the wound in Muir's leg and wondered if his herd had been driven out into the Greyside ocean deliberately, for easy hunting.

She forced her attention back to the seedling, which

was growing fast – too fast. She took a breath and forced herself to slow her magic. *Steady*, she thought. Not too fast, or too slow. Gradually the vine grew, spreading out in a network of tendrils across the wet black cobblestones of the market. Nearby, the Prof was doing the same thing. Their two vines split into many, many different branches, each one delicate and almost unnoticeable in the dim light of the hanging lanterns. Each tendril snaked towards a cage, towards a lock. Daisy exhaled. She had hoped that the Prof could work the magic alone, but there were too many cages for that. Their plan depended on all the doors opening at the same time. She trembled with the effort of holding the whole of it in her mind.

One of the cages creaked – a vine had crawled around its bars. *Wait*, she told it. *Not yet*. Indigo was crouching beside her, murmuring noiselessly. He was speaking to every single one of the animals, telling them what was about to happen. She could tell by the sudden brightness in the animals' eyes, a look that hadn't been there before. They were poised. Ready.

'On the stroke of eleven p.m.,' Daisy whispered to herself, watching the clock that hung above the market.

Three . . .

Two . . .

One . . .

The clock hand tipped onto the hour, and Napoleon leapt from the top of a stall onto a barrel full of ivory beads.

For a moment, it teetered, then smashed across the middle of the market, sending the precious beads spinning across the paving. In that instant of distraction, Daisy let go of her control with a gasp from the bottom of her stomach. Vines swarmed upwards, growing thick and monstrous and huge – and under their enormous pressure, the locks shattered all over the ground. There were shouts of alarm across the market as stallholders looked around wildly. Then the animals, with a roar of noise and motion, surged from their cages. The elephant swung its trunk and sent the nearest Grim Reaper sprawling to the ground. A golden panther, so starved that its ribs showed through its mottled fur, leapt forward, jaws dripping. A ferocious silver dormouse the size of a thimble launched itself into a stallholder's hair and bit him on the ear. A great crocodile gnashed its teeth. Birds of paradise soared through the air, shrieking and pecking the eyes of the Reapers until they fell back, shouting and slipping on beads. And at the head of the throng was Napoleon, perched on the back of a griffon and leading the way with white whiskers aloft.

Padlocked water tanks full of dolphins and silver-clawed lobsters and priceless stingrays burst open. The sea creatures inside them sluiced across the cobbles and straight into the canal. A giant walrus careened through a market stall, knocking six Reapers off their feet before somersaulting into the canal and sending up a plume of water that crashed down on their heads. Within moments, it was gone, racing out into the freedom of the lagoon.

Daisy felt a great surge of pride and hope. For a moment, she thought that they would do it, that it was going to be okay.

Then she saw what she had done.

One of the vines had surged so far out of her control that it had crushed the cage it was curled around. One of the tiny capuchin monkeys had lost her tail. It had been sliced by the contracting metal as she'd leapt free of the bars.

Daisy gasped at her mistake, dizzy with the horror of it.

Then she heard a terrible noise. It was the sound of a mechanical bow being drawn. There was a mean, fast whoosh, swifter than thought, and the golden panther lay dead on the ground before them, a black arrow stuck in its starved ribs.

'Max, NOW!' screamed Daisy. She tucked the wounded monkey inside her shirt. Indigo was crouching beside her, tears running silently down his cheeks, but his amber eyes were open and his lips moved silently as he told the animals what to do. As one, they swelled forward, their sheer mass trampling the marketeers underfoot.

Then, Daisy saw Max toss a pinch of powder above his head. The whole market went dark. It was the kind of darkness you'd find inside a locked velvet box, close and soft and absolute. It shut out all light, totally.

There was the sound of a hundred pounding paws, slithering bellies, flapping wings, racing past in a great, bold, desperate race. There were shouts, and curses, and then the sound of something smashing, and the unmistakeable *whooomph* of something going up in flames. Gradually light began to return to the market, as the darkness powder settled in a thousand black grains on the ground – and Daisy saw a scene of desolation.

A hundred cages, smashed and empty. A hundred stalls, trampled and overturned. And a great fire rising from the centre of the market where a lantern had been overturned in the chaos. Cloaked figures were rushing around in panic, and she and Indigo slipped into their midst.

Chapter 55

The journey back to the *Nautilus* dock was one that Max would never forget. Indigo was riding on the back of a water horse, which had lowered its neck and practically scooped him up. The Prof was riding on a leopard, her spectacles blackened with soot. Max himself was on the back of a giant, mangy lion that smelled of blood, and he'd hesitated for a split second as they'd flooded out of the market. 'It's safe,' shouted Indigo. 'They know we're helping them. Quick, there's no time.' And so Max had leapt onto its back, and then looked around wildly for Daisy. She was racing out of the door behind him, almost crushed between a wombat and a stampeding elephant, a bundle of jars and vials clutched in her hands. There was a Reaper on her heels, reaching out one thin hand that glittered with the cruel edge of a knife.

Jarndyce.

'Daisy,' cried Max. He felt a thrill of terror, like iced water through his veins. Then the elephant turned back and with a sweep of its tusk it tossed the man off his feet. In the split second before Jarndyce got up, Max stretched out his hand and swung Daisy up behind him onto the lion's back. She landed with a grunt, and then they were moving with a swiftness that should have been impossible – a great bounding propulsion of pure motion that carried them through the streets of the sleeping city.

Max buried his fingers in the lion's mane and his hands vanished up to the wrist in yellow fur. Daisy wrapped her arms tight around him, hard enough to bruise, and they surged on. There were orangutans swinging through the treetops and lampposts ahead, while hummingbirds and hornbills and golden pheasants raced low through the air, and rhinos and rare tigers kept pace beside them. The

smaller animals – the salamanders and shrews and dormice – hitched rides with the stronger, faster ones, and the whole impossible, miraculous stampede of them charged through the city like a conquering army.

Lights went on in the windows of houses and boats as they passed, and children cried out in surprise and delight, but no one stopped them. They only slowed when the opera house came in sight, and just beyond it, the *Nautilus* fleet, its portholes shuttered for the night. Indigo held up a hand and the animals gathered on the quayside in a great milling mass. The players would be sleeping, thought Max – they just had to pray that the animals would be quiet enough not to wake them. Indigo seemed to have had the same thought, because he was hushing the animals, and even the elephant was practically tiptoeing as they came near the boats.

'Right,' said Daisy. 'We've got to get them inside.'

'What?' Max stared at her. 'Are you mad?'

'No,' said the Prof. 'She's right. The barges are made from flexilis wood. We just have to get the animals on board and hold our nerve.'

Indigo was already leading the elephant up the gangplank of the captain's boat, which buckled dangerously but held. Then he was leading it below deck and into their cabin. The flexilis wood of the doorway stretched and lengthened, and then the elephant was through. One by one the animals followed Indigo onto the boat, with Max and Daisy bringing up the rear on the lion.

What Max saw inside was perhaps the greatest of all the wonders he had seen that night. Even as he watched, their cabin was transforming itself into a forest. Their bunks were lost amid the foliage as rustling trees rose up from the wooden planks of the floor. They sprouted branches for the orangutans to swing through, and undergrowth for the shrews to hide in, and there was a watering hole for the elephant to drink at. It took long grateful gulps through its trunk and then showered itself joyfully with water, soaking Indigo in the process.

'How is this possible?' asked Max, looking around. A snake was unwinding itself from around the neck of the leopard it had travelled with, and was now coiling happily around a tree trunk. The hummingbirds were hovering in the air like flying emeralds, sucking up nectar from pink umbrella flowers that were opening before his eyes, while the marmosets plucked bright yellow mangoes from the trees.

'Won't it be obvious that the boat is bigger?' asked Max. 'Won't people notice that something is going on?'

The Prof shook her head. 'The wood only expands on the inside. The outside still looks the same. It's just a bit . . . roomier in here now, that's all. The forest though . . .' She frowned, closing her eyes to sense the currents of magic around her. 'I think that might be Daisy.'

Max glanced behind him at Daisy, who was still sitting on the lion's back, her head bent over a tiny black and gold monkey.

'It will be okay,' said Indigo, coming over and taking the small creature in his hands. It was trembling in shock. Indigo pulled a jar of chamomillion cream from his overalls and used it carefully on the stump of the capuchin's tail. 'Her balance may not be so good now,' he explained, watching it heal. 'But she will be okay.'

Above the sound of elephants trumpeting, monkeys

chattering, pangolins rustling and birds of paradise exchanging calls, there came a different noise. The sound of a throat being cleared with disapproval.

Slowly, the four children turned around, and through the thickets of enormous green leaves and foliage at the heart of the swaying barge, they saw the small and incredulous form of Rozaliya, framed in the open doorway.

'So,' she said, raising one long eyebrow. 'You don't think a theatre company is good enough, is that it? You want to make us the Nautilus Circus?'

Chapter 56

Daisy felt her heart rise into her throat. She was so exhausted that she didn't know whether to cry or laugh. Tears had the upper hand, though. Every time she closed her eyes, she saw the crushed capuchin cage, the lost tail. *My fault*, she thought. *All my fault*.

She stared at Rozaliya, who had shut the door behind her, and was now looking around with wide eyes. A small pygmy marmoset, about the size of a lemon, was curled on Rozaliya's shoulder, grooming her hair with tiny fingers. A tortoise with a shell made of emerald was nibbling on the fringe of her sequinned gown, and a rare butterfly was perched on her ear like a clip-on earring.

'I really hope,' said Rozaliya, 'that you have a good explanation for this.'

Indigo, Max and the Prof launched in at the same time. Daisy couldn't bring herself to speak.

'There was a market and—'

'You see, we had to rescue them—'

'We had no choice, so—'

'ENOUGH,' said Rozaliya, glaring at them. 'One of

you – please explain.'

Daisy swallowed and forced herself to meet the wardrobe mistress's frosty gaze, putting down the vials and jars she'd swiped from the market before it went up in flames. One of them was labelled 'Whipple seed powder'.

'It's like this,' she said. 'We – um – discovered that there's a black market in Iffenwild. We think it was being run by the Grim Reapers. And we realized that Pompey – you know, the Duchess's chief advisor – knew about it and wasn't going to do anything to shut it down. So we—'

'Decided you'd do it yourself. Is that it?' Rozaliya's eyes glittered dangerously. 'You decided not to ask for help. You decided to put yourselves in danger, along with the whole *Nautilus* fleet, by bringing the animals here.'

'I'm sorry,' said Daisy. Rozaliya was right. She tried to remember their logic, and it sounded foolish to her own ears. 'We didn't know who we could trust. We think there's someone at the Nautilus who's reporting to the Reapers, and if they'd found out where we were going it would have ruined everything.'

'You didn't see the market,' put in Indigo. 'We couldn't have left the animals there. We just couldn't.'

'So,' said Rozaliya. 'This is the situation. You have a menagerie of priceless animals hidden inside your cabin. We will probably have a horde of Grim Reapers coming down on our heads at any moment. And an elephant has just pooed on my shoe.' She lifted one exquisite rhinestone boot, and it came away from the floor with a horrible squelch.

'Pretty much, yes,' said Daisy. She fought the urge to put her hands over her eyes.

'Well,' said Rozaliya. 'You have done a stupid thing – but a great thing.' Daisy looked at her in astonishment. 'Yes,' the wardrobe mistress declared. 'Idiotic in the extreme, but *magnificent*.'

That was when Daisy knew it was going to be all right.

'It is true. If you had asked me before, I would have done everything to stop you. But now it is done.' The wardrobe mistress tossed her cape over her shoulder. 'Now,' she said grandly, 'I am going to *help*.'

'Th-thank you,' said Daisy. 'We mustn't tell anyone else that the animals are here. Maybe Alexei – but not the crew, or Ingrid or Marie-Claude. Or –' she swallowed – 'Gabriel.'

'You think there is a spy,' said Rozaliya. 'I do not agree. But still, we will be careful. We will tell no one. We can put ignotus leaves around the door and windows of the cabin. They will stop anyone hearing or seeing what's inside. Luckily, we only have one performance left. Tomorrow night is the final show, and then the carnival. The morning after that, we leave Iffenwild, and somehow, we will get these animals back to where they belong: in the wild. Until then –' she gazed at a pair of black crested gibbons swinging in the treetops – 'I think the animals will be happy here. Indigo, you can keep control of them, yes?'

'I can't control them,' he said. 'That would be wrong.

But I've spoken to them, and they understand. They won't attack each other or anything.'

'Good,' said Rozaliya. 'You stay here. I will bring food. You must be hungry.'

None of them noticed the raven crouched at the window of the cabin as Max removed his itching wig and they sat down to rest.

After Rozaliya had come and gone again, leaving plates of cheese dumplings and fresh bread and ripe peaches and an enormous tin of spiced biscuits; after the animals had settled, and the children (and some of the marmosets) had eaten their fill, Max looked up.

'I heard something in the market,' he blurted out. 'Before everything else happened.'

Daisy went still, and Indigo put down his sixth biscuit. The Prof, who was arranging white ignotus leaves around the cabin's door and windows, paused and pushed her glasses back up her nose. 'Go on,' she said.

'Well.' Max tried to recall the scene exactly. 'There were two cloaked figures near the door to the market. They were going past me quickly, so I didn't hear everything they said. But they were talking about the Botanists in the Amazon.' He glanced up and saw that Daisy was leaning so far forward that she was almost tipping into the empty biscuit tin. Napoleon was poised on her shoulder, his tail in the shape of a question mark.

'They said . . . something about Botanists being stripped of magic. They said that now that they had a – it sounded like a "mortal"? – something like that anyway, they could start stripping them properly. I don't know what it means, though.'

Daisy gasped. 'It's what that woman said. Remember, Prof? The one in the paper who was found dead in the Amazon. The article said that her last word was "mortal", or at least, that's what they thought she meant – that she was dying. But what if that wasn't it? What if she was talking about an *object*?'

The Prof was already flipping through her copy of *The Compleat Botanist*. 'It's not in here,' she said. 'Of course not. Whatever it is, it must be dangerous.' She rooted around in her bag and pulled out a book with a blood-red cover: *Dark Botany: A Cautionary Guide*. 'I – um – *borrowed* this from the Mallowmarsh library, just in case. It has things they don't put in the usual books, in case they give people ideas.' She flicked to the index and ran her finger down the entries. 'Here we are. I should have thought of this from the start.' Her face looked almost ashen. 'Mortle. M-O-R-T-L-E. The death seed.'

Daisy felt all the hairs stand up on her neck. 'What does that mean?'

'It's a seed that sucks magic from anything it touches,' explained the Prof. 'Sort of like a black hole. If a single seed touched the earth in a Botanical pocket, it would drain huge quantities of magic before it was stopped. And if it was held to the throat of a Botanist . . .' She paused, and Daisy knew they were both remembering the words of the article. *The victim displayed no visible signs of injury except a round burn mark on her throat, and a bleaching to the irises of her eyes.* 'Well,' continued the Prof, swallowing. 'It could drain a Botanist in moments. The shock would probably kill them.'

Max felt sick. 'That's what they're doing to the Botanists imprisoned in the Amazon?' he asked. 'But why? What for?'

'I don't know,' said Daisy, trying not to panic. She thought of Ma, and felt dizzy with horror. 'We need to get there as fast as we can, and with help. But the *Nautilus* leaves Iffenwild the day after tomorrow – and there's no way we'll persuade the Iffenwilders to come with us. We're just children. It's impossible.' She thought again of the capuchin's lost tail and her own catastrophic failure to do the simplest thing: control her own magic. She got up quietly, and left the cabin.

Chapter 57

Daisy stood on the edge of the lagoon and looked silently out across the water. If only Ma was here, with all her brilliance and her bravery. She would know what to do. But that was the problem – Ma *wasn't* here. Daisy was alone, and she wasn't good enough. All her life she had felt like an outsider: half English, half Persian, a citizen of nowhere. Not belonging in the Greyside, but still feeling like an imposter in the Greenwild. A girl without command of her magic.

Again and again, she replayed the moment when she had released her control on the vines. She had thought she'd timed it right, but one vine had moved too soon, and her mistake had harmed an innocent creature. Indigo said the capuchin would be fine, but that wasn't the point. She was just as bad as the Reapers who had mutilated those rhinos and shot the beautiful golden panther. Daisy let out a great shout that seemed to scrape the sky. She kicked the water at the edge of the lagoon, sending up a great, angry arc of spray in the dark.

Then she paused. The water was glittering where she

had kicked it, pulsing with bright-blue light that rose and fell with the waves. She kicked it again and saw the swish of her foot light up with a thousand electric blue sparkles. She crouched down and drew her hand slowly through the water – and when she brought it out, she saw tiny stars sparkle and fade across her skin.

'Sea sparkle,' said a voice behind her. 'Also known as bioluminescence.' Daisy turned around and saw the Prof, wearing her old overalls and a red headband. 'It means "living light", and it's caused by chemical reactions inside tiny, microscopic creatures in the water.'

'Really?' Daisy said, smiling despite herself. 'It seems pretty magic to me.'

The Prof shrugged. 'Magic, science. Sometimes the two aren't as different as we think.'

There was a silence as Daisy watched the blue light rise and shimmer around her ankles. She could tell the Prof was waiting for her to speak.

'I did something bad,' she said at last. 'Because I thought I could control my magic. But I couldn't. I hurt that monkey. It was me.' She told the Prof how it had happened, how she hadn't realized until it was too late.

'Oh, Daisy.' The Prof's voice was quiet. 'It wasn't your fault. It was an accident. What you did was extraordinary. You must have controlled fifty vines, and only one of them slipped out of control.'

'One too many,' said Daisy, kicking hard at the sand. It

lit up with a sparkling blue halo, and she wiped her cheeks with the ends of her hair.

'Maybe,' said the Prof. 'But Daisy, if we hadn't tried, then all of those animals would have been killed. You did your best, and sometimes that has to be good enough.'

Daisy shut her eyes. 'It's just so . . . *hard*. I know you don't like water plants, but you still make everything look so simple. You control everything so perfectly.'

The Prof shrugged. 'It's only practice. But Daisy, you have something I'll never have. Sheer, raw courage – and the kind of magic that matches it. The kind of magic that's hard to tame. The kind that can grow a whole forest.'

Daisy turned to look at her, astonished.

'Yes,' said the Prof. 'I felt you pouring your magic into the cabin. How else do you think it managed to grow an entire rainforest in the space of five minutes?'

Daisy shook her head. 'I didn't mean to do that.' But that wasn't quite true. Hadn't she wanted, desperately, to protect the animals? To give them a home and make them feel safe? She felt the hollowness and exhaustion in her own chest, as if someone had scooped out her insides with a spoon – and knew it was because she had spent her magic like water.

'Oh,' said Daisy. She drew her fingers through the surf and watched a stream of blue sparks follow the arc of her hand like a trail of sequins.

Then she heard a throat being cleared and turned to see Max and Indigo standing behind her, their glittering blue footsteps lighting up the sand.

'Are you coming back now?' asked Max. 'Only, Boris is getting grumpy because Napoleon stole his dinner, and I'm pretty sure he won't calm down until you come and sort it out.'

Daisy stifled a laugh. 'I'm coming,' she said. 'We only have two days until we leave Iffenwild. We need to think fast.'

'Okay,' said Daisy, three hours later. They were all tired and heavy-eyed, and Napoleon's tail was drooping with exhaustion. 'Think. THINK. Let's go over it again. We know that Pompey is involved with the Reapers. So, he's going to do everything he can to stop the Duchess sending a fleet of Iffenwilders to the Amazon to fight them. We know that lots of Iffenwilders don't like Pompey, but they're toeing the line because they're scared. So . . .'

'So,' said the Prof patiently, and for the twentieth time, 'we need to get him out of the way.'

'But what does that even mean?' asked Daisy. 'We're not assassins. And anyway, that would make us as bad as the Reapers.'

'Well then,' said Max, 'we need to expose him somehow. Show everyone how bad he really is.'

'But how?' Daisy sighed. 'Look. I think we need to do two things. One, we should try to get another message to Artemis and the Mallowmarsh ship. They need to know where we are and what's happening here. They probably won't arrive in time to help, but at least then they'll know about the Grim Reapers, and they'll be prepared.'

'Yes,' said the Prof. 'Let's do it now.'

Daisy wrote quickly and handed the rolled-up scrap of paper to Indigo, who attached it to Jethro's leg and sent the parakeet flying out of the cabin window.

At the last moment Daisy thought of something. 'They'll need the dandelight,' she said, 'if they're going to find the door.'

It would be a terrible gamble, sending the dandelight out into the unknown, but she trusted Indigo and she trusted his birds. He whistled and called up two more parakeets and a magnificent African grey parrot. Moving quickly, they placed the dandelight in the empty biscuit tin, packed it with spare socks, and sealed it shut with vines. Then they constructed a harness with string and attached it to the legs of the three birds to carry between them.

The trio soared after Jethro in a wobbling but determined line towards the horizon – and then, suddenly, just as they reached the water beyond the coral reef, they flashed out of existence.

'They've left the Marindeep,' said Indigo, 'and they'll find the Mallowmarsh ship as fast as they can.'

'Good,' said the Prof. 'Daisy, you said we needed to do two things. What was the second?'

'I think,' said Daisy, 'we need to pay a visit to Emil.'

Chapter 58

Daisy, Indigo and the Prof were up at daybreak, bleary-eyed but determined. Daisy tried to wake Max too, but he groaned and turned over in his bunk.

'Let him sleep,' murmured the Prof. 'He looks exhausted.'

The air outside was still cool, and the sunrise was the precise colour of a watermelon, with streams of gold and pink light pouring over the shell towers of Iffenwild. They arrived at the Jolly Fishhook before opening time and found Emil by the back door, emptying a slop bucket into the gutter.

'You're alive!' He looked equal parts astonished and relieved. 'I heard them saying that they found the secret entrance and the market in flames – abandoned, full of empty cages. I thought – I thought something terrible must have happened to you.'

'We're all right,' said Daisy. 'We destroyed the market. The animals that were imprisoned there are safe.'

'Really?' Emil looked at them and gave a sort of whoop. 'It is incredible, this thing you have done.'

But Daisy was picking over his words, piecing things

together. 'Who did you hear talking about the market, Emil? How did you know where it was in the first place?'

'Oh,' he said, tipping more water down the gutter. 'I hear rumours around the place. You know, gossip.'

'No,' said the Prof. 'I think it's more than that.' She caught his gaze and held it. Emil looked away first.

'Ach,' he said, putting down his bucket. 'I meant to tell you, many times. But I did not know if I could trust you.'

'You can trust us,' said Indigo quietly.

'Yes,' said Emil. 'I know this now.' He puffed out a breath, and it feathered the cool morning air like a steam engine. 'It is like this. My father is a member of the Iffenwild resistance. They are a group of people who are fighting to get rid of Pompey and to restore the lost prince. The Jolly Fishhook is one of – how do you say it? – one of the headquarters. I am not old enough to join, but I hear everything. This is how I know so much. I heard them talking about a market, but they had not decided what to do about it. Now . . .' He paused. 'Now, I think they will be interested in you.'

Daisy glanced at the Prof in excitement. She knew they were thinking the same thing.

'We can help each other,' she said, leaning forward. 'We can tell you about the Reapers, the people who Pompey is working with. We can tell you everything you need to turn the whole of Iffenwild against him.' And maybe, she thought, the Iffenwilders could be persuaded to join the fight in the Amazon.

*

Max woke to find a tortoise nibbling his ear. He had overslept, and the cabin was empty – if you didn't count an African elephant, four rhinos and a whole jungle of wild animals.

He glanced out of the window just in time to see Daisy, Indigo and the Prof walking along the canal towards the ship. It looked like they'd been out – without him.

He heard their voices faintly through the glass and he thought he caught the sound of his own name. After everything they'd been through together, they'd left him behind, again – and now they were talking about him behind his back. This was too much to bear.

Gently setting down the tortoise, Max left the cabin and climbed halfway up the stairs. Some impulse made him stay hidden. He wanted to hear what they had to say.

'Really, Prof,' came Daisy's voice. Max could just see her shoe from his position on the stairs. 'Can't you give the revision a break? How likely is it that we'll actually be able to take the second Bloomquist test?'

'I don't care,' said the Prof stubbornly. 'Whenever we take it, I want to be prepared. Besides, it's a good distraction.' She cleared her throat. 'Ready? What is a cumulapple and what is it used for?'

Max frowned. Something about the name rang a bell.

'Honestly,' said the Prof, when Daisy didn't answer. 'It's a tiny sky-blue apple that grows in the cloud forests of the

Malaysian Greenwild. It has wisps of real cloud inside it, and it allows the eater to fly – for a limited time.'

Max leaned forward. Yes! He'd heard his mother talk about this one with real longing in her voice. 'It's the rarest thing there is,' she had said. 'The apples only grow once in a decade, and they're nearly impossible to pick.'

'They're priceless,' the Prof was saying. 'But Emil said that the Duchess keeps a stock of them in the palace. Maybe she takes them on her hot-air balloon for safety, like a parachute. I suppose she's rich enough to afford them.'

'Imagine flying,' said Daisy dreamily, and Max nodded to himself. Yes, imagine it.

Then – 'Do you really think he seems better?' asked the Prof, as if returning to an earlier topic. Max's ears pricked up.

'Maybe?' said Daisy. 'I wish there was something I could do to make it easier for him. His mother died so he could live. I know it's impossible, but she'd want him to be happy.'

Max leapt to his feet, stubbed his toe and sprinted up onto the deck.

Daisy and the Prof were sitting on a pair of barrels, mending a pile of ropes.

'What do you mean, my mother died so I could live?' He was panting, and there was a ringing noise in his ears.

Daisy went very white. 'Oh Max,' she said. 'I—'

'This is it, isn't it? This is what you weren't telling me.' He found that he was shaking Daisy's shoulders, and her eyes were wide and very close to his face.

Napoleon spat and scratched at his legs, and he took a step back.

'Sorry,' he muttered. 'I have to know. You have to tell me.'

Daisy cursed herself inwardly. How could she have been such a fool?

'I didn't know what to do,' she said. The blood had drained from her face, and her fingertips felt cold. 'Max – I – I didn't tell you because I didn't want you to be more hurt.'

'Tell me now,' growled Max.

'Okay,' she said shakily. 'Okay. This is it, the truth. Your mother stole something while she was at Mallowmarsh. A priceless plant called a ghost-moth orchid.'

Max nodded, as if this wasn't surprising. 'So?' he prompted.

'Well,' said Daisy. 'The flowers of the orchid are edible. For each flower you eat, a year is added to your life. But at the same time, a year is taken from the life of the person you love most in the world.'

'And this is relevant because . . . ?'

'Because,' said Daisy, 'you ate the flowers your mother sent you. And the person you loved most in the world was her.'

Chapter 59

'Oh,' said Max. And suddenly he understood. He remembered the envelopes packed full of white flowers. He thought of the feeling of strength that had been slowly coming back to him day by day, like a slow-motion thrill ride.

Every flower he'd eaten had taken a year from his mother's life.

'It's my fault,' he said slowly. 'It's my fault she's dead.'

'No,' said Daisy. Her voice sounded panicky. 'Max. NO. That's not true. It was her choice, her decision—'

Max felt a sort of buzzing in his blood, as if a swarm of bees was running riot through his veins. He needed to get out of here. He turned his back on Daisy and ran out of the ship and into the network of canals that surrounded it.

Half an hour later, he found himself wandering around the docks. His mind was blank. He simply walked and watched the world pass by. Most people seemed to be discussing the annual Iffenwild carnival, which traditionally took place on the night of the final Nautilus performance. 'I hear the Duchess of Malfa is dressing up as a rhinoceros,' said one woman to another, eyebrows raised. 'I hear that they're importing the fireworks from Velupo this year,' said another. Max walked on, thinking now of his mother and what she had done.

Then he heard a snippet of conversation that stopped him in his tracks.

'. . . where the Reapers are assembling,' a short man was saying to the tall person beside him. A group of children scampered past, and Max only caught the end of the next sentence: '. . . only a matter of time.'

Max darted behind a coil of rope, breathing hard. He recognized the voice – high and emphatic. It was the man they'd seen in the alleyway on the night of the siren reed attack. And beside him was Gabriel Rose, the company's vainest actor.

An hour later, Max was still missing, and Daisy was getting worried.

'Do you think we should go and look for him?' she asked. They were standing on the deck of the captain's ship, scanning the canal in both directions. 'I don't know if—'

Then they saw him, running down the street towards them. He almost fell up the gangplank of the boat.

'I – saw – Gabriel Rose,' gasped Max, bracing his hands on his knees. He'd clearly run far and fast to get to them. 'He was with the man from the alleyway – the one we thought was mixed up in the black market. He said something about the Reapers assembling.'

'What?' The Prof came out from behind Daisy. 'Are you sure?'

'I'm sure,' said Max impatiently. 'How many men who look like Gabriel do you think there are wandering around the streets of Iffenwild? It was him, and he wasn't being forced to be there or anything. They seemed really pally.'

'Oh.' Daisy felt herself slump. She paused, thinking. 'If Gabriel is secretly a Reaper, well . . . that would explain a few things, at least. Like how they knew where to find the *Nautilus* fleet before we passed through the gate into the Marindeep.'

'But why would Gabriel do this?' asked Indigo. He looked winded, as if someone had knocked into him from behind. 'I mean, I know he's a bit self-absorbed, but why would he be helping the Grim Reapers?'

'I don't know,' said Daisy bitterly. 'They probably told him that he had pretty eyelashes.' She felt hollow with disbelief. It didn't seem possible that any of the *Nautilus* crew, with their laughter and their music and their kindness, could be working with the Reapers. 'It's like Artemis kept saying. We can't trust anyone.'

'So, what now?' asked Max, looking uncertain.

'We've got to tell Alexei,' said Daisy, with conviction. They went and found him at once, standing at the wheel with Annika propped on his hip. But when they told him what Max had seen, he didn't seem worried.

'Ah, well,' he said philosophically. 'I expect Gabriel was trying to get hold of some dark-market face cream. You know how obsessed he is with his looks. Greenness forbid that he should get a wrinkle!'

'But . . .' Daisy looked at him, nonplussed.

'I shouldn't worry about it,' said Alexei, handing Annika a rusk. She bashed it up and down a few times, and dribbled all over his shoulder. 'I know Gabriel, and I know that no one on this ship would betray us.'

Chapter 60

Max couldn't stop thinking about what Daisy had told him. Again and again, he saw the white flowers on the floor of the basement, the note in his mother's handwriting. He missed her desperately, with a deep slicing pain that felt like glass in his lungs. Every breath seemed to hurt. More than anything, he wanted to see her just one more time.

He crept down to the storage room as soon as the others were asleep after that night's performance. Afterwards, he wished he hadn't. It was a memory he'd kept buried so deep that he never wanted to look at it again. But the leaf hadn't let him look away.

It was the day of the kidnap. The last argument they'd had.

'You cannot go to school,' his mother had said, brushing out her long golden hair in front of the mirror. 'You're not well enough, Max.'

'I can,' said Max, sitting up very straight in the hotel room chair. 'I am.' He ignored the pain in his chest that told him that he wasn't. They were in London to try a different hospital, a new treatment, and he would be checked in tomorrow. 'I want to go to school.'

'No.'

'You don't understand!' cried Max. 'I want to be normal!' His anger made him want to hurl furniture across the room; but the bed was too heavy, and the hotel chair seemed to be bolted to the floor.

'Oh Max, my darling boy.' She turned towards him, and a jewelled dolphin clip glittered in her hair. 'You *are* normal. You might not be able to do all the same things as other people, but that doesn't change anything about *who you are.*'

'No,' said Max, and he was too angry now to hear anything she said. 'You don't ever let me do what I want. I hate you! I hate you!' He spat the words at her, and a fleck of spit landed on her cheek. He watched as she wiped it away, and the look in her eyes made him step back.

Thirty seconds after that, the first attacker burst into the room. Those were the last words he had spoken to her before they were separated.

Now, in the darkness of the storeroom, Max curled over in agony. *I hate you! I hate you!*

He wanted his mother to place her hand on his forehead and say, 'I forgive you.' But there was only silence.

Max went back to his bunk and spent the rest of the night staring at the wall without seeing a thing.

*

Disaster struck the next morning, just as they were finishing breakfast on the deck of the captain's ship. One moment Daisy was asking for a second piece of toast, and the next, a dark shape dropped down from the rigging, knocked a blow to Max's head, tossed him over his shoulder – and was gone over the side of the canal boat.

Alexei gave a roar and chased after them. Daisy sprinted behind and skidded onto the street in time to see Jarndyce go flying over a string of sticky vine that Alexei had cast across the exit of the nearest alleyway. Jarndyce landed on his back and two seconds later Alexei planted a foot on his chest. A few seconds after that, Max was free of his attacker, his powder smudged and birthmark showing, and had sprinted back to the gangplank of the boat.

Jarndyce gave a groan and covered his eyes with his hand.

'Game's up, Jarndyce,' said Alexei, levelling his sword at the man's chest. He was already in costume for that morning's rehearsal, and he looked particularly splendid in his red trousers and velvet cape. 'Tell us who you're working for and what you want with Max.'

'I'm not telling you anything,' spat Jarndyce.

'Oh really?' said Alexei, pressing the tip of his sword into Jarndyce's chest. 'I sharpened this blade a few hours ago. I advise you to talk.'

But Jarndyce only grinned; a terrible pulling back of his lips from his teeth to reveal wolfish yellow canines. 'I don't think so,' he said casually. And then he twisted up like a great muscled fish, wrenched the sword from Alexei's hand, and drove it through the huge man's chest.

Daisy heard herself cry out in horror and saw Alexei choke and look down at the sword protruding from his chest. He clutched a fist around the hilt and for a moment there was a confused expression on his face, as if he couldn't quite believe what he was seeing. Then he crumpled where he stood and fell to the ground.

Rozaliya gave a piercing cry and flung herself over his fallen body, even as Jarndyce turned, reached the end of the alleyway, and was gone.

Chapter 61

'Oh no oh no oh no.' Max fell to his knees beside Alexei's body. It couldn't be true, he thought. *Not Alexei.* He bent his head and let his tears fall on the great man's face.

'Hey there,' came a familiar, deep voice. 'You're getting my shirt all wet.'

Max opened his eyes. Alexei was sitting up and smiling, the sword still sticking out of his body.

'But – I – what – how?' Max could barely form the words to ask his question.

'Ah,' said Alexei, looking around at them and pulling the collapsible rapier from his chest. 'This is a theatre. You didn't think this was a real sword, did you? I thought it best to let that rat go for now. He'll be back, I'm sure. But we'll be ready for him.'

'But you – I saw you fall – you were, you looked—'

Alexei sat up properly and gave a great booming laugh. 'That, my child,' he said, 'is why they call me the greatest actor of my generation.'

After that, Rozaliya insisted that they all have a second

breakfast, to help with the shock.

Daisy pulled Indigo, Max and the Prof aside afterwards. 'This is proof,' she said. 'There must be a spy on board the *Nautilus*. How else did Jarndyce know about Max's disguise?'

It was a good thing they'd had a second round of pancakes, because it turned out to be a long and exhausting day. Emil turned up just before lunchtime. 'I have news,' he said. 'The resistance is spreading the word about Pompey and the market. Everyone in Iffenwild is talking about it. The people are angry. Yes, decidedly we are angry. And there is more to do. We will turn this city upside down.' Emil raised a fist to the heavens and Max glanced around. A few children were bowling hoops down the end of the street next to the opera house, and a little old lady was passing by with her shopping trolley. It didn't *look* like a city on the brink of revolution. But appearances could be deceiving.

'Also,' said Emil, 'my aunt Josephine, she is a maid at the palace. She is working for the resistance too, and she says that the Duchess is walking around the palace all night; the servants think she's going mad. Also, she is locking herself in her study and opening the safe in there. My aunt,' he said, proudly, 'watches through the keyhole.'

Daisy's heart began beating fast. 'Does your aunt see what she gets out of the safe?'

'No,' he said. 'But she says the Duchess is acting scared.'

'I bet it's something to do with the death of the king

and queen,' said Daisy. 'I bet she knows that Pompey was responsible, and now she's afraid for her own life. If we can find proof he was behind their deaths, then it might just be enough to free the Duchess from his power.'

'What kind of proof?' said Max. 'And how would we get in? It's impossible.'

'Not necessarily,' said Emil, looking thoughtful. He ran a hand through his hedgehog spiked hair. 'Tonight is the last night of your play, yes?'

'Yes!' said Daisy. 'You're right. The Duchess and Pompey attend the first- and final-night shows. That means that tonight they'll be at the theatre. The palace will be empty.'

'Exactly,' said Emil, turning away. 'Oh. And one more thing,' he added casually, pausing on the gangplank. 'The resistance has found out that the Reapers are planning to capture you, Max, at tonight's performance. They know about your disguise.'

'What?!' Max stared at Emil in horror.

'Yah, I know,' said Emil, shrugging. 'It is not so good.'

'Okay,' said the Prof after Emil had left. They had retired to their cabin for an emergency Five O'Clock Club meeting, and Indigo was feeding the elephants while they talked. 'We can deal with this. We need to get you off the stage tonight, Max. Then we need to get into the palace and into that safe. But how?'

They all sat glumly. The porthole window was slightly

open, and Daisy felt the cool damp air blow in with the smell of spring. Napoleon had stolen a ball of string from Rozaliya's workroom and was batting it hypnotically back and forth between his paws. Daisy could see he was pretending not to watch a little mouse creeping along the edge of the cabin, stealing its way towards a *pryaniki* crumb that had fallen on the floor. Just as the mouse gained its prize, Napoleon pounced.

'Ugh,' said the Prof. 'Did we have to see that?'

'Wait a minute,' said Daisy slowly. 'What if we could do the same thing?'

'Don't tell me you've suddenly developed a taste for mouse,' said Indigo. 'I don't think it tastes at all like chicken, whatever people say.'

'No, no,' said Daisy, waving a hand. The biscuit-crumb bait had given her an idea. Talking slowly, she outlined her plan.

That night, the crew of the *Nautilus* assembled on deck before heading off to the final gala performance of the play.

'All right, crew,' said Alexei, looking around at the gathering. 'This is our moment!' He raised his arm and turned his face in profile. 'Not for the Duchess, but for ourselves. We're going to go out there tonight, and we're going to show Iffenwild what we do best.'

Rozaliya brushed a tear from her cheek. 'Hear! Hear!' she called loudly, and the rest of the crew cheered. 'To the

Nautilus,' cried Marie-Claude, raising a fist.

'The *Nautilus*!' the others echoed; and they set off across the square for the last time. As on every other night, baby Annika went with them to the opera house, where she would be set in her special cot backstage. Max watched as Daisy, wearing his full changeling costume, joined the throng of departing actors. They had made sure that none of the crew – especially Gabriel – knew about the swap. Daisy's long braid was curled under the hated blond wig, her cheeks were powdered, and Napoleon was hidden inside the sky-blue waistcoat, his tail just sticking out of the collar. She was slightly shorter than Max, but their builds were similar enough that the likeness was convincing. She sent the others a half salute as she disappeared around the corner, and mouthed the words, 'Good luck.'

Max patted his pockets. Inside, he had a vial labelled 'Whipple seed powder' – one of the vials Daisy had snatched from the market before it had gone up in flames. 'Hang on,' Max had said, as she explained her plan. 'Whipple tree? Isn't that the one with seeds that are almost impossible to find, because they're *invisible*?'

'Exactly,' said the Prof, cutting in. 'And – most importantly for us – the seeds can also induce temporary invisibility. The effects last up to three hours, depending on dosage.'

Now, Max shook the vial. It looked completely empty, which he supposed was to be expected.

They gave it half an hour, and then Max, Indigo and the Prof slipped away quietly from the *Nautilus* dock. This time, they went by water, paddling a small rowboat lent to them by Emil, and made their way along the edge of the lagoon towards the palace. The city was already teeming with people getting ready for that night's carnival, and there was an air of glittering excitement on every street corner.

At last, the palace came into view. Its great white towers and spiralling shell turrets glimmered in the streetlamps and flashed on the surface of the lagoon. The ramparts were patrolled, and the ornate mother-of-pearl gates were guarded by soldiers. There was a narrow portico in front of these gates, with steps leading straight down to the lagoon, so that the Duchess could come and go by private barge. The windows of the palace – and there were many, maybe hundreds – blazed with golden light, even though the flag was at half-mast to show that the Duchess was away for the evening.

'Good,' said the Prof, once they were crouched in the rowboat about ten feet from the gates. 'Indigo, are you ready?' He nodded, one eye on a small pod of porpoises circling nearby.

'Max?'

'Ready.' He lifted his chin, like a boxer before a fight.

The Prof smiled, and then she took a slingshot from her back pocket, picked up a stone from the bottom of the boat, and aimed it at a spot about five feet to the left of the main entrance.

THWOCK! It hit the wall with a satisfying impact and bounced to the ground.

'Oi!' said one of the guards. 'What was that?'

'Dunno,' the other shrugged. 'Probably some tuna. They're not so good at flying at night.'

'That's not good enough, eejit,' said the first guard. 'You cover the door while I investigate.'

Max took the vial of Whipple seed powder from his pocket, un-stoppered it and tipped it into his mouth. For a moment, he thought it really had been empty. Then he felt the trickle of something numbing on his tongue. 'Okay,' he said thickly. 'Here we go.' Then he crouched like a sprinter at the edge of the tiny, rocking boat.

Indigo whistled, and the porpoises leapt from the canal directly in front of the portico of the palace, splashing the face of the remaining guard with so much water that he was momentarily blinded, and Max – who had jumped from the boat onto the crumbling stone steps – slipped past him and into the palace.

Chapter 62

Max felt his whole body tingle with the effects of the Whipple seed. He looked down in amazement as he stood in the entrance hall of the palace. His body had vanished. The only evidence of his existence was his shadow, cast from a great coral chandelier onto the pearlescent floor. His skin felt slightly numb, but his sight and hearing were intoxicatingly sharp.

The palace was deserted, for the Duchess and her household were at the opera house watching the play. Moving stealthily, Max made for the grand staircase. It was strange, being invisible. He could not see his arms and legs to know where to place them, and once or twice he stumbled and almost lost the boundaries of himself.

He climbed through the palace, passing more guards and making as little noise as possible. The stairs were carved from ancient sea-oak, and they shifted and reconfigured themselves as he climbed them, so that by the time he reached the top, they had spiralled around to deposit him at the opposite side of the hall, and he was forced to circle back around the gallery at the top.

'Oi,' said one of the guards. 'Someone's on the staircase.' But Max crouched down behind the banisters at the top and they surged past him, baffled. 'False alarm,' said the nearest guard. 'I knew this old wood was faulty.'

Max stayed there, crouching down and trying not to breathe too loudly, until the guards had moved down the corridor and out of sight. He'd never been more conscious of his own shadow. Then he got to his feet and set off again, moving as quietly as he could. The safe, Emil had said, was hidden in the Duchess's private study, 'in the room below the tallest tower, behind a very ugly painting of an old man and his three daughters.' Emil knew this because his aunt Josephine had to go over it with a feather duster twice a day.

Easy, thought Max. *Sort of*. They had worked out earlier that the tallest tower was in the west wing, so he crossed to the far side of the building and set about looking for the nearest staircase. A guard strolled past, and Max ducked, forgetting he was invisible. The guard glanced round, as if sensing something in the air. Then he shook his head and walked on.

Max took a breath and kept climbing, higher and ever higher. The stone stairs were lined with a thick carpet of moss that was springy and cool under his bare feet (he had taken off his shoes so that he could move as silently as possible). Then he came out onto a landing, and knew he had found the right place. The rooms here were elegant and

bright, with iridescent lamps and pale, lustrous hangings. It was like standing inside a pearl. Max walked through a reception room garlanded with carved vines – and found himself confronted by a locked door.

Two minutes later, Max was putting away his lock pick and pushing open the heavy wooden entrance to a book-lined study. This was it. And there, just as Emil's aunt had described, was an inexpressibly ugly painting of King Lear and his three daughters.

Moving quickly and carefully, Max placed the painting on the floor and reached up to try the combination on the safe that lay behind it.

Chapter 63

Daisy held her breath as she waited for the curtain to rise. Her long hair was hidden under Max's blond and curling wig. She understood, now, why he had complained about it so much – it was the itchiest thing she had ever encountered. On her right cheek, just below the eye, was inked a strawberry-red mark, concealed with a thin layer of powder. Napoleon was by her feet, whiskers twitching, ready to watch from the wings.

The curtains rose. The audience clapped. The play began.

Daisy waited for her cue and stepped on stage.

She kept her gaze on her feet for the first minute before she dared to look up. At first the audience was a blur of indistinct faces. She then blinked, and there, at the back of the theatre, was Jarndyce, watching the changeling's every move.

For a moment, their eyes locked.

Daisy took a shallow breath and heard Rozaliya's words in her mind: 'Life is a theatre, child. It is important to dress for the show.'

Well, she was dressed now for the show of her life. As

the scene ended, Daisy stepped off stage, taking care to walk with Max's distinctive gait, which was proud and a little clumsy, as if he wasn't quite used to his own arms. Napoleon leapt onto her shoulder the moment she left the stage. The first act passed. Daisy's arms were tense. Then, as she re-entered for her next scene, she saw a guard hurry in from outside and whisper to Jarndyce. She saw the guard gesture towards the palace and her stomach lurched. Had Max been discovered? Jarndyce hesitated, clearly torn between going to investigate and keeping his eyes trained on Daisy.

Daisy raised a hand to her cheek, and making it look like an accident, she rubbed some of the powder away, exposing half of the fake birthmark. Jarndyce's eyes sharpened, and he began to move through the audience towards her.

If only she could keep him distracted long enough for the real Max to get to the safe and break into it, then she would have done her job.

Daisy slipped backstage, and then, moving with deliberate slowness to make sure she was seen, she walked into the dressing room. It was large and shadowy, with ornate and dusty mouldings and several portraits of men with bristling moustaches who stared down at her with accusing eyes. As soon as she entered the room, she began to move very quickly. *A quick change is a great skill in an actor*, said Rozaliya's voice in her head.

Less than forty seconds later, Jarndyce burst into the room. He looked around wildly, and Daisy saw herself reflected in his eyes: a small girl with a scrubbed face and heavy braid, calmly stroking a black and white cat. She looked up at him, her gaze limpid.

'Can I help you?'

Jarndyce gave a great roar of frustration and tore through the dressing room. Racks of clothes were overturned, tables full of props were jolted and upset as he searched beneath them, and chests full of scarves and wigs were scattered across the floor. Jarndyce stared at one particular curly blond wig for a moment and then bent his eyes to Daisy.

'Where is he?' he said, his voice low. Suddenly he was very close, and one enormous hand was clenched, manacle-like, around Daisy's wrist, pulling her to her feet.

'Wh-where is who?' asked Daisy, and she didn't need to act to put the tremor in her voice.

'You know who I mean,' said Jarndyce, practically spitting. 'The boy. Max Marina.'

Marina? thought Daisy, astonished.

Jarndyce's grip tightened on her wrist, and she cried out in real pain. Napoleon scratched at his shoes in fury, and Jarndyce kicked him away.

'I won't tell you,' Daisy rasped. She saw Napoleon stagger to his paws, fury in his eyes. The pressure on her wrist increased until it became a halo of pain, and she thought the bone would snap beneath the force.

'Please!' she cried. 'Please, stop, please, I'll tell you. He's looking for proof – proof that the Duchess is controlled by Pompey. That he's helping the Grim Reapers.' She looked up at Jarndyce with every ounce of courage in her body as she delivered the final lines: 'Max is in the basement of the theatre. That's where we were told the Duchess hides her documents.'

Jarndyce stared at her as if he was trying to see into her soul. Then, abruptly, as if he had come to some decision, he dropped her arm and strode from the room.

Without his grip holding her upright, Daisy stumbled back against the nearest wall and slid slowly to the ground, cradling her wrist. Napoleon leapt into her lap, and she wrapped her arms around him, both of them trembling.

'Come on, Max,' she whispered. 'You can do it.'

Chapter 64

Max was good at picking locks, but it had never mattered like this before. It had never been so important. He felt the tension in his eyebrows, and he reached out with invisible hands towards the combination lock on the wall. It was odd to see the dial shifting as he touched it, even stranger to look down at his feet and see nothing but a slight ripple in the knap of the carpet beneath him.

Max closed his eyes, and then he listened to the lock.

It was similar to the ones he'd worked on before, except that this one was made of some kind of hard, ivory-white wood that he suspected was magical. Thin, whip-like vines grew from the lock, coiling around the outside of the safe like steel bands. *What was it made of?* Suddenly the answer came to him, in the voice of the Prof reading from one of her hundreds of neatly written revision cards:

Adamantine: also known as Impervious Wood. Harder than iron and more invulnerable than steel, it can only be carved with a diamond blade and is often used for locks and safes. It responds best to musical notes, sung with perfect pitch.

'Right,' whispered Max. *Impervious wood. No problem.*
With hands that trembled only slightly, he began to turn the
circular dial at the centre of the lock, listening as it clicked
with each rotation and counter rotation. *It responds best
to musical notes.* Each layer of the combination must be
programmed to respond to a different note. The key wasn't
a series of numbers – it was a tune.

As the lock clicked, Max began to hum tentatively, as if
he was feeling his way along a staircase in the dark – a series
of notes that probed up and down a sliding scale. Instead of
looking at the dial, he bent his ear towards it as he hummed,
listening for catches in the mechanism as he turned it back
and forth.

A minute passed, and then another. Already he could feel
that it was taking too long. He knew that Daisy's disguise
might fool Jarndyce at first, but it wouldn't be long before
he'd realize that he'd been duped – and then he'd come
looking for Max. His hands were shaking now, and he felt
a bead of sweat snake from his hairline under his collar.

Focus, he told himself.

Another minute passed, then two, then three. Max
hummed again, and suddenly the pattern of clicks inside the
lock resolved themselves into an order that made sense. It
was the skeleton of a tune that his mother had sung to him in
his cradle, a melody that ran through his earliest memories.
He hummed it: three notes up, three notes down, sad and
lilting and beautiful. He heard the words in his mother's

voice, words he had long forgotten but which now came back to him, perfect and complete:

> *Across the sea, beyond the door,*
> *I spy a city on the shore.*
> *Its bright shell towers spiral high,*
> *Its rainbow fishes fill the sky.*
> *And through the night while whales dive deep,*
> *While players play and children sleep,*
> *Its wild sea horses love to roam;*
> *Their silver hoofbeats bring me home.*

Max felt a click-click and one of the vines around the safe snaked open. He counted quickly. Six in total: five more to go. He hummed the tune again, turning the combination lock in just the right way, and the second vine released itself. He was starting on the third when he heard a movement in the next room.

Footsteps. Heavy and deliberate and horribly familiar.

Humming as quietly as possible, Max finished the third vine. Three to go. The footsteps were getting closer. Frantically, he bent his attention back to his task and began singing the song from the start. He felt the terrible irony of it – he could only open the safe if he kept singing; and that meant giving away his location.

Nothing for it, he told himself, as the fourth vine came free. Two more to go.

He wiped his forehead with the back of his hand and saw something that made his blood run cold. The invisibility was wearing off from his fingers, and they were horribly, comically visible, floating in the air as they turned the combination lock. *This can't be happening*, he thought. But it was. With a sick rush of fear, he heard the footsteps, faster now, cross the threshold into the room.

Click-click. The fifth vine snaked loose. He needed just one final repetition for the whole lock to tumble. With a feeling of combined elation and despair, like a skydiver with a faulty parachute, Max hummed the final note of the song. It rang on the air, and for a moment everything was quite still.

Then, like a single snagged string unravelling the fabric of a long cloak, Max felt his invisibility leave him in a rush of cold air. Jarndyce – for he was the man at the doorway – gave a great shout and rushed towards him. And Max felt the final tumbler of the lock fall into place and the safe click open in his hands.

In the split second before the man reached him, Max reached blindly into the safe and scooped the entire contents into his pockets: a waxed envelope, and a single tiny sky-blue apple that was criss-crossed with wisps like clouds. Then he ducked under Jarndyce's arm, pelted for the door in the far wall, and ran for his life.

Chapter 65

Max ran down the corridor as fast as his feet would take him, and out onto a curved, sloping walkway. He had two choices: up or down. Closing his eyes, hoping desperately that his hunch was right, Max sprinted upwards. The ground began to rise fast, cool wood at first and then something quite different under his pounding bare feet: something warm, smooth and pearlescent.

The floor, he realized, was made of shell – and so too were the spiralling walls around him. Max widened his eyes.

He was running straight into the spirals of the enormous twisting shell tower.

When Max was six years old, he had found a spiralling shell at the edge of the sand on the beach. It had been his most precious thing, and it had sat on his bedside table for over a year. Often, on the edge of sleep, he would imagine that he was very small – as tiny as a ladybird – and that he was walking around and around the spirals on the inside of the shell, lost in a maze of mother of pearl.

This was exactly like that, except that now it was the shell that was giant. There were shallow steps carved out of its sloping floor, and he sprinted up them without pausing to think, hearing the shouts of not just one man but now several behind him. The spirals began to tighten as he raced towards the top, and the walls became lower and lower, shining with opalescent light, until they were open to the air and to the stars.

'Stop that boy!' cried Jarndyce.

'Stop, thief!' cried one of the guards. 'Stop in the name of the Duchess!'

Max burst out at the top of the spiral and found himself teetering at the tip of the giant and glimmering shell. In a split-second glance he saw the whole of Iffenwild spread out beneath him – the glittering canals and the wooded islands, the floating forests and shell-domed churches, the glasshouse-boats and fishing taverns. He saw the eastern waterways choked with siren reeds, and the glimmer of the coral reef at the far reaches of the navy lagoon.

Then the guards burst out onto the roof of the shell behind him, and Max did the only thing he could think of doing. He reached into his pocket for the tiny blue apple he had found in the safe – and shoved it into his mouth. Then, with a running jump and a shout that came from the very centre of his chest, he leapt off the top of the city's highest tower and out into the open air.

For several seconds that seemed to last a lifetime, Max plummeted straight down. *I'm going to die*, he thought with total clarity, as the wind pushed his cheeks against the bones of his face and the blood raced around his body faster than it ever had before. *This is the end*. He hadn't given the cumulapple – if that was indeed what it was – enough time to work before jumping off the roof; and who knew if it would be a high enough dose.

Then he felt something extraordinary happen. A sort of buoyancy that began behind his eyebrows and spread instantly throughout his whole body. He felt the air become something different – an element with substance that he could scull and control like a swimmer in water, but lighter than that, infinitely freer. Max spread out his arms and stopped falling.

Then, with the wind in his hair, he soared.

Chapter 66

In the opera house, the play was hitting its stride. The lovers were lost in the wood, magic was running wild, and the fairy queen Titania was falling in love with Bottom all over again. Daisy had made it back to the stage in time to help Marie-Claude with her next costume change, and now she was watching the antics of the village folk as they attempted to rehearse a play of their own.

Tonight, though, she could not focus on the stage. Five minutes ago, she had caught a glimpse of Jarndyce striding up from the basement, his hair full of cobwebs and his face full of thunder. She had seen him head purposefully out of the theatre door and towards the palace, nodding to the guard who had come in earlier to raise the alarm.

Come on, Max, she urged. If everything went according to plan, he would even now be soft-footing it down the grand staircase of the palace with the contents of the safe in his pockets, to meet them behind the lilac bushes at the side of the opera house. She tried to hold her nerve. She mustn't interfere, she told herself. Sprinting into the palace would only tell Jarndyce that he was on the right track. She had to trust that Max had been able to carry out his part of the plan.

The scene ended, and Daisy hurried out into the wings. 'Time to go,' mouthed the Prof, and Daisy nodded, scooping Napoleon onto her shoulder. Indigo joined them, his mouth as straight as a ruler. Together, they headed through the labyrinth of passages behind the stage and past the dressing room, where Rozaliya was assisting with three different costume changes simultaneously. Then the three of them walked out through the back door of the Iffenwild Opera House and into the starry night.

Muir was tethered where Indigo had left him, out of sight around the back of the opera house. Beside him was the water horse they'd rescued from the market. Indigo quieted them both and stroked their muzzles.

One minute passed, and then another. They exchanged nervous looks, and Indigo murmured to the horses as they pranced.

Then, some intuition, soft as a breath on the back of her neck, made Daisy turn and look up – and she saw something extraordinary.

A boy, flying.

At first there had been only fear, like cold needles across his whole body. But then he had realized that he was not going to die. In fact, Max felt more alive than he had ever been in his life.

Flying was extraordinary, a rush of pure motion and adrenaline and delight. He soared, feeling the wind rush through his hair and across his hot cheeks. He banked over the city and whooshed downwards over the shell-topped buildings. He flew low and then lower, hearing people in the streets down below gasp and call out.

'Look, Mama!' a little girl cried. 'It's a boy in the air!'

'Don't tell lies,' said her mother reprovingly. Then she looked up and her mouth fell open.

Max climbed again and then he looped-the-loop. It was extraordinary, it was amazing, it was—

A raven collided with his head, and he spun off balance. Then there were more ravens, and still more, until he was being pursued through the sky by a black cloud of birds.

Max came to his senses at last. He might only have minutes before the cumulapple wore off. He needed to get to the bushes behind the opera house to meet the others.

Max swooped back over the walls of the palace. The ravens were gaining on him, pecking with their wicked curved beaks, leaving cuts on his arms and the backs of his legs. The cumulapple was beginning to wear off, and he felt the weight returning to his body. A particularly brutish raven dive-bombed him.

Panic filled his mouth with the taste of blood and iron – and then he was falling from the sky.

Daisy watched as Max fell, tumbling end over end through

the air, pursued by a mob of birds. For a moment there was such a confusion of vicious black feathers around him that she couldn't see what was happening and she couldn't breathe. And then she saw an enormous plume of water shoot up at the end of the street, and realized that Max, brilliant Max, had managed to fall right into the middle of the nearest canal.

This time, Max knew how to swim, and he surfaced with water cascading from his nose and mouth – shaken, but alive. Daisy rushed to the edge of the canal and together, she, Indigo and the Prof pulled him out of the water, battling ravens as they went. Max landed on the bank, shivering with shock and adrenaline.

'Indigo! The ravens!' Daisy batted one away, feeling it slice her palm open with a claw.

Indigo did something with his hands, sweat standing out on his forehead with the effort. 'It's like last time,' he said. 'They've been forced. By someone like me, I think. Another Whisperer. It's hard to . . .' He went quiet, brow creased with concentration. Then one of the ravens turned in the air, and then another and another, until the whole flock massed and flew away from the square like a squadron of feathered black arrows.

'Someone called them off,' said Indigo, gasping. 'But they'll be back, I think.'

'Come on,' said the Prof. 'Let's get out of here.'

Chapter 67

Five minutes later, the four of them were gathered around a biscuit barrel in the back room of the Jolly Fishhook. Emil was out, but he'd agreed, as part of the plan, to leave the door open for them. Jarndyce knew that Max belonged to the theatre, and would go straight to the *Nautilus* dock to search for him, but he didn't know anything yet about the tavern.

The barrel made for a solid table and also doubled as an excellent snack supply, packed to the brim with slightly chewy gingerbread that tasted of treacle and spice. Everyone took one except Max, who was too keyed-up to eat. The feeling of flight was still in his veins, and also the feeling of falling.

'Well, let's see it,' said Daisy, leaning forward and gesturing at him with a biscuit. They were perched on low stools and crates, and the ground was scattered with crumbs. Napoleon sat curled around Daisy's shoulders like a very small and imperious scarf. Slowly, Max drew the waxed envelope from the safe out of his pocket. It was sealed with the insignia of Iffenwild – two crescent moons above a sailing ship. The seal stuck slightly as Max broke it, but the papers inside were still perfectly legible, if a little damp under his trembling fingertips.

'It's a birth certificate,' he said slowly, frowning as he decoded the swirling letters at the start of each page. 'Two of them, actually.' He picked up the top sheet and stared very hard at the words as he read them:

Victor Alexander Rudolph Albrecht von Auffenberg, Commander of the Royal Navy, Duke of the Nine Seas, Defender of the Coral Reef and Prince of the Realm of Iffenwild.

Born on this day to His Royal Highness Albrecht Anton von Auffenberg, and Natasha Anastasia Galina, Her Royal Highness the Duchess of Marindeep.

There followed here a date, twenty-five years in the past.

'Oh,' said the Prof, her voice hushed. 'It's the lost prince of Iffenwild. The boy who should have been king – the one who disappeared.'

Daisy nodded. 'Yes – and look, here. There's a photo clipped to the edge.' It showed a skinny, weedy-looking boy with a sharp chin and pale, shadowed eyes – impossible to tell their colour.

'What about the other one?' asked Indigo, leaning forward.

Max took it up and read the words silently:

Maximilian Ivan Nicholas von Auffenberg,
Earl of the Salt Kingdoms, Keeper of the Pearl
Chambers and Demi Prince of the Realm of
Iffenwild.

Born on this day to His Royal Highness
Albrecht Anton von Auffenberg, and Natasha
Anastasia Galina, Her Royal Highness the
Duchess of Marindeep.

The date of birth was about twelve years in the past, and clipped to the corner of the sheet was a photograph. It showed a tiny baby, perhaps only days old, with a furious screwed-up face that made it look like an outraged prune. It had a shock of dark hair and slanting grey eyes – and there, on its cheek, unmistakably, was a birthmark the exact shape and colour of a smashed strawberry.

Max sat back, stunned.

'What?' said Daisy, looking at him.

Wordlessly, he handed over the paper, and watched as she bent her head over it. Her braid fell across her cheek as she read, and Napoleon peered down from her shoulder to look. Daisy went pale, and handed the letter to the Prof, who allowed Indigo to read alongside her.

It was Indigo who finally broke the silence. 'So,' he said,

voice blank. 'Prince of the Realm of Iffenwild. When were you planning to tell us?'

'I didn't know,' said Max numbly. The crate beneath his fingers felt grainy and smooth, and he noticed a trail of ants along the floor. His mouth was cold and dry.

'Max?' said Daisy. She was looking at him in a concerned sort of way. 'Are you okay? You look like you're going to vomit.'

'I'm not going to vomit,' he said – and promptly threw up onto Indigo's shoes.

'Oh great,' said Indigo, rolling his eyes. 'Here we go again. Am I supposed to be grateful it's *royal* vomit this time?'

'I'm – I'm not royal,' said Max, wiping his mouth with the back of his sleeve. It smelled terrible. 'My mother is –' he swallowed – '*was* Marigold Brightly. An American Botanist. This is impossible. There's only *one* missing prince, not two. Maybe this is about a different Max.'

'Another Max who was born twelve years ago with your birthmark?' said the Prof, raising an eyebrow. Max shrugged weakly. Put like that, it seemed unlikely.

Daisy was sitting up and looking at Max, bright-eyed. 'It makes sense,' she said. 'The date here on the birth certificate – it's only a few days before the king and queen were killed. You would have been so small.' She swallowed and leaned forward. 'If this is true, then it could change everything. No wonder Jarndyce is trying to get hold of you. Pompey is probably desperate to make sure you never get a chance to take back Iffenwild. He might not be able to control you like he controls the Duchess. That's what he's afraid of! You could claim the throne, Max.'

Max shook his head. He didn't want that kind of responsibility. And anyway—

'It's not that simple,' said the Prof. 'You can't just march up to the palace and say you're a lost prince of Iffenwild – and not even *the* lost prince that everyone's hoping for. No one even knows you exist. They'd never believe you – and Pompey would have you trussed up in a jail cell faster than you can say "treachery".'

Max stared at the birth certificate. He opened his mouth, then closed it again. Could it be true? It would explain Jarndyce's drive to find him. It would explain why Marigold had told him that his father was dead, and nothing else. The king and queen of Iffenwild had been killed twelve years ago.

'But wouldn't someone have recognized me?' he asked. He touched his birthmark lightly to show what he meant.

'I don't think so,' said Daisy thoughtfully. She turned to the Prof. 'Didn't you say that the queen was pregnant when she was killed? Well, what if she gave birth early, and it hadn't been announced yet? No one would have seen you apart from your family. And anyway,' she added, turning back to Max, 'anytime you've been outside the ship, you've used powder on your face.'

'It explains why the kelpies like you though,' said Indigo, grudgingly. 'If you're Earl of the Salt Kingdoms and all.'

Max blinked, unable to speak. His fists were clenched so tight that his nails made dents in the palms of his hands – painful little crescents that stayed imprinted in his skin until dark.

He dredged up memory after memory, prising them up like old stones from the bottom of a muddy pond, searching for proof like a glint of gold among the sediment. She had always said she was his mother. They had the same dimple in their left cheek! But what was that to go on, really? Lots of people had dimples. He had not shared her sleek golden hair, her smiling eyes, or the fine, soft curve of her cheek. Max's hair was about as sleek as a crow's nest, and his sharp, pale face was about eighty per cent cheekbone and twenty per cent scowl. What if she had not been his birth mother after all?

That was when they heard the crowds flooding out of the opera house, a torrent of laughter and cheering. A roman candle soared into the sky outside the window.

The carnival had begun.

Chapter 68

There was another noise from outside and then Emil came skidding into the cool, dim storeroom. 'Thank greenness,' he gasped. 'You're here.'

'What?' said Daisy. 'What's wrong?' She felt fear like an icicle against her neck.

'It's the Grim Reapers,' said Emil, gasping. 'Someone in the resistance heard them talking. They're furious about the market being burned down. They're going to take revenge.'

'Revenge?' said Daisy. Then she paused, feeling a terrible swoop to her stomach. 'Do you remember what Gabriel said, that night I overheard him talking beside the barge? He said, *at the carnival*. That's where the Reapers are heading.'

'Let's go,' said the Prof. 'Hurry!'

They rushed out into the courtyard. It was empty. Everyone was heading to the main square for the celebrations. Daisy flung herself onto Muir's back and felt Max scramble up behind her. Indigo and the Prof mounted the second water horse.

'Emil,' she cried. 'Find your family. Tell them to get

out of the square. We're going to look for Pompey and the Duchess.'

The horses were prancing with suppressed energy, sea-foam manes frothing in the moonlight. Then Indigo clicked his tongue, and they reared up and surged towards the canal at the end of the street. Their hooves sent water sparking upwards from the surface, and then they were galloping straight down the middle of the moonlit canal. Daisy looked down. Napoleon was perched in front of her on the horse's neck, every hair standing on end as he clung on for dear life.

Within minutes they had reached the corner of the main square, with the palace shining above it. The square was thronged with acrobats and jugglers and crowds of happy revellers, but Daisy had a sense of foreboding so strong that it felt like a giant hand grasping her lungs. The whole city was out for the carnival, and loud whoops and cheers rang out in every direction. She heard a loud bang and jumped, half expecting gunfire, but it was only the popping of a champagne cork. There were people dressed in ball gowns and clown costumes, in seaweed crowns and sparkling hats so extravagant they would have made Rozaliya weep with jealousy. Everyone was wearing a mask. The city had become a giant theatre, the square a colossal stage, and each person Daisy saw was a performer for the night.

The crowds seemed to have accepted the horses as a particularly showy part of the carnival celebrations, cheering as they came racing down the moonlit canal.

They turned the corner of the square. The great bell tower came into view, and beneath it the cordoned-off area where the fireworks would be let off.

'Okay,' she said, taking a breath and looking around. The crowd surged, jubilant. Candles blazed inside coloured lanterns, casting diamonds of blue and red and gold light across their masked faces. Daisy's neck prickled. Any of them could be Grim Reapers. The crowds were cheering now and beginning to chant the countdown to midnight.

Ten, nine, eight . . .

Daisy dashed towards a man in a top hat. 'Please,' she cried. 'Have you seen Pompey?' He shook her off.

Seven, six, five . . .

She looked around wildly and tugged the sleeve of a richly dressed noblewoman who looked as if she might have come from the palace. 'Have you seen Pompey? Is the Duchess with him?' The woman smiled, not understanding, and pressed a coin into her hand as if she was a beggar.

Four, three, two . . .

Daisy sprinted to the fountain in the centre of the square and clambered up as high as she could, trying to see across the whole space. She saw a tall figure in a white and red mask hefting something from his belt. She saw the glint of metal.

One.

Fireworks exploded across the sky and turned the night into a festival of sparks: silver dandelions of light shot into the sky, followed by sparkling red plumes the colour of coral, and yellow-gold cartwheels like shooting stars. The cheers were deafening, joyful, hectic. People kissed each other and danced in the street and little children jumped up and down in excitement.

Then someone screamed.

Chapter 69

The noise was keen and sharp as a knife. A man was lying at the centre of the square, blood pooling around him. Tall figures in red and white masks stepped through the crowd with unsheathed daggers. Panic spread like poison and groups of people began to push desperately against each other. Daisy watched, powerless, from the base of the fountain, barged and buffeted in every direction. There were two more people lying still on the ground, trampled by the crowd as it rushed for the edges of the square. Several men and a child were pushed into the canal.

'Max,' shouted Daisy. He was ten paces away, but the roiling mass of people between them made it feel more like a mile.

Then she saw a red twinkle in the crowd. The red speck flared into a loop of flame.

There he was: Pompey. His forehead shone with sweat, and he was holding a blazing torch.

He cast it at a Mondenbaum tree and immediately its dry old bark caught fire. Flames rushed up its branches and towards the crown. Iffenwilders screamed, some of them running towards the canal and filling hats, boots and kettles with water and tossing it onto the flames – but it was like pouring a thimble of water onto a housefire. Daisy watched, powerless, as Pompey lit another torch and cast it at another tree. The tree flinched and flames raced up its trunk.

'Fire shouldn't be able to move that fast,' she said, desperate. 'It's not natural.'

'It's fireweed,' said the Prof, her eyes wide. 'I saw some at the black market. It catches on everything, even when it's cold and damp.'

Daisy was panicking now. The fire was voracious, devouring trees in gulps of shooting sparks. 'How do we put it out?'

'Water,' said the Prof. 'Lots of it. It needs to be fully submerged for at least two minutes before it stops burning.'

Daisy felt her shoulders sag. It was no use. Iffenwild would fall to the Grim Reapers.

Then she saw the Duchess moving around the edge of the square. She was hurrying away from the blaze and towards the royal palace, where a hot-air balloon was moored and straining against its ropes. Daisy darted after her, her throat full of sudden hope. This was the Duchess's city. She alone could stand up to Pompey and put a stop to this.

Daisy sprinted faster, skidding to a halt before the balloon as the Duchess climbed aboard. 'Duchess!' she shouted. 'Call out your soldiers! You've got to end this!'

The Duchess looked at her for a moment, head to one

side. Then she laughed. The sound was as merry and sweet as ever – but hearing it now made Daisy falter. The Duchess's glass-green eyes, always so bright and sparkling, suddenly looked like marbles: cold and round and hard.

'*Stop this!*' she mimicked. 'My dear child, don't you understand? The Grim Reapers are going to take this useless backwater and make it into something profitable. Squash out the weakness, and turn it into a place of progress.'

'W-what?' stammered Daisy. 'But you saw the coral. You said—'

The Duchess laughed, and the pearls in her hair shone brighter than ever. 'What is evidence? Anything can be faked in this world, my child.' She brought her face close to Daisy's, eyes glittering – and suddenly Daisy understood.

'It isn't Pompey who's controlling you,' she said. 'It's the other way round.'

'Very good,' said the Duchess, as if Daisy was a gifted pupil. 'I have his family imprisoned, so he does what I say.'

Pompey's family, thought Daisy distantly. *Of course*. He had supposedly sent them away for safety three years ago – and they hadn't been seen since.

'Yes,' said the Duchess. 'It's very simple, really. And while everyone is busy hating Pompey, I've been making a deal with the Reapers. Their army, in return for the proceeds of the richest kingdom in the Marindeep.'

'The pearls,' said Daisy. 'That's where they've all been going.'

'Very good,' said the Duchess again. 'But why confine it to a hidden market? Why not turn it into an industry? An empire of commerce? We have sea-gold to mine, and pearls and marsh-rubies to plunder. I've never much cared for the sea, ever since it became clear I didn't have blue magic, unlike my precious brother. He was always the special one, always praised, while I was ignored.' For a moment, her face flickered and Daisy saw her as she must have been as a child. For a moment, Daisy felt sympathy like a fishhook in her chest. Then the Duchess laughed, and the feeling slid away.

'Lots of people have hard childhoods,' said Daisy. 'That doesn't mean they go around killing their brothers.'

'It was worth it. Soon I'll be the owner of the wealthiest nation on earth.'

'But you don't own it,' said Daisy. 'No one *owns* the land or sea. And anyway, you're only the regent, remember?'

'Ah yes,' said the Duchess. 'And yet, I don't see the lost heir of Iffenwild coming to claim his throne. As for the spare –' she nodded her head towards Max in the crowd behind her – 'he's done a good job of escaping so far. But I think the Reapers will take care of him for me now.'

'So,' said Daisy. 'You were the one who wanted Max—'

'Dead?' said the Duchess. 'Yes, of course. So much more convenient that way.' She looked at Daisy thoughtfully. 'And I think the same might apply to you.'

While she'd been speaking, the balloon had been filling

up with air and the Duchess had been casting off sandbags from the side until it was straining against its tethering ropes. With the last word she spoke, she drew out a dagger and slashed through the final rope that kept it grounded.

The balloon soared into the air, its propane burner flaming white and blue and roaring like a jet engine. Daisy was clinging to the outside of the basket and within moments she was five feet in the air – ten feet – twenty – thirty – too high now to let go; the drop would kill her. Napoleon was tucked inside the front of her jacket, trembling against her chest. Daisy hung on with desperate fingers, her feet braced against the merest millimetre of ledge around the outside base of the basket. Her arms felt no stronger than twigs, brittle against the immensity of the space that yawned beneath her. Already the square was no bigger than a tea-tray, and curling along the edge of the city she could see the frothing white line of the sea breaking against the shore. Her eye snagged on a flashing sequin of light at the furthest reach of the coral reef. Something about it seemed familiar.

'A nice view, isn't it?' said the Duchess, wrenching Daisy's attention back to the balloon as they rose higher. 'I find it so peaceful up here. Seeing the whole world laid out like a stage-set.'

'That's not how the world works,' said Daisy. Her left foot slipped from the ledge at the base of the basket, and her shoe went tumbling down and down and down through the endless air below, until it vanished. The air yawned hungrily beneath her. Daisy tightened her fingers, but they were starting to go numb. She was shaking so hard that her teeth chattered.

'Isn't it?' said the Duchess. 'I find that with both life and the theatre, it's only a matter of knowing how to . . . direct the action.'

Then she took a dagger out of her pocket, and calmly she raised the blunt hilt and brought it down on the back of Daisy's hand.

Chapter 70

The world was burning. Max saw trees blazing like giant torches and buildings going up in cracks of flame. The heat was like a giant sledgehammer, the air filled with the cries of people trapped in the centre of the square. Everywhere the Grim Reapers were taking control. All the guild members who had been on the platform watching the fireworks were bound and gagged. Others were still trying to fight the Reapers, but the fire drove them back. The flames rose higher and higher until Max thought the whole of Iffenwild would burn to ashes around him.

He remembered the Prof's words. *Fireweed needs to be submerged for at least two minutes before it goes out.* They would have to flood the square. It was completely impossible.

'Max,' shouted the Prof. 'Do something!'

'But what?'

She raised her eyes to the heavens. 'Seriously? You're a prince of Iffenwild. Call the water from the sea and put out the fire!'

Max remembered his efforts with the glass of water in

his cabin. He had made tea slosh out of pots and summoned a child-sized tsunami in a tin bathtub. But something on the scale of what the Prof was suggesting was too huge to contemplate. He felt the flames licking at his feet and leapt back. The exit of the square was blocked by Grim Reapers. Hundreds of people were trapped with no way out, and the fire was spreading. They were going to die.

No, he thought. He heard his mother's voice in his head. *You are going to live, Max. You are going to LIVE.* He closed his eyes and felt for the water that ran through the veins of Iffenwild. He felt it twisting and sluicing through the dark canals of the city. He sensed the water of the green and shining lagoon. And further out, much further, he touched the deep unknowable darkness of the sea.

Max fished in his pocket and pulled out a piece of string. He held it between his fingers, and visualized again the wild weight of water that surrounded the island kingdom he had come to love. Then he began to twist the string, so that with each twist it became shorter and shorter, tighter and tighter. As he did so, he hummed: a low, deep note that rose and twisted into a melody as old as the ocean itself. Then Max Marina opened his mouth and sang the song of the sea.

For a moment, nothing happened, and he faltered. Then, all around him, the water began to rise.

It started with a wave deep out in the sea beyond the lagoon. It rose slowly from the ocean floor, and it gathered strength and momentum as it rolled through the blue emptiness. It grew as it travelled, lifting phosphorescent squid to the surface and casting them down again into the depths. It crossed the lagoon in a great rolling swell, and the canals of the city began to rise. Water slopped over their edges into the streets, until the very ground shook with the force of it. And then in a great swaying steeple of water that rose and seemed to touch the very sky, the wave broke and fell over Iffenwild. Buildings were inundated; boats rose high towards the clouds and were left marooned on top of houses; people were swept up and found themselves seconds later in the crooks of drenched trees. And in the main square of Iffenwild, a great flood crashed over the ground and surged high enough to cover the burning buildings.

Max felt the pressure rising in his chest like a second wave; he felt the enormity of the sea, so ancient and essential that he almost lost himself in it. But he pulled himself back and kept singing as the trees and the buildings in the square continued to blaze beneath the water, eerie and flickering below the surface. One hundred and twenty seconds, that was all he needed. He began to shake with the effort of keeping the water high. It had come to his call, but the hard part, he realized, was not calling a wave, but holding it suspended at its peak. Every molecule of water begged to be released, to be allowed to rush back out to sea.

Fifty seconds.

Sixty.

Max took a breath and felt his lungs burning as he sang.

He twisted the string tighter between his fingers and felt blood begin to trickle out of his nose.

Eighty seconds.

Ninety.

His vision turned spotty at the edges, and he braced himself against the wall behind him. One hundred seconds, and then ten more. He saw Grim Reapers sprinting towards him. The Prof stood up, slingshot in hand, and a stone whistled through the air. One of the Reapers fell into the water, and then another.

One hundred and twenty seconds.

Max saw the flames beneath the water begin to flicker and gutter. The first tree went out. Across the square, the fire died.

He gasped, then collapsed face-first into the water.

Chapter 71

The hilt of the dagger met Daisy's fingers like a sledge-hammer. Her whole body flinched with the pain, and she gasped so hard that she coughed. Her hand let go of the basket and she was left dangling by her other hand above the emptiness below. The very air seemed to gape. The city was spread out, toy-like, beneath her. The grand square was the size of a piece of toast, the streets leading out from it as narrow as pieces of string, and the glittering canals like fine necklaces of blue beads. Beyond it was the vastness of the navy-blue ocean, with tiny white waves chasing each other over its surface like frills of lace, and mysterious shadows moving slowly through its depths.

Even as the Duchess raised the hilt of the knife to strike again, Daisy gave a great heave and grabbed the side of the basket with her injured hand. The balloon swayed violently, sending the Duchess tumbling backwards. Daisy felt a jab in her pocket and realized it was the needle Rozaliya had given her – the one threaded with a thin sewing vine.

The next moment, Napoleon leapt from Daisy's jacket and landed on the Duchess's head. He raked his claws across

her eyes, and she shrieked and fell back. For a moment Napoleon was poised there, triumphant.

Then the Duchess reached up and caught him with a savage blow. The cat flew across the basket and Daisy heard herself cry out. He hit the far side with a terrible thump, and lay still. There was a split second of silence, broken only by the roar of the balloon valve jetting flame into the inflated silk above them.

Then Daisy roared and with a surge of strength she didn't know she had, she called the sewing vine from her pocket and cast it over the edge of the basket. The thin green cord only held for a few seconds, but it was long enough for Daisy to grasp it and swing herself inside. The Duchess had found her feet again. Blood was running into her eye, and this time, there was no messing about with the hilt of the dagger. The blade was out, and it was pointed at Daisy.

'Enough,' she spat. She moved towards Daisy and slashed the air. Daisy only just managed to leap out of the way, and the blade caught her upper arm in a long, shallow cut that burned in the thin air.

'There's nothing to help you here,' said the Duchess. Her eyes glittered in a way that seemed unhooked from reality.

Think, Daisy told herself. She forced herself to look away from Napoleon, who lay still and impossibly small on the floor of the basket. She leapt sideways as the Duchess came for her again. *Think*. If only she had a cumulapple, if only she—

Then she knew what she had to do, and she didn't need to think any longer. She remembered the Prof's perfect command of the balloon ropes that day in the Mallowmarsh library. She would have to be precise. Better than at the market. She would have to control her magic like never before.

Working as fast as she could, she called to the vines that bound the great orb of the balloon to the basket. Each one burst out with hundreds of green shoots and leaves; and then the greatest of the shoots uncurled with devastating precision and tripped the Duchess so that she fell nose-first to the floor of the basket. It rocked precariously, and Daisy tried not to think about the ground a thousand feet below, swaying through the chinks of woven willow beneath her feet. *Willow*, she thought, and she called to each slender branch until they too burst to life and wound their cords around the Duchess's arms and legs, binding her in place.

Then Daisy rushed towards the valve that controlled the burner and turned it down, so that the balloon began to sink rapidly through the clouds. Wind whipped around them, and the basket began to shudder with the speed of the descent. A raven flew at her face and raked its claws across her cheek, and suddenly she understood.

'It's you,' she said, looking at the Duchess. 'The other Whisperer.'

Suddenly the black market, with its rows of trapped animals, made a horrible kind of sense. How many of them had the Duchess forced into their cages? Daisy felt a rush of anger so cold it burned. She should have realized it sooner.

The Duchess laughed and within moments the balloon was surrounded by the vicious birds. 'It's been ravens all along, hasn't it?' said Daisy. 'That's how you knew where the *Nautilus* fleet was. And how you worked out Max's disguise – the birds snooping around the boat.' Daisy tried to beat the ravens off and the effort was enough to break her focus on the Duchess's bonds. The woman pulled her arms free and lashed at the other bindings with her knife. The basket tipped dangerously from side to side. Again, Daisy saw a star-bright flicker at the edge of the lagoon. Then the balloon itself tilted, and the flames that roared from the burner tipped dangerously close to the inflated white silk.

'Careful!' cried Daisy. 'Stop, or we'll—'

But the Duchess was beyond listening. She gave a great roar of fury, and charged knife-first at Daisy. The balloon tipped disastrously. The fire from the burner caught on the fine white silk of the balloon. And it went up like a great red tulip, flaming against the sky.

Daisy stared at it open-mouthed for a split second. Then she grabbed Napoleon's body, tucked it inside her jacket, and leapt off the edge of the basket like a diver into the deep blue sea.

Two seconds later, the balloon exploded into a fireball that consumed the willow basket like a snack. And with it went the Duchess of Iffenwild and all her greed and ambition.

*

Daisy felt the explosion like a great suction of the air around her, and then a shower of sparks and scraps of floating silk that twirled above her like ribbons in the wide-open blue of the sky.

But Daisy wasn't looking at the sky. She was too busy falling.

Chapter 72

When Max came to, he found that he was being carried tenderly on the crest of a small wave. It lifted him softly onto the third-floor windowsill of the Sailmakers' Guildhall, then retreated with the rest of the great outrush of water back to the sea.

Max rubbed the salt from his eyelashes and looked around.

The fire was well and truly out, and the sacred trees of Iffenwild smouldered in the wreckage. The Grim Reapers, like half-drowned rats, were still fighting, and there was hand-to-hand combat on the rooftops of the square. He looked up and saw that Alexei was battling a Grim Reaper with muscled arms.

Max's heart clenched. Alexei was fighting for his life.

The battle looked equally matched. Alexei was bigger, but the other man was faster. Max saw Alexei beginning to tire. One lucky thrust could be enough to kill him.

Max scrambled upright, balancing on the thin edge of the windowsill. Then he clambered onto the top of the window frame, and from there, onto the roof of the building.

Maybe, he thought, it was time to stop hiding. Maybe it was time to be seen.

He reached the rooftop and stood square on his feet. 'Oi, you,' he called breathlessly, waving his arm at the other man. 'Why don't you pick on someone your own size?' The water had washed the powder from Max's face and his birthmark stood out more clearly than it ever had against his bloodless cheek. The Reaper paused and turned, and that was enough for Alexei to lunge forward and knock him unconscious. Then Alexei's eyes widened at something behind Max.

Max turned and saw another Reaper coming towards him, sword raised. It was Jarndyce, lips bared over sharp teeth. There was no time to move out of the way, no time to do anything.

Max closed his eyes and what happened next came almost too quickly to understand. He felt a rush of air as a body moved past him. He heard a cry and a thud. And he looked around to see that Jarndyce had collapsed, with Alexei's sword through his middle.

'Max,' said Alexei, and when he smiled, blood came out of his mouth. Then Max saw the terrible truth. There was a blade through Alexei's own chest. He had been stabbed by Jarndyce before he had fallen himself.

'No,' he said. 'No, no, Alexei.' Max scrambled down to kneel beside him as he collapsed. Alexei's skin was very pale and there was sweat on his forehead. 'It's not a real sword,' said Max. 'Right, Alexei? It's not a real sword. Because you're the greatest actor of your generation, you're—'

But he broke off as Alexei coughed, and more blood came from his mouth, staining the white of his shirt. 'Max.' He clasped Max's hand between his own. 'Listen to me. My name – my real name – is Victor – Alexander – Rudolph – Albrecht – von Auffenberg.' His breath came in pants, and he paused between each word. 'You are –' he pressed Max's hand – 'my brother.'

Max was stunned silent. Bewilderment hit him like a punch to the jaw. 'I don't understand.'

'I was the heir of Iffenwild,' said Alexei. His breath sounded scorched. 'Now . . .' – this pause was longer than the others, and his last words were very quiet – '. . . you are.'

He closed his eyes, and his chest fell. It did not rise again.

'No,' said Max. 'No, *no, no*. This can't be happening. Alexei!' He shook the man's arm, still warm. He waited for him to sit up and laugh and pull the fake sword from his belly. But it was too late.

Alexei – prince of Iffenwild, father of Annika, captain of the *Nautilus*, joker of the pack, greatest actor of his generation – was gone.

Chapter 73

Daisy fell for long enough to have two thoughts. The first was that she was going to die. The second was that the scene beneath her seemed to have changed. Instead of the square with its unforgiving flagstones, there was . . . water. A great rolling wave of water that was being held in the air like a transparent mountain, glittering with treasure inside it – shoals of colourful fish darting back and forth inside the wave, the spars of wrecked sailing ships glinting with peeling gold paint, and a giant squid held suspended in the green transparency.

The surface came closer and closer – and then with an almighty impact Daisy smashed through the surface. It was salty as tears and cold as the open sea, and it saved her life.

Daisy plunged down until her feet hit the bottom and she realized that she was touching the submerged flagstones of the square. All around her, beneath the water, she saw trees and buildings burning with ghostly fireweed.

Then she pushed herself up, up, up, with aching arms towards the surface and broke the top of the suspended wave with a gasp. Her spine and her shins hurt from the impact of hitting the water, and the cut on her arm stung from the salt.

Then, with a sudden rush like a release of held breath, the water surged back into motion. There was a noise like a suction cup being released from a blocked drain and the sea began to flatten and race back towards the open lagoon. Daisy was pulled along with it, paddling desperately to keep her head above water. She managed to catch a floating spar as it bobbed past and clung to it for dear life.

'DAISY!' She heard a familiar voice call from behind her. It was the Prof, steering one of the tiny dinghies from the harbour – not much bigger than a shallow bathtub with a single sail. Beside her was Emil, and between them they yanked Daisy over the side. She heard screams, smelled smoke, felt the overwhelming rush of water against the prow. Then the boat slammed into the open lagoon on the crest of the breaking wave and into the heart of a battle.

Daisy felt something graze her ear and ducked just in time. An explosion hit the water near the boat, sending up a fountain that rained down until they were nearly blinded. Seagulls cawed in outrage, debris spun around them, and the waves surged high as houses.

'Watch out,' cried the Prof, as another arrow zinged past Daisy's cheek. Hails of arrows went flying overhead from the rooftops of the square, while the Iffenwilders fought back with tridents and sticky vines cast from a fleet of tiny boats. The Grim Reapers were everywhere. This was far bigger than the battle Daisy had seen at Mallowmarsh. This was a war, and even as one attacker was cut down, a hundred more came streaming down the canals in sleek black boats, or running along the tops of the buildings with arrows that glittered as they moved.

Something came to her then with sudden clarity. The sequin of light she'd seen from the hot-air balloon. She knew why it was so familiar – and she knew that she needed to get to it before it was lost and broken on Iffenwild's great barrier reef.

'Where's Indigo?' she shouted, looking around in the chaos.

'There,' said the Prof, pointing. He was galloping towards them on Muir's back, spray flying up from the sea horse's silver hooves.

'Indigo,' she shouted. 'I need to get to the Reef – to the gate. Now!'

He didn't stop to ask questions. She reached out a hand as he came close and swung her up behind him onto Muir's back. She landed hard – and then they were galloping across the expanse of the lagoon, half blinded by sea spray, flying too fast for arrows to find them.

'Want to explain what this is about?' he yelled.

'You'll see!'

A moment passed – and then there it was, visible at last on the far side of the Reef.

It was a ship with an oak-tree mast and white sails

that billowed in the wind. It was a ship with two figures silhouetted at the prow as it surged towards them. The first had sheets of thick silver hair, and she stood at the wheel, steering the *Great Mallow* along the edge of the Reef. The second figure was short and round with bright red pigtails, and clasped in her lifted hand, blazing out a path of light like a lighthouse beam across the waves, was Daisy's dandelight.

'Acorn!' cried Daisy, as the younger girl waved from the prow of the Mallowmarsh ship. Then she came to her senses. 'STOP! You'll be wrecked if you try to get through the coral.' The sentry boats had joined the battle in the lagoon, which meant that the coral was without guard or guide. Any moment now the ship would be pierced by the knife-thin pinnacles of the Reef. 'STOP!' she cried as Indigo galloped closer. Finally, Artemis seemed to hear. She lowered the sails and the ship slowed.

'The coral is dangerous,' shouted Daisy, looking at the silver-haired figure high on the ship above her. 'You'll have to follow us through, carefully.'

Artemis nodded and signalled to show she understood.

Indigo wheeled about on Muir and then – slowly, carefully, looking down with each of the horse's hoof-steps over the surface of the water – they guided the *Great Mallow* through the Reef.

Acorn cheered when they reached the open lagoon, and Daisy laughed out loud with joy and relief. It made her giddy. 'You came!' she said.

'Oh yes,' said another figure from the deck. Madame Gallitrop's voice was magnified by the loudhailer she was holding, and she was leaning eagerly over the side of the ship as if she couldn't wait to join the fray. 'We came. And I am going to enjoy this very much.'

Chapter 74

Max watched as the Mallowmarshers leapt into the thick of the battle. He saw a woman with silver hair fighting single-handedly with two Grim Reapers and binding them with vines, hands and feet. He saw a fearsome old lady impale the edge of a Grim Reaper's cloak with a sharp knitting needle, so that her companion – a man with tufty eyebrows like two white caterpillars – could cut him down. He saw Pompey scurry away down a side passage like a mouse into a hole, ducking an arrow. Everywhere Max looked there was fighting, and it seemed to him that at last the tide of the battle was turning. The people of the two pockets, Greenwilders and Marindeepers, joined forces and fought back-to-back to protect Iffenwild. The *Nautilus* crew was right beside them, Marie-Claude casting vines that tangled around the enemy's ankles, Rozaliya yelling obscenities in Russian and – Max saw with amazement – Gabriel fighting hand to hand against the Reapers.

Then Max heard a sound like hoofbeats, and turned to see something that no person had seen in many years: a herd of water horses galloping over the waves from the west with the glow of the setting moon behind them. He saw the light glittering on their sea-foam manes and on the silver-green of their coats. He saw Indigo and Daisy, riding on the back of Muir, leading the charge, as the herd swept across the lagoon and trampled the Reapers beneath their hooves.

And then, most astonishing of all, Max saw a glittering black tentacle emerge from beneath the water. It was a creature of the deep, disturbed by the great wave he had called from the depths of the ocean. It was a leviathan, bigger than nightmares, blacker than midnight, many-tentacled and large as the opera house itself. It swam into view and filled the whole lagoon with its bulk and the glitter of its thousand eyes. Some of these eyes were on the ends of its tentacles, which came swarming up to the surface, where they caught the last of the Reapers and pulled them down into the depths.

The coral reef, when the divers returned to it the following spring, was full of new bone-growth, and rich with bright, staring pearls.

Indigo galloped over to their boat at the end of the battle and dismounted from Muir's back, chest heaving, straight into the belly of the dinghy.

'Indigo!' cried the Prof. 'That was amazing!'

He shrugged. 'I talked to Muir, and he wanted to help. So did the others. Iffenwild is their home too.'

Daisy swung off the horse after him

and collapsed into the boat.

Indigo looked at her sharply. 'What's wrong?' he said. 'Something's been wrong all this time, I can feel it.'

'It's Napoleon,' she said. Her voice cracked on his name. And with infinite tenderness, she took his small, bedraggled body from inside her jacket and laid it at the bottom of the boat. He looked impossibly tiny, and one of his whiskers was crumpled.

Indigo knelt down and bent his head towards Napoleon's chest. There was silence – the longest of Daisy's life, as she waited for Indigo to shake his head. Then, 'He's still alive,' said Indigo, 'but barely. He's badly hurt.'

Daisy felt a leap in her chest like a flicker of lightning. 'Can you do anything?'

Indigo frowned and closed his eyes. His hand was too big, but he placed two fingers on Napoleon's chest.

Daisy felt rather than saw a flicker of energy pass

through them. There was a smell like a thunderstorm wetting warm stone at the end of a long summer day. *Whispering magic*, thought Daisy.

For a moment, nothing happened, and she hung her head.

Then one of Napoleon's whiskers twitched. He opened a single silver-green eye, inexpressibly grumpy and offended. Slowly, with effort that shook his paws, he stood up.

'Oh Napoleon!' she cried. And the tiny, imperious cat allowed himself to be swept into her arms.

Chapter 75

The Mallowmarshers didn't only bring help in battle. They came with other things too. Some bad: news of the Grim Reapers advancing across the Greyside with more and more brazen confidence; news of forests felled, flocks of parakeets killed, whole swathes of ocean drowned in slicks of oil. But there were small, good things too: news of pocket after Greenwild pocket defying the Bureau of Botanical Business and rising up to join the Mallowmarshers on their journey to the Amazon. The joy, for Daisy, Indigo and the Prof, of being reunited with friends from home.

And, for Max, a letter from his mother.

'She left it with us for safekeeping,' said Artemis, who, Max had learned, was the commander of Mallowmarsh. 'We found it after she died.'

Max swallowed and took the envelope from her hand. It was marked with a single word: his name. Max took it, but he didn't think he could read it yet. He tucked it inside his jacket for later, when he felt strong enough.

That afternoon, there was a soft knock on the door of their cabin, while Daisy and the others were still up on deck. It was Rozaliya, holding a small round lamp, which she set down by the door. She was wearing a purple turban and a dress with silver sequins, and her shoes had glittering buckles shaped like leaping dolphins. They cast sparkles of light onto the wooden floor with every step she took.

'Max?' Her voice was oddly hesitant.

Max was lying on his bunk and didn't look up. He was remembering playing ninepins on the rolling deck with Alexei; the way his hands had dwarfed the skittles and the ball. He was remembering baby Annika – his niece, he realized – in her sling across Alexei's chest, looking like a furious doll with her little mouth screwed up in outrage, and the way Alexei had laughed at her until she laughed back. He had been like a great, friendly bear – so different from the scrawny boy in the photograph Max was holding in his hands. The only similarity was in the tilt of the nose and the wide, light eyes.

Rozaliya came further into the room, and Max felt the slight give of the mattress as she perched like a tropical bird on the end of his bed. She took a breath as if gathering her courage.

But Max got there first. 'You knew,' he said accusingly. 'All this time, you knew.'

Rozaliya closed her eyes. 'Yes. It is true. We knew that Alexei was the lost prince. We knew that he was organizing a rebellion. Some of us helped. But we did not know that you were his brother. He was the greatest—'

'Actor of his generation,' said Max dully, hiding his face with his hand. 'Yeah. I know.'

Rozaliya looked anxious. 'You need to understand, Max. He was a good actor, yes – but he didn't lie in how he treated people.'

'Oh right,' said Max, rolling his eyes. 'So he just *forgot* to mention that he was the crown prince of Iffenwild and that he was my brother.'

'That is not fair,' said Rozaliya quietly. 'He might not have told you everything, but he loved you. He loved to spend time with you. He never lied in his feelings. He never lied in *here*.' She thumped her chest.

Max shrugged, but he remembered how Alexei's face had lit up every time he walked into the room. Not just the first time, but *every single time*, even after Max had been rude or pushed him away. Alexei had always, always been glad to see him, and that seemed, suddenly, like a very great gift indeed.

'He was very glad you found your tree, you know,' said Rozaliya, as Max gave a start. 'Oh yes, he knew about that – it's his ship! He had a tree of his own, once. The old captain gave it to him, when he first joined the *Nautilus* – so soon after he had lost his parents. Alexei saved a seed in case someone else needed it. Feirg seeds have a way of finding the people who need them most.'

Max didn't say anything, but he nodded. 'How did it

happen?' he asked instead, keeping his eyes fixed on his feet. 'I mean, how did Alexei end up with the *Nautilus*?'

'Ah,' said Rozaliya. 'That boy loved the theatre. Each year from when he was tiny, he would sneak away to our boats every chance he had. He was hiding on the ship when we fled, on the day the old king and queen were killed.' She glanced at Max. 'That is what saved his life. If he had been in the palace, he would have been killed. We took him in as a lost child. Eight years later, he became our captain.'

Max imagined his brother as a stowaway, alone and scared, his parents dead. They had been through such similar things, and never had a chance to talk about them. He thought of Alexei's bear-like size, his bone-deep kindness. The only person in the world apart from his mother who had known who he really was, who had recognized him by the mark on his cheek. Who had known what he looked like when he was a baby.

'I've lost everyone,' he said, so quietly that he wasn't sure Rozaliya would hear. 'I have no family.'

But Rozaliya heard him. 'No,' she said fiercely, grabbing his chin. 'You have Annika, Max. She's your family, and she is going to need you. I'm going to look after her, but she is going to need her uncle. And —' she cleared her throat and adjusted her purple turban — 'and you have me. This theatre is your family too, Max. You will be needed in Iffenwild, but you are also one of us now — for your whole life, if that is what you would like.'

Max swallowed again, and a single tear spilled from each eye and ran down his cheeks. 'Yes, please,' he said. 'I would like that very much.'

Chapter 76

'So you got my letter?' asked Daisy.

Acorn was sitting across from her on the deck of the captain's boat, perched on an upturned barrel. Her hair was as fiery as ever, and she had, thought Daisy, grown a little taller. She was feeding her pet caterpillar, Albert, with a lettuce leaf that Rozaliya had donated from the kitchens. Indigo and the Prof were sitting to either side of her, and it made Daisy's heart swell to see the three of them together again, the way it was supposed to be.

'Yes,' said Acorn, looking very pleased with herself. 'We got the letter all right, and the dandelight. Those three birds you sent to carry it were exhausted, I can tell you! We had to feed them with a special seed mix for two days before they recovered, and Tuffy said we were lucky they made it at all. Anyway, as soon as Artemis saw your note and understood that you'd found a way into Iffenwild, she was ready like a shot. We sailed from Rome – that's where we ended up after the battle at Moonmarket, putting in repairs to the ship – and we came all the way to the door you described. The dandelight showed us the way, just like a compass. It was amazing!'

She handed it back to Daisy now with a slight air of reluctance, and Daisy slipped it into her pocket. Napoleon was curled around her ankles, licking his paws and yawning ostentatiously. It had taken him less than a day after his near-death experience to return to his usual snooty self. He had hissed at Miss Tufton like a tiny feline ruffian, and she had been so pleased to see him again that she'd given him an entire kipper to feast on. He was now very full and sleepy.

'Well, you came just in time,' said the Prof, taking a sip of tea. 'For a moment there I thought the Grim Reaper army was going to take Iffenwild.'

Daisy nodded, slowly, taking a slice of chocolate and ginger cake from the plate in the middle of the table. It was spicy and warming, and dissolved on her tongue as she sipped her hot tea. She felt warm all over.

There was only one thing that bothered her. 'I still don't know if the Iffenwilders will agree to come with us to the Amazon. And that's the most important thing.'

There was a noise from the stairs, and they looked up as Max came onto the deck. He was pale and tired-looking, and there was a scrape across his cheekbone. Daisy had introduced him to Acorn the previous day, and they had taken an immediate liking to each other. There was something about Acorn that had that effect on people. The younger girl's face, with its snub nose and galaxies of freckles, was so funny and nice that it was impossible not to feel cheered by it. Daisy had missed her.

Max smiled at them now and took his place in the last empty seat at the table.

'You were talking about the Iffenwilders,' he said.

'Yes,' said Daisy. 'Will they come with us to the Amazon? Who's in charge now that the Duchess is gone?' She swallowed, thinking again of the hardness in the Duchess's eyes as she had tried to send her plummeting to her death.

'Ah,' said Max, looking awkward. 'That would be me.'

For the first time, Daisy noticed that he was dressed in the tunic of an Iffenwilder, and his hair was swept back from his face in a mostly unsuccessful attempt at neatness. He had made no effort to hide his birthmark, and Daisy realized now what was different about him: the way he carried his head was so confident, so assured, that it made him almost magnetic to look at.

'Yes,' he said quietly. 'And the lost heir, the older boy. That was Alexei.'

'Alexei?' said Daisy, shocked. 'Our Alexei?'

'Yes,' said Max, closing his eyes. The tears slid down his cheeks silently, and he wiped them away without comment.

'But that's impossible,' said Daisy. 'He was the captain of the *Nautilus*.'

'Yes,' said Max. 'But he was also the lost heir. And he was working with the Iffenwild resistance, planning an uprising to take back his throne.'

'How do you know all this?' asked Daisy.

Max's mouth twisted slightly. 'Rozaliya,' he said. 'Though it seems like the whole *Nautilus* crew was in on it. That's why we saw Gabriel sneaking around. He was the messenger between Alexei and the resistance. His whole self-obsessed idiot act was the perfect disguise – we never suspected. When we saw him talking to someone in the alley, he was giving instructions to one of the rebels.'

'Oh,' said Daisy, as the pieces fell into place. 'Indigo, the Duchess was the other Whisperer. She was the one controlling the ravens. There was no traitor on the *Nautilus*. There was only the Duchess and the birds she sent to spy on us. She must have been helping the Reapers a lot, actually – remember the ravens who tried to intercept Ma's letter?' It was a deep relief, somehow, to know that the *Nautilus* crew really were what they seemed: a family who would never betray one of their own.

Max nodded. 'Exactly. Alexei had been planning a rebellion for a long time, working with the resistance, waiting until they were strong enough. Rozaliya says he planned for it to start during this year's carnival. But the Grim Reapers beat him to it. They've been supporting the Duchess's government for years, in exchange for pearls from the Iffenwild reef. After the black market burned down, they decided to take revenge by attacking the people on their night of celebration.'

'It all makes sense!' said the Prof, pushing back her hair. 'We were wrong about Pompey, but we were right that the person in charge knew about the market. The Duchess must have been practically running it.'

Daisy nodded, and immediately thought of something else. 'Max, if you're the baby in the photograph, then that means that Alexei is . . .' – she swallowed – '. . . was your brother.'

'Yes,' said Max, and his face twisted. 'And he never told me. When I think of the time we could have had – the things we could have said . . .' He pressed his fists against his eyes, and his next words were muffled. 'It's my fault he's gone. Alexei was trying to save me. He jumped in front of Jarndyce's sword.'

There was a silence. 'It's not your fault, Max,' said Daisy at last. 'Alexei knew what he was doing. He made his choice.' She paused, hesitating. 'So did your mother. Marigold Brightly made a choice to save you, Max. She knew exactly what it meant. She gave you her life with her eyes wide open. She wanted you to take it and *live*.'

Max said nothing, but he didn't look convinced.

There was another silence, broken only by the sound of Albert munching on the juiciest part of the lettuce leaf.

At last, Max spoke again. 'Anyway,' he said, sitting up a bit straighter. 'It means that now I'm the prince of Iffenwild. Actually, the council wants to crown me next week, which means that then I'll be the king – assuming the coronation ceremony works. You have to be sort of . . . chosen by the sea, I think.'

'Oh, it'll work,' said Daisy, remembering the wave in the main square.

Max shrugged uncertainly. 'If it does – well, I'll have advisors of course, to help me learn everything.' He looked anxious, his forehead creased. 'But I've spoken to the guild leaders, and they agree we need to end our isolation. The Grim Reapers are too great a threat for us to ignore. We're going to open the doors of the Marindeep back to the Greenwild. We're going to come with you to the Amazon.'

Daisy stared at him in amazement, barely able to believe what she was hearing. Then she stood up and threw her arms around his neck.

Max blushed to the roots of his dark hair, but he didn't push her away. And when Daisy stepped back, she saw that he was trying not to smile.

Chapter 77

There was much to think about; much to arrange, councillors to meet, burned trees to be replanted, guild members to placate. The head of the Sailmakers' Guild, a man called Franz Graf von Wimpffen, wanted Max to resolve a long-running dispute with the head of the Ropemakers' Guild, a woman called Gertrude von Pock. It had something to do with an insult to someone's great-grandmother, and the details were making Max's head hurt. All the same, there was one thing they agreed on.

'Our entire stock is at your disposal for the journey to the Amazon, m'boy,' said von Wimpffen, chewing his moustache.

'Oh yes,' said von Pock. 'Depend upon it, your highness. We're picking out our best and strongest ropes as we speak.'

At the end of another busy day, Max remembered the letter in the pocket of his jacket. He had never forgotten it. Without really meaning to, he pulled it out and looked at it. Inside the envelope was a sheet of paper, and Max had to close his eyes for a minute before he could read it.

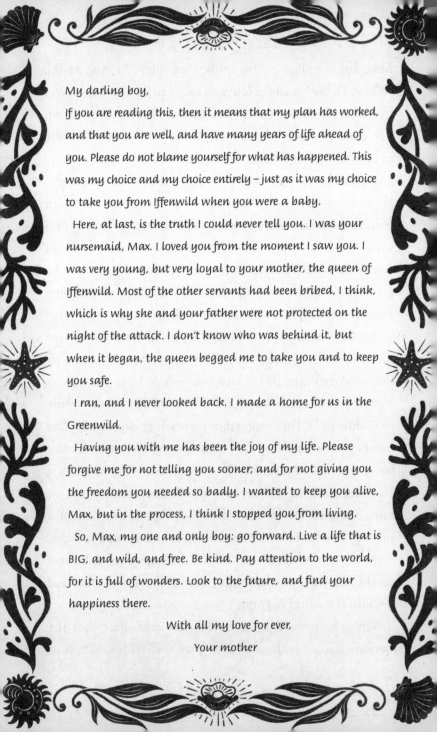

My darling boy,

If you are reading this, then it means that my plan has worked, and that you are well, and have many years of life ahead of you. Please do not blame yourself for what has happened. This was my choice and my choice entirely – just as it was my choice to take you from Iffenwild when you were a baby.

Here, at last, is the truth I could never tell you. I was your nursemaid, Max. I loved you from the moment I saw you. I was very young, but very loyal to your mother, the queen of Iffenwild. Most of the other servants had been bribed, I think, which is why she and your father were not protected on the night of the attack. I don't know who was behind it, but when it began, the queen begged me to take you and to keep you safe.

I ran, and I never looked back. I made a home for us in the Greenwild.

Having you with me has been the joy of my life. Please forgive me for not telling you sooner, and for not giving you the freedom you needed so badly. I wanted to keep you alive, Max, but in the process, I think I stopped you from living.

So, Max, my one and only boy: go forward. Live a life that is BIG, and wild, and free. Be kind. Pay attention to the world, for it is full of wonders. Look to the future, and find your happiness there.

With all my love for ever,

Your mother

Max lay sleepless on his bunk that night, staring at the ceiling. He had read the letter so many times that he knew it by heart. He thought of his mother as she had always been: fierce as a panther in her protection of him; sharp as a knife in his defence; ruthless in the ferocity of her caring.

At last, he got up and crept down to the storeroom, where his memory tree was taller than him now, and covered with glittering black leaves; dozens and dozens of memories: some good and some bad, but the greater part of them complicated, like most things in life. For an hour or two he sat in front of the tree, dipping into one memory and then another, staring at his mother's face in each.

At last, Max took a breath. He had needed the tree desperately, but perhaps now he could let it go. He could let the memories take their place back inside him, precious as diamonds but much less sharp. He stood up and the whole tree shivered. Then something amazing happened. The tree began to bear flowers – tiny flowers like silver cherry blossoms that bloomed with a smell like wind through a green meadow at night. From the flowers came a gust of tiny, glittering silver seeds that rose around the tree in a shining halo of light. Then the whole tree turned to light, and Max was blinded by it. He felt the seeds against his wet cheeks, blowing through him, across the storeroom, and out into the world beyond.

When he opened his eyes, the tree was gone. But the memories were with him. The grief was with him too; it

was part of him now, and would be always. But for the first time, Max could imagine a future in which he would be all right.

He felt the old breathlessness in his lungs. It would, he thought, probably never leave him. No cure was perfect. But he knew now what his mother had given him. It was life – and he was determined to live it.

Chapter 78

Daisy sat on the edge of the deck, her legs swinging down over the water and her face turned towards the sea. Towards the Amazon.

'So,' came a voice from behind her. 'Your mother was right, Daisy.'

'Yes,' said Daisy, not looking around as Artemis lowered herself with a small grunt to sit beside her. 'She usually is.' Leila Thistledown wasn't the best journalist of her generation for nothing. She knew, more than anyone else, the trick of finding the truth and holding it up to the light.

'She was certainly right about Iffenwild,' said Artemis, settling herself on the deck. Her silver hair fell over her shoulders, twined with white roses that opened and closed slightly in time with her breath. 'We do need their help. Things have not been good in the outer world while you've been here, Daisy. More Botanists have gone missing. Others are turning up dead. And the Amazon rainforest is being destroyed at a rate that the world has never seen before. Green magic –' she swallowed – 'green magic is dying. The systems that have kept it alive for centuries – the forests, the oceans, the ice peaks – are being weakened beyond endurance. For all its splendour and glory and strangeness, the Greenwild is rooted in the outer world. We are pockets of the Greyside – and if it falls, so do we.'

Daisy swallowed, thinking of the bleached coral and dead soil she had seen, as Artemis went on. 'The Grim Reapers are strong now – stronger than we could possibly have imagined. We'll never be able to defeat them with our green magic alone. The Amazon is a rainforest: a realm of water. The blue magic of the Iffenwilders – well, if they join us, it will change everything.'

'Oh,' said Daisy, savouring what she was about to say. 'They're joining us all right.'

'What?' Artemis leaned forward, eyes very blue and bright.

'Yes. Max – I mean, Prince Maximilian – says that the Iffenwilders are coming. He put it to a vote yesterday and the people have agreed. It helps that he told them all about the Reapers being behind the black market and the attack on the night of the carnival.'

Artemis sighed and sat back. 'That is good,' she said. Then she turned her keen blue eyes on Daisy. 'Did you find out what the black market was run on? Their main currency?'

'Yes,' said Daisy, nodding. 'It was pearls. Huge pearls from the Iffenwild coral reef.'

'Ah,' said Artemis. 'That makes sense. Those pearls are

made from the eyes of drowned men. They have the power to store a great deal of magic – like magical batteries, of a kind.'

Daisy jolted upright. Fragments passed through her mind like slides across a magic lantern before coming together in one terrible, undeniable certainty.

She looked at Artemis in horror. 'The Reapers are stealing green magic. They're using the pearls to store the power of stripped Botanists.'

Realization dawned on Artemis's face. 'Oh,' she said. 'That explains . . .'

'What?'

'It explains how the Reapers have attacked so many pockets in the last few weeks. It explains how they infiltrated Moonmarket. If the pearls are being used to hold the magic of dead Botanists . . . then they'd affect Greenwild doorways like people with magic. They'd work like a key – like a crude sort of dandelight.'

'Oh,' said Daisy, remembering something Max had once told her. *Jarndyce drew a sort of doorway in the air using this glowing white rock.* Not a dandelight, she realized, but a pearl. A giant black-market pearl, full of the magic of a stripped Botanist.

This changed everything, she realized, looking at Artemis. This was the evil that the Duchess had allowed – all for greed. This was what Alexei had lost his life fighting. She closed her eyes, pushing back tears. He had been given a state funeral the previous day, befitting of a king of Iffenwild. Daisy had watched alongside the rest of the city as his body was laid in a carved ebony boat and surrounded by coral; as the Nautilus players wept and Annika wailed from Rozaliya's arms. She had watched as the boat was set alight by a single flaming arrow, and sent sailing over the horizon until it became part of the ocean that Alexei had been born to command.

There was a long silence as Daisy wiped her cheeks with the heel of one hand.

'So what happens next?' she asked. 'What do we do?' Napoleon looked up from her lap and pricked up an ear.

'Well,' said Artemis. 'If the Iffenwilders are coming with us, then there's no time to lose. We cannot travel by Moonmarket. After the attack last full moon, the market has been taken over by Reapers – we barely escaped with our lives. We'll need to travel across the Greyside and find the doorway into Amazeria once we reach Peru.'

'I know a better way,' said Daisy, straightening her spine. 'Have you ever heard of a Mondenbaum boat?'

Chapter 79

Departure was set for the following day, but in the meantime, there were two things to be seen to. The first was unexpected, and came in the form of a roll of papers carried by a pair of official-looking parakeets.

'The second Bloomquist test!' said Artemis, unrolling the papers. 'I asked the academy to address your copies of the exam to me on the *Great Mallow* – and here they are.'

She had supervised as Daisy, Indigo and the Prof spent a morning sitting at desks set up in the cabin of the wardrobe ship, timing their progress.

Daisy felt a knot in her stomach as she turned over the exam paper. The Prof was already scribbling away beside her. Then she saw the first two questions.

1. *What is willow-silk and why is it useful in sailing?*
2. *Describe the cumulapple and explain its effects.*

Daisy smiled. Perhaps the test wouldn't be so bad after all.

*

The second thing that happened wasn't unexpected at all. Max's coronation took place on the shores of the lagoon, and the whole population of Iffenwild came out to watch. This, Daisy knew, was the moment of truth. If the water responded to his call, his kingship would be confirmed. If it didn't . . . well, Daisy wasn't sure what would happen. Max looked very small and skinny against the majesty of the shell towers and coral turrets behind him. Then he raised his hand over the waves, and suddenly he seemed to grow taller.

'I call the water,' he said, his voice ringing out over the heads of the crowd behind him.

There was a hush as they waited. Daisy chewed at the edge of her nail.

Then the waves at the edge of the lagoon stirred, and they rose up in a glittering column around Max's outstretched hand.

'And the water answers,' cried the jubilant crowd, in the words that had been handed down through a hundred generations.

'I choose the water,' said Max. 'To protect for as long as I live.'

'And the water chooses you,' chorused the people of Iffenwild. 'To protect for as long as you live.'

Daisy watched as the water rushed up around him in a great glittering fan of silver spray, and for a moment he disappeared from sight. When it fell back, Max emerged soaking wet, and blinking, and there was a crown of coral on his head. It was, Daisy thought, the most beautiful and wild object she'd ever seen – the colour of a sunset, sharp around its edges, and set with rough pearls that seemed to shift colour with the sea, from blue to green to white.

A great cheer went up from the crowd. Daisy watched in astonishment as, with a rumble like the heartbeat of the ocean itself, blue magic returned in full force to the people of Iffenwild.

Fountains of spray rose up from the hands of old ladies, and small children stomped gleefully in the giant puddles. Fishermen called up whirlpools from the lagoon, and water rushed at full spate through the canals, turning cartwheels as it came thundering through the city and sending up sprays of rainbow light where it caught the sun.

After that, the party began. It was the greatest party Iffenwild had seen in years. Tables were ranged beside every canal, groaning with platters of food that every cook in the kingdom had been working all night to produce. There were great round dishes of oysters and champagne, and braided loaves of fresh bread crusted with sea salt, and tiny glistening herring caught fresh from the sea. There were flasks of apple cider and twists of cardamom pastry, and an enormous, spiced chocolate cake with chocolate dolphins leaping from the icing, its surface piped with four words in white buttercream: *Long Live King Maximilian*. Max had looked embarrassed at this, but Daisy thought that he was secretly rather pleased.

Now, she took a thick slice of plum cake and watched as Indigo tucked gleefully into the desserts. Napoleon was dispatching a plate of sausages under a chair, and the Prof was sipping a glass of kelp-flower cordial, looking like an aristocrat in overalls. There were tables set out on terraces that looked out over the glittering blue lagoon, and the air was filled with the smell of salt and flowering orange trees. Then someone pulled out an old fiddle and suddenly there was music everywhere. The Nautilus players got out their flutes and drums and began to play an old Traveller tune. Iffenwilders drew out their violins, and joined in the melody, adding depth and harmony. Rozaliya was the first to start dancing, moving to the middle of the square and beating out a Moon Traveller dance that set the buckles on her shoes glinting in the evening light.

The *Nautilus* fleet wasn't going to come with them to the Amazon, or at least not right away. First, they had a giant cabin-full of rescued creatures to return to their rightful homes. It would be Marie-Claude's first voyage as the new captain of the *Nautilus* fleet. 'It will be our greatest performance yet,' she said, smiling at Daisy, red-eyed. 'I think it's what Alexei would have wanted.'

Now the music swung itself into motion and suddenly the square was flooded with people. Daisy saw Ingrid dancing with Acorn, and Artemis dancing with Indigo, her silver hair falling down her back. All the Iffenwilders had joined in, and for the first time in living memory the square became a mass of green and blue as Greenwilders and Marindeepers joined hands and danced, enmity forgotten. Daisy had never seen the Iffenwilders so happy, and goodwill flowed as freely as the ale from the barrels that were rolled through the streets.

The Prof was looking happier than Daisy had seen her in a long time, buoyed by the prospect of setting off towards the Amazon – and her grandfather. Daisy had found her the previous day experimenting with a water pansy and making it bloom underwater. She was still nowhere near as good as Max, but for once she didn't look worried about it.

'Maybe I don't always need to be the best,' she said, shrugging. 'Sometimes, teamwork means knowing that other people are better at something than you are.'

Daisy raised an eyebrow at her.

'Only sometimes,' said the Prof. 'Let's be clear. Ninety-eight per cent of the time, I remain unsurpassed.'

Daisy had grinned, and stifled a laugh.

Now, the Prof was playing poker with an old Iffenwilder and beating him hands down. Acorn was dancing with Emil and his little sister Anna, who was clapping her hands in time to the music.

Only Max was not part of the crowd. Daisy saw him standing at a corner of the square, looking out over the lagoon and towards the sea. The sun was setting like a white pearl, with streaks of coral stretching across the horizon.

'How does it feel?' she asked, gesturing towards his crown.

He touched it self-consciously. 'A little strange,' he admitted. He paused. 'I can feel the sea, you know. It's beautiful, but it's so deep and dark. It excites me. It scares me. Both.'

Daisy looked at him, a level look that took in his high cheekbones and the fine lines of his nose and his long eyelashes, and the shape of the mark on his cheek. For a moment, she felt she would never stop looking at him.

'Sometimes I think that's the best way to feel,' she said. 'A bit scared, and a bit excited. That's how you know you're doing it right.'

He smiled at her, a brilliant smile that creased his whole face and brought out the dimple in his cheek. 'Yes,' he said. He touched the edge of his crown. 'I think maybe that's true.' He looked back at her for a moment, and she glanced away.

Then someone from the crowd grabbed their hands and drew them into the dance, and there was no more time for talking.

When the stars came out and the lagoon began to glow with the light of a thousand phosphorescent jellyfish, the Iffenwilders lit fires along the shore, and they sang ballads and sea shanties. The Nautilus players cleared a space in the centre of the square with lanterns to mark the edge of the makeshift stage, and they launched into a new play – one that Daisy hadn't seen before, about a storm and a shipwreck, and an enchanter called Prospero. Daisy sat with her back against the wall of the square and watched the story unfold. As soon as the ships were ready, they would sail for Amazeria, to face the Grim Reapers and fight the evil that was spreading over the two worlds. But tonight, there was firelight and an island full of sweet music, and magic as rich and strange as the sea itself.

She looked down at Ma's letter, which lay unfolded in her lap, and read the words for the hundredth time. When she looked up, moonlight was falling across the sea in a flood of silver, and a herd of water horses was galloping along it towards the horizon.

'I'm coming, Ma,' she said, watching the spark of their silver hoofbeats on the waves.

Behind her the play finished, and applause rose up from the square into the dark night.

About the Author

Pari Thomson's debut novel, *Greenwild: The World Behind the Door*, was published to critical acclaim in 2023 and won Blackwell's Children's Book of the Year. Pari's original fantasy adventure was inspired by the extraordinary wonders found at Kew Gardens, a botanical garden that features everything from giant lily pads and freckled orchids to hairy pink bananas. A tribute to the beauty and wildness of nature, *Greenwild* also draws on the various natural settings that Pari lived in and experienced growing up, including misty pine forests in Pakistan, colourful gardens in India and pomegranate groves in Iran. Half Persian, half English, Pari studied at Oxford University and now works as editorial director for picture books at a children's publisher. She lives near the river in London, not far from Kew Gardens.

The final installment in the Greenwild series will be published in 2025.

Acknowledgements

Writing this book was an unexpectedly joyful experience, and I owe the greatest thanks to many people for making it so.

To my bold, brilliant agent Claire Wilson, for telling me to start writing – and for loving Max from the beginning.

To my endlessly kind, creative and patient editor Emma Jones, for making the book so much better (and shorter!) than it would otherwise have been.

To the whole team at Macmillan Children's Books for the enormous tide of support, with special thanks to Charlie, Amy, Anna and Cheyney. To Mireille Harper, my authenticity reader, for lending your expertise and grace to the story. To Ross Jamieson, my copy editor, and Fraser Crichton, my proofreader.

To Janine O'Malley and everyone at Farrar, Straus & Giroux: Allison, Gaby, Teresa and so many others – I am so proud to be published by you in the US.

To all my foreign language publishers: thank you for bringing Daisy's story to so many wonderful new places.

To my US agent Pete Knapp and everyone at both Park

Fine and RCW, for continuing to champion this series.

To Elisa Paganelli: there are no words to do justice to your beautiful illustrations. You saw inside my imagination and brought this story alive. Thank you.

To my parents, for bringing up a bookworm child with such tolerance, and for your unwavering belief and love.

To Lily and Daniel, my funny and kind and generous siblings, for making life better every day.

To my magnificent English and Iranian families all around the world.

To my brilliant friends, for everything.

And to Tom, for being beside me through all of it; for long walks and inspiring conversations and endless kindness. This book is for you.